The Last Literate Man

By J. Arthur Weber

SRCLB Press

This is a work of fiction and satire. Names, characters, businesses, places, events, locales, and incidents are either the products of the author's imagination or used in a fictitious and satirical manner. Any resemblance to actual persons, living or dead, or actual events, past, present, or future is purely coincidental and quite possibly a figment of the imagination of a massive ego.

Acknowledgements

Thank you to my mother, Patricia, for teaching me how to read before I even got to school, for taking me to the library, and for giving me a love of stories that has lasted my whole life and driven me both as an English teacher and a writer.

Thank you to Sherry Ransford-Ramsdell for encouragement, general advice, editing, and proofing.

Dedicated to my parents,

my first fans.

"The western hemisphere was ripe for a new
feudalism, given their short cultural memories
and the fact that slavery of the peoples of
Africa was a cherished cultural tradition."
How America became the World
by Tajhi Ramhero

I

The clock on the wall showed blue.

It was still a "clock" but it wasn't the clock that Dunne's great-grandparents would have known. They might have still recognized symbols like Arabic numerals, but that ability faded with each generation that led downward to his current one. Lack of use meant skills were lost. Lack of need meant only the barest elements of the old style clock remained. It had only a color on its face.

Dunne rose to a tall hunch from his partitioned space next to the belt reeking of salt brine and joined the rest of his shift trudging toward the chlorine showers. Blue meant that it was time to eat. Workers had ten minutes to wash off accumulated filth and grime and eat their few grams of sustiwafers or gray food paste before the line started moving again.

His back hurt. He was taller than most of his fellows, despite their shared malnourishment. His thin brown hair was trimmed short. Shades of occasional auburn shone in spots in his thin beard when the sun hit it at the perfect angle. He was dirty. His dirty features revealed pale skin and light freckles if he scrubbed hard enough in the chemical showers.

Dunne worked at a factory filled with powerful engines that belched thick black smoke and pulled long heavy plastic nets from the bottom of the nearby sea. The machines trawled the former Irish Sea for thousands of kilograms of accumulated plastic wastes that were then processed into machine parts, clothing, and sustenance - in that order. Dunne was fortunate to have a job on the line sorting out the unsellable biological debris from the trawled plastics.

The plastics had value on the machine market, but the biodebris was riddled with arsenic from unregulated precious metal mining run-off. Then inevitable tumors formed as the biological entities that depended on the water for life attempted to accommodate the high levels of synthetic chemicals. The netted biomass was sometimes collected and processed into machine lubricant, but it was poisonous to living things. Outcasts who sometimes stole it to eat in fits of hunger were often found dead, their corpses convulsed in their final throes of agony. Dunne had seen more than a few locked in their final grimace on the beach.

He worked on a sorting line with countless others in the seaside town of Salynog in what was once an independent republic. After the final dissolution of the European Union and years of a slow and gradual national takeover by business interests from the USA, it became the fifty-first state as a result of the Spence-Jonson Accords during President Spence's short reign. Shortly after that, the current President For Life was voted back into office for a third and seemingly unending term as the successful Constitutional Convention of 2029 had repealed the twenty-second amendment limiting the ability of the people to elect a candidate for more than two terms of office. It was only a few years later that the popular vote was rendered symbolic by the amendment that gave the ruling political party the ability to choose their own president. Dunne knew nothing of these things. He didn't have to.

Most of the things he knew were giant flashing multi-color, animated images projected on the concrete walls of the factory or the many connected telescreens, alternating between motivational messages about work and advertising meant to inflame the desires of the workers to spend themselves further into debt to the company bank.

The work was mind-numbingly repetitive: each worker concentrated on the high-speed conveyer line in front of them pulling out pieces of biological waste retrieved from the sea to be burned or reconstituted into food or other workable products for consumption. Their days dragged, but the messages on the telescreens over their heads were just as monotonous to Dunne. Screens that offered entertainment or distraction to others only mocked his awareness. He and his fellows welcomed the end of their work shift, even though for him it meant trading one monotony for another.

The telescreens were in every room of the factory, as inescapable as the temperature. Similar devices filled the walls of their dormitory hives and dens as well and many workers carried leased pocket screens. Images and sounds splashed over them constantly in a rapid race of advertisements, entertainments, and news that were indistinguishable from each other.

At the end of each shift, Dunne and the rest of the workers shambled through the chlorine shower line near the worker exit. The constant video feeds projected above the shower heads portrayed scenes of the number one rated entertainment program. It was a series that detailed the ongoing childhood and young adult adventures of the President for Life who by popular symbolic vote controlled their fate and that of the world they inhabited. *The Chosen*

One Adventure Hour was the most popular animated television show of all time. Everyone watched the full sixty minute program daily, running repeatedly the same thirty minute episodes with thirty minutes of advertising for products branded with the leader's name and likeness. Even the nutrient greypaste and the sustiwafers had his likeness on the plastic wrap.

Among other things, it detailed how he invented the popular meat sandwich, the "hamberger" when he was just a boy of three, not long after he learned how to drive and just before he made his first million by selling off the bits of horn of the last unicorn that he had defeated inside a cave in Upper Manhattan in a bout of mortal combat. The program detailed all of the exploits of the boy who became the most beloved leader that the world had ever known.

The Orangeshirts who ruled the factory loved the program even more than the workers, but then they loved all of the programs that featured their idol and leader, the President for Life. Most workers were well trained in the same devotion. Dunne was atypical, but he hid his lack of love for the leader behind a facade of empty-eyed adulation that mirrored that which he saw in the eyes of everyone around him.

Dunne looked toward the screen and instead daydreamed about places he would never see in person. He couldn't imagine specific things as they were or as they might have been for him. Instead he imagined a place where the water was blue and the landscape wasn't covered by garbage, like the ones where the wealthy frolicked on the reality shows and commercials on the screens. Shades of green and brown and blue colored his daydreams.

4

He had never seen blue water in person, but he had an image in his mind of a sea off the coast of his home that was blue, even if he didn't know the origin of his mental image. Likewise, the local landscape in his head was nothing that he had ever seen, but imagining his world as unspoiled and colored with greens, earthy browns, and blues made him feel better than watching the computer-animated people on the tele-screen narrate the amazing adventures of the boy who would become the savior of the free world while selling products adorned with his name and image.

Dunne looked back to the Orangeshirts. They were distracted by the screens as well. In the annals of hidden history, they had worn brown and black uniforms cobbled from stock of the old defense forces and civil peace officers. Repeated launderings in the polluted waters of the island's water supply bleached their clothing to an uneven dirty orange. The subjects of the island who hated them called them "Orangeshirts" out of disrespect. With time, the militant group claimed the nickname meant to disrespect them and made it their own. It became a badge of honor. These "Orangeshirts" proudly controlled the working classes on the island in the name of their glorious leader across the ocean. By comparison, the workers' clothes were all tattooed with the logos of their employers. Dunne and his co-workers wore the bull emblem of their corporate master proudly in the center chest, and the sleeves were decorated with the logos of other corporate sponsors. The Orangeshirts uniforms were made of expensive cotton weave that was meant to last longer than the workers' polyester uniforms which dissolved into tatters after a few days of normal wear.

The Orangeshirts were the self-selected volunteer police force of the state used by the ruling class to maintain order. They were a self-regulated and self-policing group of proud men and boys united by a common admiration and love for the President for Life. These like-minded fans controlled all aspects of public life and acted as a hand of the state apparatus. They banded together in common admiration for all that their leader across the sea represented and to demonstrate their misplaced loyalty to the man they adored. In addition to financial credit for the their work, they were guaranteed other worldly benefits.

They were given access to the best of the Sexdollies for a low debt charge. The Sexdollies were manufactured to embody the new hyper-masculine culture's feminine ideal. Their shapes were perfect with exaggerated butts and breasts to resembled the surgically altered models on the telescreen, their oversized eyes stood out on the their babydoll faces and they never said no. They were programmed to be the perfect plastic mistresses for the majority male population. The dolls had become popular during the President's third election celebration when he advertised them during his inauguration, standing with them at his podium as he welcomed the cheers of his people.

Orangeshirts also had the exclusive privilege to entirely compose the athletic and sports clubs by government ordinance. Men were encouraged to join the Orangeshirts to play sports because membership meant access to higher levels of stims and roids on the unregulated markets to give them the winning edge. There were sports clubs of Orangeshirts with names like "The Rods" or the "The Green Straps" who played the violent super-modern version of the old island games against each other. They beat each other with their hurls and gaffs, and tried as much to pummel and punish as they did to score goals in show of masculine dominance. Concussions and casualties were just a part of the game, and a player's reputation and credit value could rise or fall depending on the injuries he doled out to foes on the playing field as well as on the streets.

Dunne had no desire to commit acts of violence in the name of sports or for the President for Life. He had a dark and deeply hidden suspicion. He suspected that there was a time when the man was old and withered, but the tele-screens that beamed his face on the news and the adverts showed no marks of time or toil. To the public, the God-ordained President for Life was ageless and all-powerful. Rumors held that even before he took his lifelong office, nanotechnology and gene therapy had become a normal routine for the chosen people like the president and his followers who held the upper echelons of society. Dunne couldn't possibly remember an aged vision of the man, because those images were wiped from existence before Dunne was born. He could only believe that they were images of his own imagination, like the vistas of white clouded blue skies meeting glittering blue waters on far-flung horizons. His current reality was the only one that he could ever know.

Dunne wasn't an outcast, but he had no friends. He simply kept to himself. He knew the lines to toe and kept his eyes where they were supposed to be. He knew the value of compliance: it kept him alive. There was food to eat (on credit) and shelter provided by his employer. Even if the food was mostly artificial vitamin enhanced sawdust sustiwafers shipped in from the dwindling forests of the American

7

protectorate of Canada, at least it made his belly feel less empty. It allowed him to stay alive. It didn't matter if he didn't own any of it and paid for it with credit. Staying alive was all that could matter.

The days felt long to Dunne, but he couldn't measure how long in any meaningful or relevant way any more. The colored face of the clock was nonsensical to him. The colors never seemed to correspond to schedules or even the path of the sun. He could imagine a day when the clocks measured units through symbols instead of colors that told them what to do, but he had long since forgotten what those units were or what the symbols on those old clocks might have meant. They had lost meaning in a world where the only things that mattered were how much work could be wrought to demonstrate loyalty to the president and the mind-numbing entertainment used to escape the monotony of existence.

Orangeshirts sometimes referred to the President as "The Don" in a thinly veiled reference to his telescreen-program mafia-style manner of leadership. None of the workers took the same privilege, except in hushed tones away from the screens and cameras that covered the interior and exterior of the factory. The moving projections on the walls outside were of a three dimensional leader repeating some of his slogans and catchphrases that had been popular for the last few decades of his rule.

They were messages that he could not escape, words that burrowed into his consciousness and invaded his dreams, preventing him from finding a respite from the constant buzz of distraction that spun and bounced around his head like a metal ball in an old-fashioned arcade pin machine.

Wireless speakers on every building pushed phrases in a silky, smooth auto-tuned twang and echoed over and over again between looping programs that advertised the leader's products, his history, and his way of life. Ofttimes, the displays on each building were not synced with any other on the same street. Taken together, the cacophony was almost more than Dunne could bear. The only way to lessen it was to sit directly in front of one telescreen or another where its volume would block out all the others from reaching his ears.

The latest thing that had gone viral were two video games that allowed the player to be the "President for Life" in a bloody first person perspective gun and sword game for the "big" kids (over age seven) and a side scrolling platform game that featured the muscular protagonist jumping on and over enemies to collect dollars to buy the properties displayed in the game scenes for the younger fans. Some fortunate older children of the more privileged Orangeshirts got to play them in VR while millions of fans, including Dunne, watched on telescreens. People could take debt credits to watch the players play live and uninterrupted by advertising, but Dunne thought that activity was much less than worth the cost. The lowest cost way to enjoy a game was to watch someone who watched someone else who was watching the game on the monitor as the athlete played.

Dunne, like everyone else, was deep in debt. Living so far in the red on the debt curve troubled him for a reason that he couldn't articulate, and he felt like taking on more was akin to wrapping another layer of heavy anchor chains around his thin and sore neck. He wondered if anyone else in the factory labored under a similar metaphorical weight, but after watching the way they stared vacantly into whatever moment

9

was directly in front of their permanently empty eyes, he decided that the odds of them having any hidden interior lives at all was rather scant. The wonder left him almost as soon as it came. Most deeper thoughts did, chased as they were by flashing lights and sounds that demanded his attention in the present moment.

It was not that the seeds of deeper thought fell on stony ground, it was that there was no water and no sun to nourish them. Hopes and dreams were watered by imagination and fed by inspiration that only existed in the fringes of free time, and if there was no free time spent unexhausted, then there was no imagination or inspiration to consider better things. The long work shifts six or seven days a week had a way of preventing any sort of meaningful life outside of work. The typical schedule was continuous, but workers could buy a day off using their credit if their rating allowed it.

Dunne tried to focus on an internal monologue as much as he could while sorting out the bio-debris from the plasti-petrol nets. It wasn't a job that required a tremendous amount of focus. He had done it without thinking nearly every day for years. The muscle memory was real. There were days that he closed his eyes on the sorting line and simply let his hands do all the work. Those were dangerous moments though, as his hands could have easily become caught in moving parts that were near breaking point and in need of repairs.

The catchings from the nets fell down into huge chutes that emptied onto conveyor belts that ran by Dunne and his fellow coworkers in the sorting factories. There were so many petrochemicals in the biological specimens that machine eyes had trouble sorting the plastic bottles from the ocean life filled with plastic. It was left to the humans to pull the organic pieces out for further processing. Those went into large bins that were then wheeled into another area of the factory where the gutter crew worked to skim as much plastic from the creatures as was possible. Then the remaining biological wastes were refined into grease for machine lubrication. Other workers cleaned the plastic caught in the nets. On rare occasions when the net was accidentally torn by one of the machines, the whole mile long net was cut from the drag lines to sink into the sea for future recycling and then replaced by another gigantic net from the factory that produced them in the south of a westerly neighboring island ruled by the last functioning monarchy on the planet.

Dunne's job on the front of the line smelled bad, but those jobs further down smelled worse. At least open windows and crosswinds blowing through his level could carry away the roadkill scent of the drying matter they cleared from the nets. Biological rot mixed with the chemical odor left many of those working in the back or lower areas asthmatic and chronically short of breath. Nostrils and sinuses burned and dripped. Cuts and scrapes on hands became infected and oozed. There was danger in the work they did.

There were many things in the world that could leave a man feeling ill and short of breath, and there were no extra precautions taken. Depending on the winds and the weather, the outdoors wasn't a true respite either. If the winds were high and storms were settling, then the smoggy miasma of burning turf from the power plants would blow off the highlands and coastal areas. If not, then being outside could be just as noxious as being inside.

When the workers weren't sequestered inside on the separating lines, they could walk outside the rending factory. During the rare waking moments when Dunne wasn't working, his walks outside could easily leave him winded. He tried to get as far away from the factory as he could, because he felt better out there. The exhaust stacks were nearly level with the roof, and the air outside was chronically thick and heavy. The gray mists hovered there when the wind stalled. They weren't the gray mists of olden days, when the water vapor caused by warm land heating cool air moving in off the sea kept the air heavy and moist; these were dark hovering clouds of civilization, of man's constant drive for profit.

When the men of the west decided that the world was going to end shortly and that Jesus would "come quickly," they set about ruining everything in the name of short-term profit for the advancement of everlasting redemption. They believed they were bringing the second coming of the savior on sooner by creating the environment of the "end of days."

That mentality took a bit longer to reach the island of Dunne's recent ancestors, but after the President for Life from across the ocean took his third term, it diffused rapidly from his office and through the new fifty-first state. The economy of the southern part of the island took a tumble with the northern part's exit from the Euro-Union Alliance, and the only way through the economic crisis was a stronger alliance with the economy from across the Atlantic.

The country across the sea was God's chosen land, populated by God's chosen lambs. The rulers there were the richest of any in the world, and the success of their cultural influence upon the rest of the world was proof of God's favor. Years of trickle-down economic policies that hadn't yet trickled down had given the wealthy a financial power that easily translated into political strength to create a brutal blend of old-style feudalism and neo-capitalism. The obvious and easily observable fact that God favored the rich by making them richer was a strong argument for their growing control, as well as the perfect tool to power the movement for the change they wanted to see in the world.

There was nothing to deny the truth of it all. Power created the truth, manipulated it, controlled it, shaped it, and used it to pull the strings of thousands of puppets up and down the line. The status quo made "the right people" strong. There were no "deserving" or "blessings" to be had by those who did not possess wealth. The wealthy who were elevated by the status quo then manipulated that status quo to keep their "blessings" — to cement them as a simple matter of God's providence. God rewarded those who pleased him and punished those who did not.

Each generation had that truth and also its own nostalgias for its particular generation's cherished past. People would reminisce about the "good old days" before cancer was an inescapable fact of life, back when married couples could afford to take on the debt of raising a child, or even when the average citizen on the island could afford his own home — but none of them had ever witnessed such days. Those times were immortalized on telescreen programs that sold them faces and products that promised a return to the better days of the past as long as they went into debt to buy them.

Dunne knew these things because he was told to know them, but he wondered if he truly believed them. He had spent most of his life daydreaming about being anywhere but where he was. His head was always lost in the clouds, seeking comfort from the world that wounded him daily.

No tool was more important than
the internet when it came to socializing
the masses. It replaced classroom
education during the first great
pandemic of the 21st century.
Education: The Mass Opiate of Failure
by Jon Okada

II

Nix grew up surrounded by screens in his parents' flat. They showed him everything. His only memories were of screens, boisterous flashing scenes of moving wonderment. Nix loved the telescreen programs, even as an infant. His first warm memories were of bathing in its radiance and having the rest of the world washed away in the loud, bright blasts of light and sound emanating from the screen. It was always there. It shone down upon him when he fell asleep, and he awoke to the same strident brightness each morning. It was there when he ate. It was there when he took his mood pills, drank his "President for Life!" brand soda and ate his processed, breaded meat patties. The screen was there when he urinated and defecated. The things he learned from the telescreen were constant and myriad.

The stories from the box were steady and consistent. They were the subtext that every viewer absorbed day and night through the images and the sounds. They laid the foundation for the replication of the culture that Nix and his ilk were to spread around the world. Day and night it echoed the same message until it became innate to those who absorbed it. It was like the nighttime crickets of a former age before their extinction, or the sound of waves on the shore where only the rich and privileged could afford to live. The backdrop of his existence was the telescreen.

It held songs, it held pictures. It held heroes and villains. It told him what to believe and made it so very easy for him to decide what to do. It told him what to drink and what to eat. It told him when and how to demand the things that it told him that he deserved. He knew about sex and how to take it by force before he was seven. He knew about alcohol and pills, things in syringes and tabs, and to take hold of girls by their most tender places because if you were an Orangeshirt, they would let you. The telescreen taught him much of the ways of his world long before he had any thought to the whys.

His parents drank to fall asleep every night. They slipped him a bit of whiskey each night when he was colicky, putting the bottle to his lips and tipping it for him, pouring enough to sedate him. By following their example, he had his first hangover before he could write his name. The telescreen taught him about the importance of sex, drugs, and money; more than any of those things though, the telescreen taught him about power. It taught him about the raw strength of the electronic pulpit. He understood implicitly that the people on it were gods, and the knew that he wanted to become a vessel of their divine powers. He believed in his destiny to have a holy mission for the President for Life.

Cruelty excited Nix. Watching it was euphoric, but committing it rocketed his pleasure to the next level. He had seen so much violence by his teens that he was already bored by the constant flood of rapes, murders, and explosions on the telescreens. He craved the real thing in the same way that predators craved meat after being caged downwind from a slaughterhouse. He would stay up late just to see his father return home from work to visit violence upon his mother. He watched from dark doorways from behind the couch and would smother his gleeful giggles as his father attacked her in one of his regular drunken rages, each impact of his fists upon her face and body provoking further giggles that had to be stifled from his hidden viewing spot, lest his father visit the violence upon him as well. And sometimes, his father did just that.

Nix changed from a pudgy, soft toddler to a pudgy, soft child, then to a pudgy, soft teen of average height. As Nix grew, he reenacted his father's violence against his mother in his own ways. When she didn't respond to his demands for more food or more entertainment quickly enough, he verbally berated her. He hit her with his toys. He flailed at her with his fists and feet in imitation of his father's violence. She accepted it because she knew her place as a woman.

In his mind, he was sure that he was special and destined for a greatness of his very own, and his experiences confirmed it despite his averageness in every way, shape, and form but for his lust for cruelty and violence. His father had some measure of power, given his own position as a chaplain in the Orangeshirts paramilitary force. He was a bridge between the bullets and the book of the faith and held an unassailable position of power that bound the Orangeshirts at their very core. They all believed that the Bible foretold the President for Life.

Nix's father was the intermediary for their faith in the president-savior, the transmission signal between the world of the Orangeshirts on the island and the leaders of the movement far across the sea in North America. His paramilitary status as chaplain transcended its powerless origin in the American military many decades before and was a vehicle for control.

Nix's father's position meant that he had privilege that his son could not understand. Nix only knew entitlement. Nix was more bully than bullied as a child, which was normal for someone who was chosen to matriculate into the Orangeshirts. There was never a doubt with his parents that he would carry on the proud family traditions, donning the faded brown uniform to signal his control over the lower classes through coercion and violence. By following in his father's footsteps, he could ensure that some day his own offspring would become the next generation of leaders on the island.

First though, he had to do his time in the lower ranks. Everyone had to learn their place through subjugation, and through that, to learn to subjugate others. Those were the dues to be paid. Orangeshirts learned their place through the violence visited upon them by other Orangeshirts. They also learned early on that they could buy respite from the violence by offering bribes to higher ranking Orangeshirts. This paved the psychological path to proper utilization of the messianic structure that directed the surrender of all power and profit upward to the supreme leader so that he might visit it down upon his subjects as his whims drove him to.

Nix's ancestors on the island had been significant for as long as it mattered. His grandfather had been the CFO for the island's number one government media content and service provider, Err. He had also been one of the first among the elite to adopt the ChipIn service as a means to demonstrate the safety of the implant and demonstrate brand loyalty for all of the lower class workers on the island to emulate. The company's board of directors had asked him to volunteer for the first round of in-service testing of the device, and he was more than happy to do it for the bottles of Jimson's whiskey that he was paid with.

Nix remembered his grandfather's incoherent but intensely racist ramblings when the chip ignited inside his skull and burned part of his brain from the inside. The mutterings made Nix laugh. The whiskey lessened the old man's burning pain, and it cauterized the wound it left on his temple as it burned through the flesh. He wore that scar for the rest of his life as a sign of bravery and brand loyalty. He often bragged about taking part in the study when the fog lifted from his brain enough for him to feel pride.

The ChipIns were still the normal enhancement for citizens. After the first generation technology improved, the implant was much less likely to ignite randomly under the skin. Implantation of the ChipIn varied by social class. The Orangeshirts and their families took them in their skulls. The workers took them in the meat of their hands. Like all citizens, Nix was chipped at birth. The ChipIns were used to monitor locations and habits so they could be tracked, their habits sold, and their lives monetized fully by the corporations that owned the world.

Becoming an Orangeshirt was academic for Nix. He was marked for it by family status at birth, but his inherent and instinctual cruelty made him ideal for the work they did. The ChipIn in his frontal lobe also increased his cruelty, nestling as it did where an inhibition against cruelty might have grown in other humans more capable of empathy. He rubbed the thin white scar over the implant on his head when he felt bored.

Dirt made it look like a bruise where his filthy hands met the raised tissue.

A broad, flat face and widely spaced eyes gave others the impression that he was stronger than he was, given that a heavy body was associated with physical strength. He wasn't the star of his athletic teams, but he was an adept enforcer: always ready to use his hurl as a cudgel, his cleats as daggers, and his fingers as claws when he could hurt the opposing players.

Nix aspired to cruelty as soon as he saw the power that it held over people. He was designed for it. When he came of age, his advancement was natural. He wasn't as tall or as "telescreen handsome" as some of his peers, but his blonde hair and ruddy complexion fit the bill for his place in society. His first posting was as a guard at a factory on the river that moved through the heart of the capital city. It was there that he began to refine his personal art of cruelty.

III

"Ay there, gobshite!" shouted the Orangeshirt.

He wasn't talking to Dunne, but whenever an Orangeshirt spoke, everyone paid attention. If they didn't snap their eyes to the Orangeshirt, they could be struck or worse. The Orangeshirts derived their power from a ruthless sadism and increased its intensity by engaging witnesses to each cruelty. More eyes on their actions increased their power to wield it against their victims. Any attention he captured was good attention because it was another power over the audience.

This man was an Orangeshirt through and through. He pulled his handgun from his crotch where it was stored in his bulge holster and waved it around in the air. "You feckin' gobshites are up for it!" He looked around as if he had lost his train of thought. The workers stared at him through his pause, then the rest of his thought came out of him jarringly in spurts. "I just mean that brown stain... that looked at me wrong... when I didn't have me pistol..."

All the workers in the rending factory looked away at once. He chuckled, gurgling the spit in his throat. Fear was an aphrodisiac, and seeing the workers' reaction to his threat of violence made him hard beneath his ill-fitting pants. A threat of violence was all it took to increase the feelings of power, the sense of control — but he desired this time to take it further to its logical climax.

He choose the worker on the line who was three bodies over to the right and two in front of Dunne. It was unclear from where Dunne stood whether the worker was male or female. The Orangeshirts preferred to rape the biological females, but when it came to making a bloody display of power, sex was a simple sideline. They'd violate a male just as freely as female. They found pleasure in the power, not in the sex.

"Whud the feck are you gobbos looking at?" he shouted as he pulled the worker off the line and out through one of the wide doors nearest the workstation to mete out his punishment for the imagined infraction. Dunne tried to focus on the task at hand, but a gunshot rang out from just beyond the wall. Screams followed the gunshot, almost as piercing to his ears as the sounds of the gun's report. The rest of the Orangeshirts in the factory laughed loudly at the murderous inside joke. Then there was more muffled shouting as the outdoor Orangeshirt exercised rights given to him by his station and his weapon. The fact that Dunne could hear that over the sound of the machinery that pulled the nets was impressive.

Two more shots rang out, and the Orangeshirt returned, his shirt spattered with a muddy red. He pulled two more workers from the line and forced them outside to drag the remains of his exercise in power to the rending pile down by the water to be washed out by the tides. Dunne knew exactly what was going on without turning his head to look. It was spectacle that was repeated often enough to have lost its inherent shock value. Human life reduced to its lowest value was no longer worthy of any attention, let alone the outrage that the loss of it should have provoked. Dunne was incapable of outrage and numb to death.

He looked up from the line moving along in front of him again only to check the time. The clock on the wall was yellow. He thought it seemed yellow. But in the low light, it was almost greenish-yellow. Dunne and the others had to be careful of leaving before it was fully green. If it was still only partly green, they would receive hurtful shocks through the metal grates in the floor. Dunne had only done it once.

It was one of the few things he could fully remember. The clock looked fully green that day, but it wasn't. He left his work station early. The initial shock administered to him caused his leg muscles to spasm and drop his body fully onto the electrified floor. The rest of the alternating current cycling shocks either pushed him into unconsciousness or erased his memory, he did not know which. The next thing he could remember after the intensely painful shock was lying soaked in his own urine on the metal floor grate and feeling burned bodily from the inside out. It was dark. Yellow was the rot brought up in the nets as well as the color of work, but that day yellow was also the opening of pain that led to red. The red spots in his vision and the taste of blood in his mouth as he blacked out. From the redness of the pain and the darkness of the environment now came first the green of the clock. He was still facing the clock and it was unmistakably green. None of his fellow workers remained. They had all left the processing plant, some of them stepping over his shuddering, convulsing body as if it were only so much of the same garbage that littered the concrete and asphalt outside. The third color he remembered from that day was orange. It was the Orangeshirts that came for him and lifted him out of the stench of the brine-soaked plastic and his own urine.

After that day, he learned to stay where he was on the line well beyond the changing of the clock's color. Dunne waited until others left the line first. They were all slow, all uncertain if the green on the clock was green enough. They went out through the cleansing chlorine showers again, just like the processed meats that were shipped from across the sea for consumption. The showers became standard practice after it was discovered that bacteria from the polluted things pulled from the nets was killing nearly fifteen percent of the workforce in any given fiscal year. After the clock was safely green, the line of exiting workers would spread wearily out from the sorting factory to return to their company housing across the square or to the hive above the factory.

Dunne, like all the rest of the workers, was in debt to their company due to the high cost of their housing and their company-provided sustiwafers. Everything that they wore or ate was provided by the corporation in its own benevolent fashion — but it all came at a cost. Just like the telescreen projections and entertainment on the walls of their dens and sleep pods. Nothing that held value was available for free.

All employees were housed on the manufacturing site to increase shareholder profit through lease debt. They were in a state of near constant default on their leases, and the company exercised the right to charge them daily penalties with interest to drive their accounts even further into arrears. Employees didn't work for pay, they worked against their debt to the company.

Their living quarters were called "dens" or "hives." They were petrofiberboard constructions with walls made of compressed shredded plastics which were unfit for other reclamation projects, but the walls bled grease and stank of dirty oil. The dens were shabby and shallow buildings built with honeycombed sleep creches embedded lengthwise into the walls and centered by a communal bathroom and dining unit with a rubbish burning incinerator to provide heat and cooking services. They sat within the foundations of older buildings that had been destroyed or deconstructed in days gone by.

A licensed vendor might set up shop using the cooking surfaces to warm sausage-like tubes of shadowy rank-smelling meat encased in edible plastic. This rendered the food-preparation spaces unusable by the tenants, but given that most of them ate cold processed carbohydrate mush or the sustiwafers from the company store, there was little need of the warming plates. The venders had the ability to charge tenant's imbedded ChipIns in exchange for the warm sustenance. It provided the only warm food on chilly nights when the winds from the east swept the refuse from the otherwise barren hills of the city.

The ChipIns were a necessity of the times. They were cheaper, simpler and smaller than the chips implanted in the higher social classes — a descendent of the old RFID chips of times past. The President for Life had told them all that financial fraud was too easily perpetrated, so the ChipIn was embedded as part of the personal identification debt program for the working class. Wealthier citizens received the ChipIns as a class rite of initiation. Workers saw it as a necessary pain they traded for survival. The ID program meant that terrorists and domestic dangers could be tracked and processed early on — people who were deemed greater risks for terrorist behavior like immigrants or non-natives were swiftly arrested and processed before their anti-social behavioral tendencies could fully manifest. The authorities no longer waited for potential criminal behavior before taking action.

Dunne walked from the factory into the fading daylight, squinting into the sun setting over the murky lowland slums to the west. The large city to the west beyond the poorest areas, built over a dark pool thousands of years ago had been partly overwhelmed by that dark pool as the polar regions melted during the years of forever summer. The sun burned hotly even through the smoke and mist that lingered when the seaside winds weren't blowing. The sting of the chemical showers still numbed him slightly and he blinked rapidly to clear the rheum from his eyes. A whirlwind of dust spun and eddied over the broken pavement and rippled the banner of the President for Life that hung on the side of the hive under the color clock. Shortly, it would show blue again, and everyone would know that it was time to rest a short night before they awoke once more to its changing colors which signaled the start of the next workday.

The hive that Dunne and the other workers lived in had once been a grocery store with a parking level beneath it in the days long before any of them could remember. It was a shelter of plenty in the days before the President for Life came to global power, but it was reduced now to a den of cold, miserable hunger on top of the rending factory it housed.

Dunne's belly rumbled. It was the rule of the land that no worker ever got enough food to fill their bellies, and none were ever allowed to be comfortable. The people had to stay hungry and uncomfortable, or else they'd have no reason to commit themselves to a life of unceasing work. People who struggle to live are people who are willing to fight each other to live, and the struggle for the scraps that trickled down from the wealthy was the rule. Conflict made the ruling class rich, and their wealth was the only thing that mattered. There would never be enough of that zero-sum commodity of quality living to be shared with the poor and the debted.

Dunne was fortunate to have the hive for shelter. He saw many people living without the same resources. There was the class of unhoused who had exhausted their debt ratings and were too much at risk of defaulting, thus costing the banks or businesses more than they could profit by employing or sheltering them. They lived among the ruins, scavenging subsistence off the wasted leavings of the wealthy owner class. Even though people starved, there was always so much waste left behind by the wealthy. The workers still believed in the myth of upward class mobility. That kept the workers inside dedicated to the task of maintaining access to debt acquisition. Their dedication ensured profit for the owners of the banks and the corporations who controlled everything. Dunne and the others still needed their jobs, lest they be allowed even less than their meager existence.

The former grocery store that had become their hive was less inviting than a rodent cage, but it operated as a giant Skinner Box with the clock lights on the walls. As Dunne and his shift entered every day, another shift filed out in the other direction with the changing of the clocks. They shared their bunks, sleeping in shifts, each bed space filled with the sweat and unwashed stink of the others who shared them. There was no privacy. Every nook and cranny of the building was filled with dank bodily odors and sounds. Dunne never slept well.

He was always hunched with fatigue. No one sane could find rest.

Unrested people were unhappy people, and unhappy people were better consumers. They would consume more distractions to escape unhappiness. The key was to keep a perfect balance where they were distracted from their misery, but too distracted to learn to do anything about it. That was all that mattered in their engineered society.

*"The tragedy of egalitarianism is how
brief it was in any society: like a firefly
seeking a mate before it was crushed
by a speeding auto windshield."*
Making the World Move
Hussein Al-Hassan

IV

Nix may have been a mid-level Orangeshirt at the factory on the river, but he was on his way up. He lived like most childless Orangeshirts his age, in a spartan barracks that was full of sweat, noise, and other men. Orangeshirts were afforded more comforts than the average citizen: one of those important comforts being personal space. Each man had nearly unlimited space to share within the barracks compared to the claustrophobic walled hives the workers lived in.

The economics of the island's system were kinder to the wealthy. Like the factory workers, their health was left to the free market, but Orangeshirts had access to better priced drugs and health centers. Nix's lower debt burden allowed him a sense of freedom not allowed to the wage-serfs on the factory floor because they kept him floating near an economic level where he could actually see the principal on his debt decrease when he wanted it to.

Nix worked long shifts, but fewer than the factory rats. His job controlling the factory workers was easy in relation to theirs. Victimhood was their lot in life. He knew how fortunate he was to be a part of the managing class, even though he didn't understand how his society worked. He couldn't see the lives of the people above him who pulled his strings, but he could watch the reality programs on the telescreen that showed

29

him the best parts of their pampered existence. He knew with certainty that he wasn't on the bottom rung, and that was truly all that mattered to him.

His father's status gave him more freedom than the average guard. Most days Nix was stationed outside the main door of his factory. It was a preferred post because it freed the Orangeshirts from the dank rank of the inside with its festering buckets of salvage from the drag nets and the near combustible heat that the line pickers worked in during the summer months. From his position outside the door, he could still see two large projected telescreens across the square. They mostly displayed a rotating series of product adverts, but during the afternoon shift they also flashed scenes from the leading sporting and sex programs from the night before as a way to entice viewers to watch again the next night. His personal pocket screen was in his locker. Not even the Orangeshirts were allowed to use them on the job. He watched the screens and scratched his scar absent-mindedly.

The job was still boring to Nix. Everything was boring. There were times when he tried new things, new drinks, new stims, new women... but the fun never lasted long. Things never felt as good as a they should have, never as good as they looked on the telescreen. And they never lasted as long as he wanted them to. That was why he began taking the stims during his guard shifts. They sped things up.

When he felt unwell, he knew exactly how to change it. He knew that he was no one's victim. He had no idea what privilege was, but he was the closest to privilege that almost anyone born on the island would ever be. Nix preferred the cheaper, bootleg stims available on the black market. They made him feel just as good as the others from the online stores, but the extra added feeling of acting in defiance and breaking free from the constraints of order was a high that he was also addicted to. He didn't realize that he was getting extra additives that weren't sanctioned or monitored by the manufacturers in his stim packets, which meant that he was as likely to get rat droppings or detergent as he was to get his stimulants. He didn't care regardless, so long as he felt the way he wanted to. Either way, the black market stims gave him a high that was preferable to the regulation packets available — probably due to those custom additives. His stomach rumbled as he stood guard at the door. He looked from one large telescreen on the square to the other. It wasn't long until he could eat.

He had access to all of the processed foodstuffs he could ever want, boxes and bags of processed bars and packaged meals awash in salt and sugar — the only catch was that he was expected to remain stable in his debt scores. Orangeshirts had to keep their monthly debts between one hundred to one hundred and thirty percent of their monthly income. That meant that his spending had to slightly outstrip his earning as a junior Orangeshirt. They always had to incur debt at a constant, controlled rate. Whenever they earned raises for promotions, they also earned the requirement to spend more to maintain their debt profile and power. It was an ideal arrangement because it recognized the nature of the addictions that saturated the culture, as well as the cost to satisfy those addictions without breaking or destroying the citizen who held them. As soon as the need or hunger was sated, it grew to new outsize proportions for the next round. Every man, no matter his position in society, was expected to allow his gratified desires to outstrip his means in just the proper measure.

It wasn't difficult for Nix because his spending was tracked and the offers made available to him were balanced to keep him just within the debt threshold established for his rank. He was tracked through the ChipIn and the offers were personalized for his desires and addictions. The creditors discovered decades ago that too great a debt burden caused by addictions run wild incited some in the management caste to exercise their frustrations destructively on the working caste. Too many workers died during that fiscal period to maximize profits per shareholder. It wasn't just the violence of the Orangeshirts. Citizens who felt too overwhelmed and hopeless about their debt tended toward suicide instead of simply working longer and harder. Debt opportunities were fine-tuned by the banks through the monitoring of the ChipIns. The financial chains had to weigh the workers down, but not crush them to suffocation under their weight. A certain kind of cultural hypoxia was necessary to keep them gasping for air and unable to think deeply. The empire was dependent on people who would believe what they were told by celebrities, and the leader was the greatest celebrity who had ever lived.

Nix had grown up immersed in a sea of faces, bodies, and guns on flashing screens. His religion was the one that had come from across the sea: one part celebrity worship and one part evangelical Christianity. His mother was a woman who engaged in Orwellian "doublethink." She believed that women had no rights, but that other women had fewer rights than her. The middle caste privilege she exercised was not shared with lower caste women. In the mathematics of humanity, she believed herself exceptional, but they were "less than."

Nix's mother was married off to an Orangeshirt with power because his power protected her from other men. It was the best marriage that her parents could buy for her. She knew that men with power had the right and the authority to do whatever they wanted with her whenever it was convenient to them, unless another powerful man could stop them. She was the white daughter of an Orangeshirt Chaplain who married another Orangeshirt Chaplain. She dyed her dark hair blonde daily and used the orangest skin creams she could. She also spit on the lower caste women begging for scraps outside the factories when she traveled to her own job as a corporate social media influencer. She made photos and videos in the most scenic locations available to promote goods and services in exchange for free things that did not affect her credit score.

Nix could remember that his mother sometimes experienced bouts of incoherence and an inability to walk. When he was a wee cub, he didn't know that she was drunk. He would never know that she often drank while he was in utero. It was a habit expected of a woman of her caste. She asked for a snifter of whiskey when she delivered a boy with small, widely-spaced eyes and a flat face bearing a short upturned nose. Nix's father didn't see him for his first week. He was on holiday with one of his mistresses.

Healthy, live births were already a rarity, and Nix's was certainly was unexpected, but his features were merely regarded as a progression of his own family's ongoing genetic inheritance. After all, his father had small wide set eyes and a flat face, and his mother had a small, upturned nose and a thin upper lip with a wide philtrum. Such features were considered desirable and attractive among the Orangeshirts and the people they lorded over.

Nix was colicky. In his infancy Nix cried unless his mother rubbed a bit of whiskey on his lips and gums. She traded his adult problem-solving ability for his immediate quiet by dosing him with alcohol until he stopped crying. The only faces he could remember from his childhood beside the President for Life who visage was on every screen were those of his mother and his father, in that order. The former, because it meant food, and the latter because it meant pain.

Later, this sometimes violent boy grew into a teen with no impulse control, poor judgement, and a tendency toward violent rage. He was normal. Nix was often coddled by his mother, but he was as often beaten — because to spare the rod would spoil the child, and spoiling the child would spare the rod that was given by the Lord for ensuring righteousness. The rod was more than a simple parental right, it was an obligation. Rods were used to make blades and arrows for the righteousness of the Lord and his ruler on earth. Nix was a blade, forged against the anvil of existence where his cruelty and ignorance were blended by hammer until he emerged a brittle razor-sharp bludgeon of willfully belligerent violence to be wielded by others in the interest of power.

He matriculated early into the ranks of the Orangeshirts because of his father, but his inability to follow even the most basic of orders from his higher officers and his desire for violence for its own sake marked him as one who would forever remain below the office of those who pulled the puppet strings and manipulated matters of local governance. He couldn't be a Chaplain. Chaplains were rods who shaped and directed the blades.

Nix didn't know it, but he was trapped as a lower level member of the Orangeshirts unless someone with more influence lifted him up. He needed someone to push him to the top, but he had little to offer in return to anyone who might promote him. His current position was one he achieved by simply being born to his parents. The Orangeshirts, pawns as they were, had no meaningful political or economic strength — but they were useful interlocutors between the powerful and the powerless. They held the space between those families who held true power and the 99 percent whose labor powered their neo-feudal aristocracy. Nix and his parents believed that they did have control and power, but theirs was a useful delusion taught and reinforced through the telescreen by their own puppet masters whom they admired and loved.

Nix lived in a world where his immediate wants were gratified so he could be more easily manipulated, but only if they did not conflict with those of his betters who controlled him. He had *some* illusion of choice. He "chose" not to participate in the forced education of his age cohort, so he was allowed to be home schooled as the children of Orangeshirts often were. His father ignored him unless he needed to be beaten, and his mother ignored him beyond schooling unless she needed him. His fortune and destiny were written by people who didn't know he existed as an individual, but who nonetheless molded him and the men of his caste into perfect tools for controlling others.

At fourteen, Nix was still illiterate, but reading wasn't needed for his place in the world. It meant little in a society that was built entirely upon the lower class's ability to do what the screen told it to do and to think what the screen told it to think. Yet, very little was denied to him beyond love and affection, and despite his learning deficits he learned the boundaries about what could and could not be his after relatively few corrective beatings. Most of the beatings from his father that he endured simply had no lesson in them besides teaching him that violence was a useful means of control.

He joined the Patriot Scouts, the children's version of the Orangeshirts, and made his name quickly by using violence against his peers. Typically young men (even sons of Orangeshirts) had a three-year period of duty in the scouts to determine candidacy for becoming an Orangeshirt officer at the age of sixteen. Nix took only two.

His brutal bearing and his lack of empathy made him a prime candidate for early matriculation into the ranks of the adult Orangeshirts, and he moved quickly ahead at a young age. He was the human equivalent of a hurley used to settle disputes in the back alley — a violent bludgeon without remorse or care. His superiors learned to simply point him at an object or a person and tell him what to make it do. As long as it was only a one or two step process, he executed orders efficiently and with no small amount of visible glee when his orders demanded violence. When orders had more than two steps, he would short-circuit and shut down, growing more and more frustrated until he lashed out at those nearest to him. His masters learned to use his tendency for frustrated violence as a tool. Nix didn't care. He couldn't imagine any further than his next moment of gratification.

The Orangeshirt barracks that Nix lived in were similar to living quarters for anyone else who lacked the means to bootstrap themselves into the upper class, but they contained slightly more square footage. Physical space denoted power and social status. Those with more had more. The Orangeshirts, like those beneath them, had no way to know what they were missing beyond what they were sold on the telescreen. Those who ruled them from above made sure to keep the depraved depths of their extravagant lifestyles a sheltered secret from anyone with the eyes to be more envious of the freedoms that wealth granted them. They lived on the opposite side of towering walls in enclaves built by mountains of money meant to seal them off from the cares, concerns, and contempt of the worm-like masses that sustained their lives of excess through mindless work and existential drudgery. The illusory lifestyle options of the wealthy (promiscuous sex with beautiful slaves of questionable maturity, lavish parties, amazing technological toys) were dangled in front of the unwashed masses on the telescreen, but were always just beyond their poor, unprivileged reach.

Nix and his ilk were the small end of a ball peen hammer. He was the blunt force used to shape the people below him. Ultimately, there was nothing exceptional about him. He was just another tool in the box. The wealthy were the machinists. The media they controlled were the hands that wielded the blunt or sharp objects. Nix and the Orangeshirts were simple tools, and people like Dunne were part of the raw materials that were worked into profit.

Nix's rending factory was near the dark pool on the river at the city center. Its location made for easy disposal of manufacturing wastes, and his home was a common one shared with hundreds of other Orangeshirts on the north side of the river in a former military barracks and museum. He crossed over the river in the single passenger autocab that he rented daily for transport. Autocabs powered by burning plastic resins from the rending factories ran the streets picking up riders and charging credits, belching black particulate smoke behind them. It was a short ride through the crowded and filthy streets and over the toll bridge where Nix was automatically charged against his account again, but it was usually enough time to watch a quick recap episode of his favorite telly program that focused on barely clad women frolicking on a beach. Each viewing added to the cost of the trip, so getting to the factory was a costly affair. But Nix hated boredom as much as he hated dark-skinned people, so the charges were worth it to him. The single seat car whizzed past the tourists and locals alike on the route. It could have run them down and he would have had no cognition of the event, so absorbed in the screen was he.

Then the likeness of Saint Paddy flashed at him to thank him for choosing Saint Paddy's brand cab lines and using his PaddyPay account on his ChipIn to pay his fare, fees, and toll. Nix was a Paddy fan. He'd loved the telescreen character as a child and was conditioned to continue to spend credits when he saw his likeness on any product or service.

Saint Paddy was a right proper religious prophet, a profitable icon of the grace of the great leader from across the sea, the Lord's chosen vessel of righteousness. He had the same orange complexion and blonde hair as so many celebrities and powerful people that Nix saw. Nix wanted to be like Saint Paddy and all the other celebrities: rich and famous, loved, adored, and emulated by millions. Nix already spent credit debt to buy the orange paste that he put on his face every morning before work. He gazed into the mirror of his dark reflection on the telescreen as he smoothed it into his pores. He looked stronger and more confident when he was as orange and blond as his role models. He smiled back at himself as he rubbed the whitening cream on his teeth that burned his gums and made them bleed if left on too long.

Nix's job at the factory was simple. Some days he sat on a chair viewing a bank of telescreen monitors watching the factory. Other days he guarded a door. In either place, his job was to prevent the workers inside from taking rest. He was the human link in the chain because he was cheaper than the AI, and people like him needed tasks to keep them occupied lest it occur to them how miserable they may actually be.

Nix didn't know much, but he knew who he was superior to. Knowing well as he did which of the moving, living objects before him were human gave Nix freedom that other people couldn't even conceptualize. He could do almost anything as an Orangeshirt, given that there were rarely any other humans to consider. True freedom lay in not giving a damn about the sub-humans that surrounded him, and Nix was free.

Nix's days never changed. The Orangeshirts imagined they were the very important "cogs" that the machines of society ran on, but "wheels" would have been more apt. They were the contact point on the "pavement" that was the workers. They were chewed up by the rough, patchwork surface and were often replaced because they were made to be worn down. The workers were the raw material that generated capital for the factory owners. They lived in a world where those with a particular taste for power and dominion over others floated higher in the water that drowned so many others because they were willing to stand on the bodies of the drowned.

Nix returned to his barracks across the river after every shift. It was cramped and filthy, but not to the degree of the worker hives. He had access to better quality foodstuffs — but the quarters and the food were incidental to the enjoyment of the job. The true draw was the power over others. That was the part that Nix particularly relished. Enduring the practiced cruelty of superiors was a small part of the cost of being a citizen of the island state. Nix accepted the cruelties because he had the power to pass them down on others. Then one day, Nix's pattern of life began to fall to pieces.

Nix had been invited to a party at the old lodge once in the mountains above the city, called "The Hellfire Club." He had gone there, traveling in the back of a small cargo van with a dozen other off-duty Orangeshirts. Their post commander called it a "bonding" — a team-building exercise. He provided several liters of muddy brown and yellowish liquors to them and sent them with two of their commanding managers to bond over their shared supremacy above the workers.

Nix drank two of the bottles himself that night, without the help of his peers. He remembered only bits and pieces after the first bottle. The rest was a haze of vomit and violence.

There were chanting and name calling, provocation, mockery and threats of violence. All of the usual initiation rituals of their cultic existence. After they were drunk, then occurred the Orangeshirt ritual of truth sharing: a dare contest where each member of the group tried to outdo the others in telling horrific things they had done. Every single man tried to outdo the last barbarism divulged to the group by another.

The alcohol made everyone feel at ease, as if it were a great and righteous unloading of unfortunate truths. These rituals built with alcohol and humiliation built trust among the members of the Orangeshirts, established camaraderie and forged bonds of shared experiences among the men who had committed acts of incest, rape, murder, or theft during their formative years. It was an act of confession that wasn't led by a priest, and there were no acts of contrition to make amends to their sallow, obese-faced God from across the ocean. These acts of violence would have been proscribed in another age before cruelty became ascendant, but now they were social currency, and the repetition of the acts in story form gave power whereas previously it would have brought only shame.

"I robbed from a grocer."

"I took my little sister to bed."

"I raped my neighbor in front of his wife."

"I killed every dog in the village."

It didn't matter if their statements were true or not. Each gave the person who committed the acts a form of enhanced social currency among the group. Before long, they were all piss drunk and shouting to outdo one another. They were going further and further which each declaration: incest, rape, and animal cruelty were merely the start, and each man had a litany of accomplishments that should have made the perpetrator blush in shame, if not collapse in painful regret, and cause the audience to shun them or even to call for their imprisonment. Shame did not exist outwardly among these men, even if some semblance of the feeling still existed internally. Those feelings were redirected and focused outward in an expression of violence.

The men toasted each other's horrific acts and each admission brought forth another. It was the most awful drinking game ever invented, but it validated their cruelty and their hatred. The gathering was a good analogy for the rest of Nix's life. Drunkenness, violence, feelings of camaraderie between the men, followed by a reward for horrible acts, then the repetition of said cruel acts, then the duplication of the whole cycle ad infinitum until death.

Nix was pulled in a spiral that moved in only one direction, and each day diminished his already significant lack of humanity. He was not aware of that loss in any meaningful way. An outside observer could have looked at his life and seen it for what it was, but Nix had as much ability to see himself from the outside as he had to empathize with the workers whose lives he was employed to control: None.

It was after the night at the Hellfire Club on the hill that Nix began to notice more people than average becoming ill around him. It may have been spreading before that, but he didn't notice. Nix's view of the world was very myopic and narrow. If something did not entertain him, he did not attend to it.

When Nix left for the city after the partisan party on the hill, he had a hang-over that bordered on alcohol poisoning. Neither he nor any of his mates had been cautious in their consumption. Two of them that he barely knew had not yet awoken in the scene of the drunken debauch. They laid face down in beds of cold vomit and Nix didn't know or care if they would wake. He had to get back.

Once he got back to his home factory, he noticed that the Orangeshirts weren't the only ones who were moving more slowly and with more problems than usual. Many of the workers looked like they had gotten into some cheap, semi-poisoned drink as well. They were slow to move in work and the Orangeshirts — dulled by their own excesses were slow to punish that day. But then when the dullness of his excesses washed away, he noticed that some of the workers were falling down. They seemed to be on a deleterious progression of that state over the day even as some of his Orangeshirt mates' violent attacks on the workers were progressing upward. As the violence increased, the workers slowed even more and were less able to rise from their beatings.

Usually the workers responded positively to the violence in the form of closer adherence to the task before them and increased speed, but that day took shape in the exact opposite fashion. By afternoon, the workers could no longer return to their feet after being knocked down. Nix stood guard over the remaining workers while three of the soon-to-be corpses were dragged down to the river's edge to die. It was the normal thing to do: throw garbage in the water. And these workers were already less than human, barely removed from garbage on their best days by Nix's estimation.

Near the end of the work shift, the first Orangeshirt went down. He was guarding the open door to the outside where some of the Orangeshirts took their cigarette breaks. Nix watched him throughout the day from his position in the factory. He started out standing with a heavy slouch at his post. Then before mid-day, he was leaning against the door in defiance of basic orders. The commanding Orangeshirt paid him no heed though, because he was also suffering the after effects of the night drinking on the hill.

As the light on the clock shifted to release the workers, the man by the door slumped to the floor, his back sliding down the door and wiping a smudge clean with the sweat that had soaked though the back of his uniform. He was gasping and wheezing for breath, but as soon as he dropped to his haunches, he started coughing. They were full body coughs, the likes of which Nix could not recall seeing. The man gasped for breath on his knees and then fell forward onto his face.

Nix laughed at the ridiculousness of the sight. An Orangeshirt on his face in the mud and garbage! Nix didn't understand irony, but even if he had, he wouldn't have appreciated that he had been an Orangeshirt face down in the mud the night before. A black-out was simply something that came along with the drinking for him; it was all a part of the fun. Perhaps this man who looked to be drunk on the floor by the door was simply taking his own fun "too far." Nix didn't like that phrase. It felt like an excuse to be weak.

Outside, many of the workers had left the shop and the hive altogether at the end of the shift and were hovering in small groups, looking down the river and out to the sea. It was low tide, so the ruins of many buildings were visible in the garbage shallows of the river, flirting with the ripples.

His own shift over, Nix returned to his barracks, where he shared a large space across the street from a plasticine clothing manufactory in a den that was once a building supply store. Each man had an individual bunk, and there were enough telescreens spread throughout the building that each of the popular channels were all playing simultaneously in a shrill cacophony of noise. It could be overwhelming for others living there, but Nix had no problems getting to sleep with a handful of downers that he picked up from an old pub and drug den downtown. It was just one of the many pills that he and the others took to alleviate the daily symptoms of being human.

His drug and medicine regimen was unregulated. The laws were sponsored by the pharmaceutical conglomerate owned by one of the president's many descendants. Their commercials were shown constantly as backdrops of the celebrity reality shows on the telescreens. He couldn't avoid the adverts for Nightol, even though he and the rest of the crew were already on it. When they awoke in the morning, it wasn't to the island's famous "fry" breakfast, it was instead to a cocktail of low-grade amphetamines that gave energy and a craving for more of the same.

Each night, they cleaned their teeth with a jelly paste that was sweeter than any of the "fizzies" or candies that they consumed regularly. It whitened their teeth and made their gums bleed. They took uppers to wake, downers to sleep. Penis pills to give them erections. They took laxatives to make them defecate and anti-diarrheals to stop their bowels from gushing, anti-psychotics to drown out the voices in their heads and hallucinogens so they could dream an internal monologue. The older Orangeshirts took the same pills and slathered their testicles with testosterone salve, but they found that doubling or even tripling the testosterone replacement was necessary to achieve the desired physical effect because of the estrogenic plasticine chemicals bleeding into their food from packaging. A good many of the Orangeshirts that reached their fourth decade without taking enough of the blue and orange pills grew protuberant breasts. Nix suspected his own father of hiding breasts in a plastic girdle under his clothing.

Drugs and their side effects were nothing new to Nix and his cohort. They'd been steeped in pharmaceutical drugs since they floated peanut-sized in their mother's amniotic fluid. From birth they were constantly assailed by adverts for every conceivable "cure" as the telescreen had taken over early for the crib mobiles or any kind of involved creche care. It was simply cheaper to lay every infant down under a flashing screen than it was to pay a caregiver to watch over them while their mothers were at work.

Nix's mind had been bought and sold since well before he had ever conceived of having a mind. Every child in the state was a subject of propaganda from the womb to the tomb. They were told exactly what they should think and feel about every potential topic of thought, even their own self-images. Every human on the island was a constructed product created to be consumed by someone or something else.

Nix took some of his pills, doubled his sleeping ration and laid down on his mattressed bunk cot. Even though he was nodding off, his erection throbbed in his pants from the pills. He considered masturbating there in the crowded barracks before passing out into a deep and dreamless slumber.

He awoke two minutes late the next morning. Late because he had forgotten to set his own alarm on his pocket screen and late because it took his three closest healthy bunkmates ninety seconds to fill their long tube socks with assorted objects hard enough to beat him into wakefulness. They hooted like bonobos in a mating frenzy as they pummeled him before and after he rolled over instinctively to protect his head and begged them to stop. One of the first blows had been struck to his scrotum, and he was unaware at how lucky he was that his semi-rigid penis had protected his testicles from the full force of their wake up call.

That morning, nine of the fifteen Orangeshirts assigned to their factory didn't report for duty. Several of the workers didn't come in either. They would be dealt with later. Nix and the remaining Orangeshirts had to make sure that production went on as scheduled.

A newsflash came across the telescreen shortly after the start of the shift, but it gave a very incomplete picture of events transpiring outside his small, confined environment. The orange blonde woman on the telescreen with her breasts nearly fully bared assured viewers that a handful of workers across different factories around the island were "demonstrating a poor work ethic" and needed to "pull themselves by their bootstraps," and that due to lowered overhead costs, the number of Orangeshirts deployed to certain factories would be lowered. No one questioned it.

The day after, almost no one showed for work, but Nix was not nonplussed. There was always something that he could do. He picked up his rifle from the armory that morning, along with his allotment of bullets and walked out to the street. He slotted the clip of bullets into the gun and took aim at the side of the building. It was already collapsing. There was no penalty for vandalizing it. He fired his weapon into the crumbling bricks. The shots echoed. He thought it was someone else shooting at him and he dropped to the ground in shock. He'd never heard an echo before.

When he realized that there was no one else around him, he emptied his weapon into the rubble. The bullets were his to shoot. He was given new ones every day as part of his rations, and there was no point in saving them. Shooting at other Orangeshirts was forbidden, as long as there was a superior to report to. Nix looked around. He was alone.

It was never quiet enough until now to hear the sounds of echoes off the metal and stone structures that surrounded him. It wasn't until then that he noticed that the traffic that generally zoomed past on the road by the riverside was much diminished. The light rail line that ferried the tourists up and down the coast was quiet as well. It was an eerie sort of quiet, but the high strangeness of it wasn't the thing that struck him. It was simply the lack of noise. He was accustomed to the constant cacophony and struggle of society as a soundtrack to his existence. The sound of men subduing other men and nature was the ambient noise. Its absence was a vacuum that threatened to suck something else in to replace it, something alien. Something dangerous.

V

Dunne felt worse than normal at the end of his gruelingly boring work shift at the plant. He slunk back to his honeycomb pod and drifted off to sleep. When the alarm called him back to work that next day, he was too weak to respond. A virus or something from the sea nets had gotten into him. He was going to be charged credits for time missed on the line, but it was insufficient motivation to overcome the sickness, and he remained prone and listless despite the insistent rhythmic alarm shocks applied for two minutes through the filament wires woven into his bunk pad. He lay in a daze pondering his own mortality and the world that he lived in.

He felt so sick. He wondered if he had cancer. Dunne knew that cancer was in his future. It was as inevitable as aging. Everyone got it — some sooner, some later. There was no avoiding it and no one knew exactly why, but they all accepted it as a simple fact of life. They were told that it was God's punishment for sin, but it was still hard to make the connection between sin and cancer. What was a sin, and what wasn't? How were the wealthy and the the powerful who never got cancer so perfectly without sin? Some of them actually had multiple children from different wives or mistresses. It was public knowledge. It seemed to Dunne that some sins were simply a matter of social class, like so many other privileges that he observed. Children could be a product of sin, or a reward of virtue, but he couldn't imagine how the people who had them could tell the one from the other.

The sleeping pods were segregated by sex. No women were allowed in this part of the den. Their spaces were even smaller, due to their smaller bodies, and tucked in the other side of the building. In the days that Dunne knew, the women he worked among didn't have children. Fertility was a fragile gift not often blessed upon those near the bottom of the status quo. Neither was athletic skill or ability, those things that in the past had given some from the underclass an opportunity to rise out of their accidents of birth. Like children, those things had become the providence of the blessed — the same as their wealth, their property, their homes, their tools, and their technology. Dunne never got to see their things or their events, except on the telescreen. He never had God's favor. Now he felt he was being punished by the divine power and couldn't understand why. Wasn't his life suffering enough?

He could see the telescreen in the common room from his sleep pod. A sporting event was on. Dunne stared at the screens as vacantly as anyone else at the sporting events. It was often the only escape available from the drudgery of work. The brightly colored players, clad head to toe in adverts, flooded onto the playing field, each clutching his own oxygen breather. There were those who could remember when the iOlympics took place outdoors and athletes competed in clear, clean air without needing bottled oxygen and bronchial relaxants, but Dunne had never watched sports competitions on the telescreen without seeing the performance enhancements go hand in hand with the competition. They were as much a part of every sport as sponsorship logos and protective padding. All of the iOlympics and other athletic competitions took place indoors in climate controlled domes named for corporate sponsors but paid for by the payroll deducted taxes of workers like Dunne. The athletes were genetically-crafted and drug-honed human anomalies who wore their own corporate sponsorships on their model-perfect faces while they spouted professionally machine-crafted word memes for products at every interview. Every two minutes, the game was paused so the athletes on the field could promote all of the products that gave them a winning edge or provided their spectacular look and performance.

Now he couldn't breathe. He wondered how much further into debt he'd have to go to get his own bottled oxygen. He couldn't afford the brand the athletes used anyway, not unless he could get a corporate sponsorship, and certainly the factory wouldn't sponsor him as a no-show on a work day. His mind drifted over the facts of the world as he descended into a state of fevered delirium.

The nation was a corporation and each corporation was an individual — with lawfully protected voting rights. Dunne didn't know that, but he was suspicious of the rules behind the facade of lawful society. They were the props under the mirrors which combined with the media smokescreen to keep eyes off the maneuverings and the manipulations that supported the neo-feudalistic market world that he existed in.

He certainly didn't experience the rules of life in a manner he comprehended as manipulation. He felt them differently, as if possessing an awareness deep in his genetic memory.

He rolled in the sheets, tearing and fraying them more in his fever. He could not remember his childhood; or at least that which he remembered was not what people considered a childhood. Trauma, stress and electrical shocks had erased large swathes of his memory. He remembered working in the factory when he was much smaller. His earliest memories had been of sorting waste plastic to be reused or burned for power generation in the factory itself. There were other things in the corners of his mind that sometimes revisited him in his sleep. Faces, feelings, events with no foundation in truth. They were neither the dreams he'd been told he could have, nor memories.

He remembered strange dreams of a woman who treated him with kindness and compassion, a woman who cared for him. He couldn't remember such a person in his waking life, and images of her were so indistinct and fuzzy. Such dreams do not materialize from nothing, though. Even a dream about monsters has to be spurred by a real event. Dunne had never even heard stories of a "mam" treating others with kindness and love. The mams of the stories on the telescreen were cruel and manipulative.

Once he heard in hushed tones from another fellow worker that she was worried that she might become a "mam" after being forced into copulation by an Orangeshirt who supervised the plastic reclamation factory. But a fullness in her belly turned out to be only a cancerous tumor, and she never delivered anything except blood that was a sign of her impending doom. Her hemorrhage lasted far longer than a few days and turned out to be a greater loss of blood than her body could survive.

She lay there upon those rocks outside for one more day after she ceased outward signs of life before a worker was forced at Orangeshirt gunpoint to drag her to the refuse pit for organic wastes. There she was composted. Four days were allowed to pass between being a human being and being a piece of discarded capital. He fought to concentrate through his fever: how long had he been here? Would they drag him to the refuse pits soon?

To Dunne, 'mam' should not have been a word that invoked a swollen, distended belly and an agonizing death on the rocks between the factory and the waterline where the woman was forcibly removed to from her sleeping dormitory and left to lie prone and moaning after she failed to report for two consecutive work shifts. In his mind though, the word brought forth the old dreams of comfort and kindness. Things he craved now as he became sicker and sicker.

There was something else in his head too, not a memory but another dark thing in the recesses of his senses. There was yet another "mam" hidden in the shadows that he could not drag into the light. It was something that he knew without knowing, in the same way that a trout knows how to navigate upstream to its breeding grounds. His illness deepened. He drifted in and out of delirium until his thoughts and memories felt alien.

He felt emotions that he could not possibly have known, but he had been taught for years not to trust his own inner monologue. Those thoughts drifted away from him, were disregarded and lay dormant in his skull until some experience triggered their reemergence into his waking world. They were difficult to disregard, but dismissal had gotten easier with practice, and now in his delirium things passed unrestricted to and fro through his brain. He drifted off into a fevered and dreamless state.

He woke from his stupor in the middle of his work shift and forced himself to slide out of his ragged covers onto the dirty floor. He could barely breathe and it was impossible to swallow. His lymph nodes had nearly closed off his throat and his nose dripped orange bloody mucus that had crusted over and closed off his nostrils. He crept awkwardly to the communal water font and tried to turn the tap on to get water. He found that his credit score was already too deep in the negative for missing work that day and the alarm over the font went off and flashed red. There would be no water for him. At least not from this font.

He smacked his dry lips and tried to use his tongue to push some moisture from his mouth to his lips, but they were already cracked, and his salivary glands had quit working. He weakly stumbled out the door of the hive and sat down on the dirt facing the filthy sea. All that water, and not a drop to drink. If the accumulated pollution wasn't enough to kill him, the salt content would. He tried to swallow what little saliva had formed in his mouth from the deeply humid air mass he breathed, and the effort brought an audible snap from his throat. It hurt worse than anything else he had imagined. He fell to the ground, broke into a breathless sucking sob and buried his head between his knees.

As Dunne sat in the filth near the water sobbing weakly, trying not to swallow for fear of choking, a hand lightly touched his shoulder. Or so he thought. He reacted quickly and turned to the touch as though stung, but there was nothing there. It was merely the wind kicking up as a brown misty squall swept in from the sea, disturbing the dust and the mud before unleashing a downfall of reddish-brown tinted rain upon his weary head and ragged clothes.

Dunne looked up at the clouds over the water. What kind of life was this? He was uniformly miserable, even when he wasn't ill. Being sick made everything feel so much worse. The wind off the water stank of benzene and crude oil. It burned his swollen throat. He couldn't help but begin to sob again — this time long, ragged, sucking breaths drew the miasma into him and caused him to fall into a coughing fit. His caustic coughs became more and more intense with each paroxysm and he doubled over in full-body spasms, writhing in the dirt. It pained him unimaginably.

Tears ran down his cheeks and collected the grime in narrow tracks. He wrapped his arms around himself to hold the racking cough that came between the sobs. The world grew dark and the raw, scraped, dry feeling in his throat spread into his chest. He couldn't take a full breath and started hyperventilating — a panic attack on the rocky refuse-strewn shore. He squeezed his eyes tightly shut and braced himself against the pain that convulsed his chest and throat. He wanted to die. Then darkness came over him fully and suddenly.

He didn't wake for a long time. He had no idea for how long a time. His eyes were crusted shut and his nose was filled with an earthy, musty scent. This place was warmer than his bed and smelled less like human waste, yet there was the unmistakably odor of humanness. He regained his dull sense of consciousness in the darkness every so often in his fits of coughing. Then he could feel a warm hand lift his chin and pour a hot liquid down his upturned throat. He'd choke and gag and swallow it painfully down and slip quickly away into the darkness of sleep again, warmed by the fluid. He felt heat on his dirty skin when his consciousness drifted back and forth near the surface, a warmth unlike the sun or the burning garbage he was accustomed to. His consciousness bobbed between wake and sleep like a piece of plastic trash floating on the sea. But, he was somewhere safe. He slept.

It could have been days or weeks when he finally rose back above the surface of his watery consciousness again. There were long periods of dreamless darkness and internal depths between having his head raised and a fiery tasting liquid poured into his swollen throat before he sank back down each time. This time, he brushed his eyes clear and he saw his location. As he slowly rose up from the depths of illness and unconsciousness to a bit of light in his physical environment, he saw something that he could not have imagined.

He was in a close, low-ceilinged space. The floor was worn, and walls of packed earth and stone stood just a few meters away from where he was lying on suspended frame of fabric. He was wrapped in a bundle of blankets and cloth that seemed to be a denser weave than he was accustomed to. He brushed his fingertips over the material next to his skin. It was soft and dense, thicker and softer than anything he had ever experienced. He was warm and comfortable. It then hit him: someone had been taking care of him.

His eyes adjusted and he was able to scan the space in the low diffused glow. It was much bigger than his sleeping space in the hive. He couldn't tell yet where the dim, hazy light was coming from. It suffused from everywhere — the surfaces, the air. His eyes couldn't yet find focus. He felt so warm, so perfectly wrapped in soft comfort. A wave of sleep overwhelmed him and he submerged into slumber again.

He rose gently and slowly toward the surface of wakefulness. When he emerged this time, he felt a presence in the chamber. He sensed its eyes upon him. He breathed deeply in the moist air, relishing the painless inhalation before he realized how different it was from his last clearly remembered breath. He opened his eyes to see a human-like shape peering at him in the low light from across the space. More light strangely seemed to be coming from its eyes. He stared at it, unblinking for a few moments before attempting to speak. His voice came out in a low croak, sounding like nothing so much as one of the long-gone amphibians of the old days. His coarsely-clad form resembled a toad in more than just voice.

His exhalation caught on phlegm in his throat and he started coughing and reflexively spit into a torn remnant of his old clothing clasped in his hand. He looked back up to the human shape a few feet away from him, and he felt a warm blush wash over his face.

Out of the human shape with eyes of light came a voice like nothing that he'd ever heard. He had heard rumors of outcasts from society, living in the undeveloped midlands of the island state, who spoke a different language, a "brogue" he'd heard the Orangeshirts call it. It was recognized by them and their kind as a provocation to administer a severe beating. It was a sign of the old ways, of a people they called "culchies," and of those people whose traditions had been purposefully washed away by the tide of progress brought about by the leader of the capitalist western world. Dunne held no such ill will toward the speaker who had saved his life.

The brogue said, "You should'ave died."

Dunne didn't know if the voice implied disappointment or surprise. He coughed again in the damp space. His throat felt new, as if it needed to stretch. The figure before him held out a large dusty glass bottle. The dim light diffused through the nearly clear liquid. Dunne looked at the outstretched arm, confused.

"Poitin," the brogue cracked at him.

He thirstily took the bottle without thinking and tipped it into his mouth, even though he didn't know what a Poitin was.

He gagged slightly at the taste, but recognized the feel on his lips as the bottle that he'd been fed from while he

59

lay in unconscious repose in this dark space. Sometimes it had held water, sometimes it held this potent stuff that flamed his throat and nose. He passed the bottle back to the figure. His throat burned.

His head swam from the contents that wet his throat and warmed his chest, but he took stock of his growing self-awareness. He was clad in a robe and covered with blankets of woven cloth fragments and soft, greasy sheep's wool. In the dim absence of light, it all looked brown or earthy green.

His sense of self was coming back through his skin. The warmth of his slumber receded and he felt the touch of the clothing and sensed a boundary of skin that he'd lost until that very moment. That skin felt more sensitive and alive than it had in memory. He could feel a hundred small knots in the regular pattern of the woven fabric up and down his arms, upon his chest and back. His feet and hands tingled warmly as if returning to life from a cold hibernation. His head felt light. Neurons that had been dead in the factory were coming back to life and throbbed inside his head like glowing, growing points of light. He flexed his hands, balling them into fists that cracked and then stretched the fingers. His body muscles popped and strained after a long slumber.

The person with the bottle stepped to the side and Dunne could see the low light of an irregularly shaped aperture from behind. Perhaps the light from the person's eyes had been a hallucination. He felt drawn toward the door and rose unsteadily to step toward it. The air now felt less stagnant and more mobile than when he had first awakened — he sensed light breezes upon his uncovered face. It moved in chill zephyrs that quickened his heartbeat. He pressed against an unfinished wooden door and stepped through the widely opening cracks into the light of day.

He blinked and adjusted his eyes to the new brightness of the outdoor sun. His steps were unbalanced, and he fumbled his way forward with difficulty. The murky, smoggy coast of the polluted sea that was the last thing he remembered seeing was now to his right. He could hear it. As his eyes adapted, he found that he stood on the side of a high spot, a cairn of ruins and stones. He shaded his eyes with his hand and turned again to face the sun. It was high in the east, indicating that late morning or early afternoon was upon him. The air felt warm and inviting. He heard shuffling behind him. He turned back to find there was nothing except boulders and ruined mounds of garbage. Wherever he had come from and whoever had helped him had disappeared.

Dunne felt energized in an odd way, yet he still wanted to close his eyes and return to the slumber of the dark, quiet space. He stood blinking in the light and was overcome by confusion as he sought to make sense of his recent memories. He didn't feel like he had climbed upwards even though he knew he had arisen up out of the earth, and he could see no caves or cairns from which he might have emerged. Wherever he had been was now gone. As the winds wound around him, he felt those healing moments from the warm place slipping away from him as if they were nothing more than the remnants of a fever dream.

His vision had adjusted well enough so he could now see the top of the building where he had lived and worked in the near distance to the south. He wondered if he was still dying on the shore and if everything since then was a hallucination. He kicked at a small stone amidst the plasticine garbage by his foot and felt the pain ring through his weak shoes, into his toe, and up his shin. Wherever he had been, if he had been in a dream, he wasn't dreaming now. The pain was real.

His head became light and began to swim again. He felt himself bobbing as if floating in that debris-filled sea. The bottle he was given must have held some powerful drug — that "poitin" the woman had called it. Yes, he thought now, it must have been a woman. He sat down on the rocks from which he had emerged. He laid his heavy head upon his knee, with his arms gathered around the green robes he had awoken in and fell immediately into a deep sleep.

He awoke in the twilight that directly preceded dawn the next morning with a sore bottom and a rumble in his belly. His head was still resting softly on his knee. He sat upright and looked about for a sign of what to do next. There was only one place where he knew to get food, and even though he knew that he had no credits because he hadn't been working and had slipped too deeply into debt to afford food regardless, he thought that perhaps someone would take pity on him and allow him to eat against his future wages.

He stood and walked slowly in the direction that he knew the factory to be, relative to the sound of the waves and the slowly increasing light. The wind blew an unfamiliar scent to his nose, or rather a lack of the scent that he had known all his life. The wind wasn't strong enough to explain the absence of the odor that he'd come to associate with work and the products of man's labor upon the earth. He couldn't smell burning plastic. Something felt different.

He was so accustomed to looking down at his feet as he walked that he had to remind himself to look up into the distance, even the tightness in his back and neck that he'd always felt from hunching over at his job was gone, and he felt no worse for having slept bent over on the cold stones the night before aside from his sore buttocks. He was still wearing his mysterious greenish robe of light, strongly woven fibers. He found that it had an attached cloak and hood as well. It had kept him comfortable both under the hill and during his dreamless sleep on the rock.

With each footfall, a growing awareness burrowed more deeply into his waking mind. He knew all at once that there was something wrong. There was no smoke. There were no lights. Nothing was burning.

*"The way to control anything
at all is to control all information.
Nothing else means anything at all."*
The Wealth of Wealth
Henrich Dent

VI

Nix found it easy to break into the commanding officer's stash of liquor once the old man was bedded down ill in his quarters. He took the first bottle and smelled it before downing a sizable quaff. It smelled similar to the chemicals used to clean the windows in the barracks, but it had a sharp peppery or minty finish at the end. Too much so he found, and he spit it out in a spray of alcohol and mucus.

It was meant to be taken in small shots, and he discovered the hard way that drinking a huge slug was too much even for him. He quietly pushed other similar looking and smelling bottles out of the way to reach the back of the cabinet. Surely the best stuff was hidden in the back, he thought. Nix was too unsophisticated to understand that the officer had no reason to hide his favorite drinks in the back of the cabinet because it wasn't a parent's secret stash at home. It was a commanding officer's private reserve. All of his men knew that he had one and knew where it was. They also understood that they were not to touch it, lest the punishment be severe for theft.

Nix didn't care because he knew at the moment that there were no eyes on him, that the man monitoring the cameras was probably just as sick as the rest of the men he knew and that no one was going to be monitoring, much less enforcing the rule of law.

At the back, he found a dusty bottle of colored fluid. The bottle was flimsy plastic, like every other one, but the absence of a label marked it as some of the officer's special reserve. There was a crystalline crust in the neck of the bottle where the fluid inside met the air and evaporated. Nix uncapped it and stuck his tongue into the bottle neck. The crystals tasted sweet. He tipped the bottle and filled his mouth without swallowing. The liquid burned, but he held it in because he'd learned that the burn was a positive thing; it meant that the alcohol was good. It could have been pure ethanol and window cleaner, and Nix would have believed that it was good to drink.

Nix had grown up with alcohol his whole life. His father would drink it. Then he'd hit his mother. His mother would drink it when she was hit. The other children of the Orangeshirts that he spent his youth associating with drank it as well, tipping the bottles at an early age as it was lawfully accepted that there was no prohibition on drinking age after the abolition of the laws that left the responsibility for consumption in the hands of the private individual. There was no reward for defiance when there was nothing to defy. There were other rewards for drinking as children.

Nix and his friends first got drunk when they were five or six years of age. Alcohol was commonly used by parents to calm or soothe anxious or willful children, and they were already accustomed to the flavor at an early age. Drunk children were easier to manage than sober ones. The depressant often caused them to fall asleep. A hungover child with a headache was easier to manage too, requiring nothing more than a handful of paracetamol to knock them out again. Some children that Nix knew went between drink and painkillers more than they did the telescreen and nap time. It wasn't uncommon to see drunken children left to fight each other on the rubble strewn wreckage that was their playground.

Often the adolescents who drank far too much weren't considered for the ranks of the Orangeshirts, and Nix dreamed of being one of them from a very young age, so he made certain to trim his drinking habits to acceptable levels whenever someone who mattered might be watching. Nix knew that often the alcohol was the only beverage available to drink. Their water was polluted to begin with, but the near constant breakdowns at the water treatment plants made boiling the brown tap water a necessity. During those times, it was often easier to go to the local kiosk and buy a lager or whatever was on tap from the local international beverage conglomerate. It was a market that paid the owners of the beverage companies well.

Nix sat back in the officer's chair and looked over the surveillance screens from the factory laid out before him. He touched the screen and the menu opened. A list of other factory sites opened up, and he touched one. All of the screens instantly switched to another scene near downtown at the mouth of the overflowing river. He could see the muddy banks and sea walls through the open door when he scrolled the camera into a closeup. The factory was deserted.

The alcohol burn in his mouth died, and he swallowed the mouthful. It went down easier this way. He nestled the flimsy plastic bottle in his crotch and started scrolling through the camera feeds on display. All of them empty, devoid of humans. He touched the screen again where the menu had been visible and selected another location that he didn't recognize by name. The camera views changed over yet again. Another factory. This commander had been responsible for the oversight of many factories up and down the coast and into the capital city. Nix wondered what his credit score was like.

He spent the next half hour spinning in the commander's chair and switching between the cameras on the monitor at drunken whim as he continued to empty the bottle. Each location showed the same thing: quiet, empty factories devoid of people. Nix found the repetition of imagery to be ridiculous, as if it were simply a misinformed version of his own favorite reality telescreen show.

Nix's mind wandered in ever tighter circles as he imagined the stars of his favorite program at the locations, then he realized that he might be able to tune the screens into the program and watch that episode on demand using the commander's account, but then he fell asleep with the bottle clasped between his thighs before he could work his way through the menus to locate his program.

He dozed drunkenly for a time before the bottle slipped off the chair from between his thighs to make a light hollow sound on the floor of the control room. It was enough to wake him with a start. His head felt like it had been squeezed in a vise.

He needed some pain killers. Where did the commander keep his private stash? Nix knew that the commander would have drugs that made paracetamol seem like nothing by comparison and that they would very likely be stashed nearby.

Nix lurched forward in the chair. There was movement on one of the cameras in the old quay by the toll bridge that had been taken over by the Orangeshirt road commission. He couldn't be certain at the resolution of the old surveillance camera, but it looked like a human figure walked by the doorway of the factory headed toward the water. It was the only human shape he saw on any of the cameras as he tracked through them looking for other people. He panned the camera from the touchscreen in the direction that the figure was moving, but then the view was blocked by the wall. He panned the camera back left to the open door and left it there. Perhaps the figure would walk by again or enter the factory.

Nix watched the screen while he switched two of the other monitors to the channels that he was accustomed to watching. The live streams were down. Both stations were playing streams of *XtreemDaats*, the mega-popular dating program that set up Orangeshirts selected through a lottery for sex with willing women who had been "subjected to a vigorous physical vetting process." Yet, those women were rejects from the ruling class due to fertility issues.

Women were commodities, much as they always had been, and attractive, fertile ones were most in demand. Most women of a certain attractiveness were subjected to a rite of first night by their twelfth birthday. Many were auctioned to the highest bidder, but a handful went directly to the many lineal descendants of the President for Life due to extension of his privilege. Very few people were fertile, but fertile women were passed upwards no matter their social class. Orangeshirts like Nix weren't going to get the most choice, most fertile, or most attractive women.

Nix didn't know any of that, but he didn't have to. His awareness was only the present. When he wanted to have sex, he found someone to have sex with. When he wanted drugs, he took drugs. When he wanted to commit violence, he did just that. From the beginnings of his personal awareness, he was allowed to take almost everything he wanted. His sense of history was only of the immediate and the local. If there was a world, it revolved around him, and that defined his view. He could only see one perspective: his own. He had never been asked to imagine any other. He knew his own past. He knew history only as it was fed to him. It was built in the image of its grandmasters, but they were all behind the smoke and mirrors that hid the truth.

If the President for Life ever was as malignantly cruel as the policy he birthed, Nix could never know. None of his citizens could imagine questioning how he was still so alive, so timeless, and so healthy. His handlers knew, his marionettists were aware. He was more myth than man in the island state. While it was entirely possible given the state of technology that some part of the original man was still alive in some bubbling black magic cauldron of rebirth made of blood and gold, it was much more likely that the man himself had died decades before. It didn't matter though. He was already immortal.

As Nix watched, his *XtreemDaats* program ended and was replaced by a replay of one of the President for Life's rallies on the island. His taut, orange visage appeared on the screen smirking his usual toothless smirk. Nix riveted his eyes to the screen, just as he was conditioned to, and looked upon his leader with a mix of adoration and love. He trembled in the seat, poised as if to jump and cheer for the telescreen. The master and commander of his heart ruled it from across the sea.

Videos of his presidential appearances were shown daily on the telescreens, but he ruled from overseas. When he made his visits to his properties on the coastlines of the island, actual witnesses were absolutely impossible to find. Rumor among the workers was that his rallies were attended by appointment only, and that his nearest local subordinates hand picked those only with the proper connections to be his audience.

Nix thought the rallies on the telescreen were things of beauty. Fighter jets in formation droned across the sky, trailing vapors echoing the striped tones of the national flag across the mottled brown clouds. Cheering crowds of artificially bronzed faces waved their bright plastic national flags with glittering stars in the corner and emblazoned with the logos of the regime's biggest corporate sponsors in a holy matrimony of national and private interests. Some of the island's biggest celebrities were on display, standing and cheering in positions of power and prestige nearest to the cameras with their effervescent white smiles and unlined orange faces. They bore a proudly voluminous display of affinity and loyalty to the man who had united not just the two nations on opposite sides of the ocean, but many others in an economic alliance across the face of the western half of the globe.

Nix aspired to be like those celebrities on the screen: one of the chosen to be near the President for Life. He did not understand that he was the product of a system that had worked for generations to create armies of men like him. He felt like a strong, proud individual who mattered. He believed that the work that he did providing security for the factory was one of the most important jobs available on the island. He was told that time and time again, whenever any doubts began to shade his mind about his importance.

Nix had no notion that he was tracked and controlled from conception to the grave. In his world, there were two kinds of useful idiots. Those who were ground in the wheels of capitalism and those who enforced the separation of the useful idiots into their raw material aspects. Nix was proud to be in the latter group. He and his ilk thought of themselves as elite. It was an idea strongly encouraged by their wealthy puppet masters. It was the magic that Nix and his social class would never be able to understand because they had their beliefs and values trained and pruned like hothouse bonsai into the shape most useful to their overlords.

As the telescreen program droned on, Nix's uppers wore off and the alcohol worked in. He slumped in his chair and felt the weight of fatigue. He drifted in and out of his doze, too intoxicated to care whether he had seen a man drift though the gaze of the camera outside.

In truth it wasn't a man. If Nix had run outside to confirm the shape, he would have seen nothing at all — not a person in sight, despite being near one the more populated areas of the city. He didn't know that things were wandering about that few modern men could conceive of. His was an age where myth was lost, the books that held them burned or locked away. Echoes and reminiscences of stories long forgotten had awoken on the island when the men and women who had mastered the local mythology fell down and stopped breathing.

Nix began to snore.

"Perfect capitalism is a balance: the best citizen pays as much as he is able, including credit, and the property owner charges more than the market can bear in order to maximize extraction of profit.
The 21st Century Human
Petr Mazetlev

VII

The smoke that had always hung over the den and the sorting factory from the industry to the west and the city to the south was missing that morning. Dunne stopped and stood to watch the sun rise over the hills to the east, slowly ascending untainted by smog in a way that he had never seen before. The glow was warm and rich.

The smoke had been produced by burning turf, recovered plastic, and garbage. All of the trees and bushes had long since been burned up in the quest for cheap energy. Nothing green could grow in public areas, so anything that could burn had to be burned. Everything had been reduced to ash and soot.

Dunne looked at the clear sky and wondered if finally there was nothing left to burn. He looked down at the dirt beneath his feet. He used his toe to scrape away the layer of plastitrash covering the mud, but all that he found below it were more layers of broken, torn plastic interspersed with the thick oily muck. He wondered to himself if there were any depth that he could dig to which would uncover soil that the plasticized filth had not penetrated. That led him to wonder what the land would look like if it were scoured of all the deposited trash — if a great cleansing storm washed over the island and swept it clean of man's indignities.

Dunne looked up again. If the smoke had ended, that must mean that the activity that generated the smoke had ceased as well. If the industry had ceased, then there was something wrong. Never in his life had anything stopped the burning.

Every day the smoke had poured from the stacks and billowed across the hazy sky. It was as normal as coughing. There were times during the windstorms when the smoke didn't hang in the valleys like wet hair, but then the stench from the sea filled with waste that lay to the east drifted in and settled. These were abominable facts of modern life. Dunne could not have avoided them, but now they were absent.

He turned in the direction that he knew his hive to be. There was no where else to go. Although he was thousands of credits in debt to the company for the job training that he'd received and thousands more in debt for his housing, everything else would be closed to him. There were thousands more dollars of debt on top of housing and training because of his food bill and the use of the credit toilets at the hive. No other shelter would even scan his ChipIn through the door.

Dunne knew that no employer could afford to pay a worker as much as it cost to live, but that there were better paying jobs that cost much more to train for. He could have trained for a better paying job, but would have remained as deeply, if not more, in debt. Everyone had to keep working just to stay behind. There were never enough petroplastics pulled from the oceans during his shift to cover the expense of harvesting them and separating the biomass —or so they were told. It was an ongoing equation where there was never a chance of equaling zero, much less of achieving a net financial positive.

He knew that his factory was one of many owned by one man, and he'd heard that the only thing keeping the businesses afloat were the subsidies provided by taxes that workers paid from their own wages. Without the government paying monies collected from taxation to the businesses to remain open, the citizens would have no jobs. Part of the reason that he and the rest of the working class stayed in debt was the high tax rate, but much of those taxes were paid back into the business so that he could have a job. There was a hidden math at work there.

As he walked toward his former home, he thought about how a lack of work would translate into a high rate of unemployment, which further meant a population excess. The last time that a "population excess" was created, the Orangeshirts had spent two days and two nights reducing the number of unemployed by using their firearms to create more material for the flesh rendering pits. The sides of the equation was always balanced by the free market. Humans were capital and no capital could be wasted, even if that meant converting them into something besides potential labor.

The companies owned workers liked Dunne, even though the message broadcast through the telescreens said that "every man was his own nation." They were slaves to constant debt, but since debt was a natural constant, they had no idea that freedom from it was conceivable. Without work, there was nothing for Dunne's co-workers to do except watch the omnipresent telescreens, an action which often increased their debt burden. They paid to watch their private pocket telescreens deliver a constant barrage of advertising for lives they'd never live and objects they'd never own. If they were were fortunate enough, they could lease cheap copies if their monthly credit score allowed them the privilege.

Both Dunne's and Nix's credit scores were calculated on a daily basis by machine intelligence, beginning with the time each spent at their assigned job. Figured into the mix were how much debt they already carried and the amount of free time they spent viewing the ads from the telescreens. Subtracted from the score were the foods and other goods that they consumed, including transportation and daily clothing. Failure to be at work and on task for the assigned minimum allotted time resulted in a lower score and a lessening of the quality of one's basic conditions of existence. Higher scores could afford slightly better foodstuffs from the company commissaries and better materials in one's clothes and beddings. Dunne could only achieve so much. His clothes fell apart instead of being laundered because he couldn't afford the soap, but the cloth wouldn't have made it through a wash regardless.

Those things available to him were designed to fall apart with regular use, the threads and the stitchings so thin (to increase production numbers and decrease production costs which generated greater shareholder profit) that they had to be replaced almost daily if one were to continue to appear respectable in public. His earnings never quite stretched far enough to buy something that was good enough to last more than a few days. Even though Dunne tried valiantly to save his credit, he only ever continued slipping down the same debt hole that everyone else was in. There seemed to be no escape from the treadmill he was on.

But now, there was no more smoke. As he walked toward the hive and factory, he felt an increasing sense of danger. There was something wrong with the world as he had always known it. He was not prepared for change.

He walked faster, processing his disbelief. His mind raced. What could have happened? Was the machinery broken? Were they out of fuel? Had there been some sort of purge of workers that left the factory undermanned and thus unable to function? He walked past the rubble of old homes and businesses strewn with garbage and detritus up the slight hill along the road until at last he got to the major intersection in what old broken street signs marked as "Sallynog" and saw the factory and hive. Each was ominously dark and quiet.

Dunne was incredulous. His mouth hung open. He slowed his walk and cautiously waded toward the building through ankle-deep garbage cluttered in the low spots between cracked concrete and asphalt paths and over the broken pavement. He tried not to let his fears control him. If something violent had happened, perhaps whoever had done it was still there. Perhaps the Orangeshirts had shot everyone for unpatriotic behavior and were simply lying quietly in wait for escapees and errant workers like him to come back in order to finish them off.

There was no visible movement from within the building even as he cautiously drew closer. Nothing moved outside or up and down the broken trails of pavement stretching as long and far as he could see. He could now see quite distantly compared to when the usual fog of dust and smoke clouded both the high and low lands.

The factory seemed less oppressive without the cacophony coming from within. He walked up to the ground level where the work took place in the doorless space under the pillars that supported the hive living facility. There was no one. No signs of violence. No signs of work. No signs of movement at all. It was as if everyone had left all at once with the change of the shift and not been replaced.

He mounted the long-dead cart escalator ramp that was the entranceway to the living quarters in the upper level of the factory. He paused momentarily outside the entrance at the top and listened again for any noise inside. There was nothing to hear except a ringing silence. He inhaled deeply and pushed the door open.

He was met by a sickly sweet smell, as of rotting meat. It hung in the air in advance of the typical dense miasma of human musk that typically filled the narrow halls between the sleeping cubes and the shallow kitchen area. He wished that there was a way to let the winds from outside push the smell out of the building, but there were no windows to open. He cautiously and quietly crept to the kitchen area where the food was usually kept on offer by the building's licensed sausage vendor.

The vendor's dry ice box and sign were there, but the man wasn't. Dunne looked cautiously from side to side and listened through the silence. He had hoped to get some food out of kindness and to address the space in his belly against future wages, but the man who sold the food on behalf of the company wasn't there. Dunne was painfully aware of a gnawing hunger in his belly that was enough to provoke him into actions that he never would have considered in polite company.

He opened the unguarded cooler to find a day's worth of food still chilled in the dried ice. With no one around, he quickly decided that the pain of breaking the law was worth diminishing the hollow in his belly. He seized a handful of the gray processed meats and wolfed them down, ignoring their odd, plastic odor. He couldn't help looking up and down the hallways while he ate, like a suspicious lab rat, still somehow expecting to be caught at any moment.

No one was there to arrest him. He ate his fill alone. Feelings of tension and anxiety threatened to overwhelm him, but he had to break the rules he'd known violently well in the past so that he might live now. The water to drink from the tap that normally charged against his credit for him dripped freely — almost a continuous stream. The faucet had been broken off. Dunne cupped his hands and drank again and again from his palms. Then he found a plastic bowl in the sausage man's cart to catch the sparkling drips in to bathe his face. The light filtering in from the mirrored light tubes on the roof was brighter than he'd ever seen before, due to the clear skies. He stood there patiently while the bowl filled with dripping water, draining it over and over again each time it filled, quenching his thirst with the first free water that that he had ever tasted.

The hallway to the tenant cubbies was dark and the door was half closed. The faint hint of rot that he thought was coming from the processed food abandoned in the kitchen was stronger by the door. An odd and new awareness in his head told him not to go back to where he had spent his few sleeping hours between work shifts.

He knew in his heart that his time at this place was finished. The lack of movement, the missing people told him that important changes had come. His sickness and whatever else had happened to the world around him meant that his life would not be the same, but the compulsion to see his bed one last time won out.

He shook the tightness from his shoulders and gently pushed the swinging door open. He was driven by his pessimistic curiosity and frightened need into a space that was no longer familiar. He could see in the dim light that everything that was breakable had been broken. Glass, wood, plastic. It was all smashed and mangled beyond repair. Plastic drapes that had separated the sections of cubbies lay torn on the floor. The rag-thin bedding that all of them had used was ripped to further shreds and littered the floor beneath his feet. Darkness ruled the space. Even though he was alone, he was very frightened of being discovered by the Orangeshirts. This looked like their brand of destruction. He found his own cubby somehow less destroyed than the others. He crept quietly back to the central hall.

Dunne could imagine the heavy, crashing footfalls of the flabby Orangeshirts with hard, cold faces. He could picture the icy and malicious exhilaration with which they had made all this that was not theirs into more trash for the piles, and more fuel for their sanctimonious, privileged, and ruthless sense of right and dedication to their fascistic cause. Everyone that Dunne had toiled with was gone. Every last vestige of them had been broken and shattered into nigh unrecognizable bits. The smell of rot was merely the filthy living spaces airing out, and his nose grown unaccustomed to the daily miasma. There were no bodies inside. If there were bodies, he could be numb to the spectacle, accustomed as he was the brutality of the Orangeshirts.The fact that there was nothing was much worse.

He felt an anger within him that was alien, but not wrong. He hadn't felt anger in so long. Children could feel anger, but Dunne and people like him learned that anger could get them in trouble. Anger was for the upper classes. His resentment at the mistreatment that he and others of his social class were forced to endure was buried frozen under complacence and apathy because it had nowhere else to go. Anger given voice or action would only have harmed him. Such was the way of the world that he inhabited. Anger was reserved for the wealthy.

Unlike Dunne's anger, the Orangeshirt's rage was driven by things that no longer existed — if they ever had at all. In their minds, they were the victims of the lower class. Any attempt at autonomy by those people was treated as an infringement upon an Orangeshirt's God-given rights. The owners of the island state had successfully turned its people against each other instead of against them. Orangeshirts against the workers. The poor against the poorer.

In Orangeshirt culture, power was in destruction. Even though their enemies possessed little, the Orangeshirts found great satisfaction in destroying it. It could not matter what actually was — only what they believed it to be. Even the fictional Brotherhood of Goldstein had a text that could be destroyed in an act of defiance. The working class of the island state had nothing to unite them, not even a binding idea. Nothing on the telescreen connected them as a group more than a corporate logo. They had no ideology. There was no object or text to ridicule, revile, rip to shreds, rend, or burn.

In the world Dunne and Nix lived in, humans only had value when they produced profit. Therefore, it was no real crime for the Orangeshirts to commit murder against unprofitable beings even though the laws prohibited the act. Murder could only mean "productive people" had been killed. Everyone understood the truth of the murder prohibition without ever speaking it aloud. It only applied when the victims were a part of the group that made the prohibitions.

Dunne scanned the hive. The interior telescreens were silent for the first time in his life. Their screens remained an energetic black with a rare flicker across at odd and uncoordinated intervals, like a failing heartbeat awaiting a shock to return to their rhythmic rate of perpetrating the propaganda of the ruling party. The clocks were all black. Even the schedule was gone.

Dunne walked back outside through the crumbling and empty building. The day felt raw and unmade — as if left unfinished by the absence of those who tried so hard to control it. A cold front had swept in from the east and there was a low dense fog coming in quickly over the water. The air felt colder than he ever remembered it and carried with it an intensity of a particular odor that he could remember but not name. It was death and spoiled, oily meat mixed with something mysterious and even more discomforting. That mystery was salty and rotten down by the water's edge, and the wind carried it up the shore and toward the island's interior.

There was a crackle underfoot. He looked down and saw that he was standing on an obscene footpath of broken teeth. Incisors and molars, cracked and shattered, littered the mud and broken concrete underfoot. The brown mud had an unmistakeable reddish tinge. The teeth reminded him of broken fingernails coming from under the mud reaching up for the light. The scene made him think of hands reaching for value to be extracted. His mind raced: where did these teeth come from? This must have been a place where the Orangeshirts regularly visited violence upon the workers.

The sun was still high, giving the mist a quality of diffracted light that made the landscape look otherworldly. Never had he seen the place that he lived look so strange. Scanning toward the city, he could see none of the lights that he could remember well from clear days and nights when he'd caught glimpses of the world outside his factory hive shining through the darkness.

He still had questions, even with his thirst quenched and his belly full for the first time in his memory. The answers weren't inside the hive. The answers he sought were elsewhere, maybe even in the capital city. He thought that he could find out why the people had died, if only he could find the right screen or right person in the city. He had no reason left to return to the place that was his past.

He wandered down by the tidal shallows, the place he last remembered before the cave. The wasted ruins and foundations of former shoreline towns swallowed by global sea rise in the mid twenty-first century were exposed by the low tide. Those broken foundations became catch basins for whatever floated in and out on the water. The drag nets snagged on them sometimes as the manpower tugged them ashore and as the sensor ships pulled them out each day. The old concrete and stonework was weathered by water and wind, but the nets were pulled out to the sea on an old flooded road. It traveled between fractured garden walls that had been used to separate the island over and over again into smaller and smaller spaces. First, the walls had delineated the borders between fields and pastures, then the boundary lines between estates. Then those small empires crumbled, and the land was separated into smaller and smaller parcels as it was carved up into rental properties for the workers when the wheels of capitalism created a new and short lived middle-class. Then that too crumbled to dust in the age of rule from across the ocean.

Dunne walked toward the mist that covered the garbage strewn shoreline over the concrete and asphalt path where the notches were carved by the cables that drew the nets to the sorting facility. Past the high tide mark there were shapes strewn about amongst the scattered concrete and steel ruins. Some had clearly been swept out to sea, but many had caught on the ruined brick and stone buildings with the changing of the tides. Long ago, there would have been flocks of scavenging seagulls and other carrion birds seeking easy meals of scallops or worms between the tide lines, but the birds were all dead. Poisoned by the works of man.

Dunne went to an eroded stone line that had indubitably been the walls of a rich man's house because of the space that it enclosed within its angles. Half buried there in the sands and drifting pebbles were bodies that he recognized must have been some of his fellow workers from the sorting plant. Their soft tissue features were already worn away by the detritus-filled waves.

Dunne inspected them as carefully as he dared to fearing the vapors of the dead, trying to breathe only through his mouth. There were none of the tell-tale marks of high velocity lead on their bodies. No penetrative holes formed by the explosion of gunpowder and anger. There were more bodies than could have been accounted for by the workers of his simple rendering factory, and more bodies than could be explained by a mass workhouse purge.

He moved closer to a strange looking one and found that it was the corpse of an Orangeshirt. His orange uniform had held up better under the remorseless grinding action of the constant waves and tidal pressures. Dunne inspected the body, caught facedown on the remnants of a cinderblock wall. There was no reason to flip the rigid corpse to look for an identity. Every Orangeshirt was the same. If the others were dead as well, then they had died someplace else.

The fog drifted in thick and unrelenting. Dunne couldn't yet see the water, but he could hear the waves breaking. He had no idea how quickly the tide came up the hill, but he had all of the answer that he would receive from his walk toward the water today. He had to find other living people.

As he walked back up the causeway, he wondered again about the voice that he had awakened to and the place where had been since his last memories at the water's edge. Had each of these bodies been a repeat of what had happened to him? Who had pulled him from the water's edge before the tide and waves had taken him? Everything was as clear as the mist and fog that now enshrouded him in the tidal zone.

He returned to the hilltop the factory sat on, following the trail he had walked to the water, but the fog was now as dense as he had ever seen. The wind had settled and the fog hung like thick drapes. From where he stood, he knew where to go to find the mountains that lay to the west. He thought that if he could climb them, he could find out what had happened to the rest of the people.

From the hilltop of Sallynog to the mountain, the land dipped low again. During the hurricane season that ran from the third month of the year until the tenth, the low areas would flood and form garbage bogs where the trash deposited over the years would float up from the soft ground on the high waters. There was one road that ran through it to the mountain, a road that ran over and through former estates, using their broken wall stones to bridge the marsh lands. Dunne had seen it from the factory, but he had never walked it.

When he was working at the rending factory, there was never any time or energy to leave. Everything he needed was there. His place to sleep and eat was there, and where else would he want to go? The telescreens brought the world to him. But, things had changed now. The telescreen distractions felt hollow to his memories and brought nothing. Static filled the screens of his hive and the factory both.

Despite his rest in the cave and the time being cared for, his exploration and discovery had exhausted him. His eyes were heavy again with the need for sleep. He found a pile of stone shaped like an old table rock and sat against it to rest his eyes. Later, he would walk to the mountain. From there he would be able to see the city and the shore. On the mountain, he would know where to go next. For now, he would rest.

When the wealthy owned the means of production
as well as the property, it became very simple to
dictate the terms by which capital could be allowed
to flow to anyone below on the economic scale.
The Status Quo of Wealth
Markis O'Egan

VIII

Nix woke up deeply hung over, the taste of rot thick in his throat. He went back to his telescreen and found that the same program was on even though hours had passed in his drunken sleep. It had frozen on screen, a talking head pushing energy drinks, the mouth wide open like a cave. The whole system was failing, bit by bit. Nix winced. His head throbbed to a rhythm that reminded him of his favorite music even as the music from the telescreen skipped and repeated like a broken record.

He thoughts took a long time to coalesce into something meaningful. He wondered if his favorite band still existed. They had been touring the island state doing expensive concerts just the month before. The "Trumpet Military Band" was a uniformed military group that traveled from city to city to perform at the virtual rallies the president held on a regular basis. Holographic three-dimensional images of the president glided about on the stage, repeating his most popular talking points, asking for his supporters to draw from the debit accounts to support his ongoing efforts to make the greatest nation in the world even greater. The band played and women in patriotically tasseled bikinis danced suggestively with assault rifles. It was an enjoyable spectacle that merged many of Nix's favorite things into one grand show. Normally, he never got tired of it. Every want or desire on the screen led to another, and if those things couldn't be gotten, at least there were the stims, the downers, and the drinks.

Now, there was nothing to limit his drinking and drugging except his own ability to find more that other humans had left behind. As each need was satiated immediately, it became boring in turn. Nix needed someone or something to push against. He switched screen inputs to the "On Demand!" stream and searched for his favorite program.

He found it quickly on the menu and brought it to the main screen. It was called "The Factory" and involved several enhanced women who worked in a high class manufacturing plant as Orangeshirts for a commander that they all called "The Boss." They lorded over incompetent and dirty subservient male workers who they called "cuckmucks" and serviced their leader at his whim under black on-screen censor bars that advertised dating services or adult toys to the viewers. His favorite episode was the one wherein the commander had been called away for an important meeting leaving a particularly well-endowed favorite of his in charge, and she had dressed in the boss's uniform to pretend to be him. No one in the factory had noticed the switch. It was one of the program's highest rated episodes and won a handful of daytime telescreen awards.

After this episode, he was going back into the heart of the city to find more drugs. But first, he had more urgent wants to take care of. The women on the screen were just his type. He'd never seen real women like these, but they had always populated his daydreams. He dreamed of finding them in America once he could afford to travel there. Until then, he could watch them on the screen.

Nix settled in to watch his program, never once imagining that he was to become an agent of chaos in the new world that was coming. He was not special, was not spared by an act of an otherworldly being that flitted between the scenes of a man-made world. His continued existence was as random as any roll of the dice, but there was something beyond human comprehension that took notice of his presence when other men stumbled and died. Here was a man that could be used.

Ritual was the important part,
not the intent behind the act.
Just go through the motions.
Let the cultist free-associate.
Cults: How to be One
Germain De aléatoire

IX

Dunne had fallen asleep sitting against a stone wall under a table rock. He awoke in the orange dawn light to muttering and shuffling sounds behind him. His ragged earth-colored clothing helped him to blend into the dirt and the garbage, so he turned his head and shoulders slowly to hide from whatever was making the noise in the event that it was a threat.

He saw a man-shape not unlike his own, wearing brown rags but also a headdress adorned with the antlers of a roan deer from the old city park that was cleared and asphalted over to be turned into homes for business diplomats from the US. Many years before that, the nearly tame deer there had been hunted to death for sport by the youngest son of the President for Life on his holidays to the island. Dunne had seen the docudrama about it on the telescreen. It advertised their remnants on display in the city's "Bone Zoo" and that was how Dunne recognized the horns.

The deer man was mumbling and muttering under his breath as he paced back and forth a few meters away from where Dunne had lain, sheltered from view by the darkness, the rocks, and his own ragged raiment. He watched the man perambulate back and forth, head alternately raised to the sky or turned down perfectly to his feet, chin on his chest. When he turned to faced Dunne in his erratic pacing, Dunne could see his clothing was not as filthy as his first glance seemed to indicate. His robes were dark in color, but there was a spot of near-whiteness around the front neckline covering his Adam's Apple. He was wearing a tattered stole that hung down to nearly his knees and flapped in the breezes showing a sideways X mark on each side.

The dense mist was thinning around his hiding spot as Dunne watched the man pace about. He moved more and more animatedly, seeming to gain energy from the rising sun. He could see more clearly now the man's full clerical outfit. He was dressed in the outlawed raiments of a Catholic bishop. Dunne remembered seeing them on the cartoon where the glorious leader from across the ocean had vanquished several of the church officials in mortal martial arts combat.

Catholicism had been the former unofficial national religion of the land in the years before the "Great Burn" arrived from the US, spurred by their tax-funded evangelical efforts to spread their unique version of the New Testament in the west of Europe. Just as Christian missionaries saw their faith as a justification and a tool for opening the continent of Africa to western capitalism in the 18th and 19th century, the Americans of the twenty-first knew that their specific brand of evangelism was a powerful tool to bring the straying Europeans in line with the tenets of Neo-Evangelical Protestantism that controlled the political and social forces of America.

The extant church, branded false by the American evangelicals, had hidden a series of dark scandals. Many young people throughout the island nation were left to wander like so many lost sheep. They needed correction that did not spare the rod. Even now, occasional excavations for new buildings on old church grounds still uncovered mass graves of women and children who had been culled by elements within the church. The foundations of belief without evidence were already there for a new religion. The island's people were hungry for something to believe in, and when capitalism began to show cracks under the strain of trickle-down economics, the wealthy needed a new version of an old story to maintain control. Dunne didn't know that history. It had been erased. All he knew were the telescreen stories of drunken heathens and rich saviors.

The man moved closer to Dunne, but made no move to show that he saw Dunne's huddled form under the table rock. In the new light of dawn Dunne could see that his shelter was the remnants of a doorway or front of a manor house or church that had burned down, collapsed, and been plundered for building materials. The table rock that he had slept under now formed a makeshift altar for the makeshift holy man, and that holy man was preparing for a makeshift mass.

The man was bowed forward muttering to his own feet, so Dunne slipped away from the altar and to a broken building block upon which to sit and observe. The mock priest went to the table rock and bowed, touching his forehead, then the center of his chest, then each shoulder in turn in a ritualized pattern. He then made eye contact with Dunne. Apparently, he had been waiting for the sleeping man to move away from the altar to start his mass, and now Dunne was his congregation.

Dunne looked around, half expecting to see other human shapes gathered for the service, but found nothing around them on the debris-strewn ground. He was an audience of one and a mass was now being performed for his benefit by default. The priestly figure mimed the reading of a book by holding his hands face up before him. He laid the non-existent tablet upon the flat stone and proceeded to mouth silent words to his congregation of one. He flipped the pages of his book that wasn't there and showed expressions of emotion that might have befit a parable of Christ or a letter of Paul to the Corinthians, and then smiled and closed his ghost book. Then he walked to the left of the makeshift altar and stopped in the empty space between the altar and the rocks that Dunne sat against. He mimicked the washing of his hands in the mid-air, rubbing them together: first, as if to cleanse, then to dry.

He then moved farther to Dunne's right and mimed opening a tiny door to take an invisible chalice of wafers from a non-existent tabernacle that only he could see. Dunne recognized the movements from a tele-screen show that mocked the rituals of the past by showing the formerly televised liturgy with popular celebrities in the corner of the telescreen talking over the ceremony and mocking the celebrant and his congregation. It was a program of watching people deride a program on their own telescreens, and it was a common popular entertainment pulsing on the walls in the hive after work was finished.

The cleric returned to his stone altar holding up his empty hands and made a sign of benediction over an unseen item. He then walked down an imaginary aisle in the center front of his altar to dip his left hand into the space before his right hand held out before himself, and then shook a blessed shower of water that wasn't there from his raised fist above his head around a congregation that consisted of Dunne and some ghosts.

He mimed singing, his lips moving in silent, rhythmic motion. He returned to the altar and pressed his hands together before him as if clasping something and prayed. He read from the imagined book again and then he returned to the front of the altar with his hands raised as if cupping a small chalice to dispense non-existent communion wafers from his upturned palm. He stopped after a few repetitive moments and looked toward Dunne. Dunne turned and looked behind himself, expecting that another person had materialized behind him. He then realized that the cleric was waiting politely for Dunne to stand and take his place in a shuffling imaginary procession to receive the transubstantiated body of Christ in his cupped hands.

Dunne participated in the mime show as he had seen it enacted on the telescreen and returned to his seat upon the upturned stone in the audience. Then the cleric offered a blessing to his attentive congregation and walked an orderly and slow procession down the path in front of his altar that Dunne noticed now in the rising light was suspiciously well-worn.

The man ignored Dunne and trailed off into the morning mist from which he had emerged, as silently as he appeared and as silently as he had pronounced his strange little mass. Dunne was left alone in the misty space. The sun was still low in the east, setting a soft light through the haze like an incandescent light bulb wrapped in cotton batting in a primary school science project. Dunne stared up in the direction of the light and thought about his plan of action. He'd gotten lost in the fog and low-lying clouds and had then found his way out several times already, but the city kept disappearing in the mists. His sense of direction wasn't very accurate. He had lived and worked in a very small area of the island and never had a reason to go elsewhere. There was no reason to travel, no holidays for him. He worked, and working was all there was to do.

Dunne felt hungry again. It had been some time since he'd eaten the leftover food in the kitchen of his hive. If there was food to be found, it was probably in the greater part of the city that surrounded the river. He had to go there. It was the most likely place to find food and answers about what had happened to all of the people.

There were just a few kilometers now separating him from the city, but the distance was littered with buildings in various states of disrepair and shrouded in the mysterious fogs that came and went. Much of the island state had been deteriorating slowly for several decades. The island's people had been living on credit in debt for generations and infrastructure had no public funding. The roads that led in and out of the city were paths of pressed, patched, and broken asphalt. Like all of the roads, none of them went in straight lines. Dunne couldn't get on a road and follow it to a meaningful end.

The mists were moving in from the east, and they kept shifting with the winds. It was all very disorienting to the reborn man and made it difficult to plot a straight path toward the mountain or the city that was so near and yet so far. A cool fog blew in, and he kept walking toward where the mountains pointed their shadows in the mist.

X

Across the river, Nix was lost in a city that didn't love him. The feeling was mutual. The old-country metropolis was split into districts, some for the Orangeshirts, some for the privileged rich, and some for the workers at the bottom of the profit pyramid. No higher group had any tolerance for sharing the spaces of the lower groups, and the only places they mixed were near the rivers and bridges that they were forced to share to move from one side of the river-split city to the other.

Nix was hungover and out of stim-packets to escape the heavy throbbing in his head. That made him angry. The rich and the workers both were fortunate that they were long gone from this part of the city, or else he'd be fit to take his anger out on them. He'd relieve the pressure in his brain by offering up bashed heads and broken bones to any that crossed his path. He understood that the city was empty.

He had awakened from his intoxicated stupor every so often to drink more and chase the hangover away. He woke up to relieve himself, sometimes to drink more from the peculiar bottles that he'd rarely before had access to. He had not given a second thought to anything outside of his immediate needs.

He awoke again. The chair hurt his arse. He lay down on the floor beneath it to sleep only when he had drained the last bit from the bottles in the back of the cabinet and then fell back into a state of inebriated slumber. As it was, he missed the emptying of the capital. The last of the city had emptied itself before he awoke, like both his bowel and his bladder into his pants during his hours of excess.

He sat up in the grey light of morning and promptly retched nearly a full pint of alcohol from his bloated belly. It pooled on the stain left from the urine that soaked his trousers. He needed new clothes. They were at his locker. He had to stagger back to his barracks to change his clothes and find his stash of stimulants, he discovered that he'd used them all in his altered state. Now he had to find more stims to break the effects of his rather exceptional hangover.

He staggered out of the broken barrack door and wandered into the city. His normal supplies were all gone. The dealers and stores were gone or emptied of their stimulant drugs. As the illness took hold and sank in, the people tried to overcome the symptoms with more and more stims. In short order, most of the easily accessible sources were exhausted. Regardless, all of the users eventually succumbed. Nothing stopped the relentless pace of death.

He walked to the river to trace a path into the uptown district, the shopping zone known as Graffen Street, to look for the shops where he knew dealers would keep hidden stashes of their best stuff. It was the place to add debt in the city, and tourists came from all around the world to do that very thing and increase their scores. Nix knew that some of the absolute best things that debt could purchase came from

Graffen Street, including the very best stims and downers as well.

He rounded a corner at the water wall for the river and turned left at the intersection of the Trinity training center for Orangeshirts. His father had once been an instructor chaplain there. Nix wondered if the violent old drunk had disappeared yet.

That fleeting thought was pushed from his aching brain by the sudden and overwhelming need to again empty his bladder. He walked to the main gate of the training center and dropped his pants to his knees to unleash a pinkish yellow stream of urine on the masonry wall of the old edifice. There was blood in his urine again. If it weren't such a regular occurrence, he might have thought it troubling. Instead, he spat in spreading puddle of excretia and tugged his pants back up, fastening them with his soiled web belt. There wasn't far to walk now. If there was a good thing about downtown, it was that it was walkable for almost anyone.

The tourist shops hawking cheaply made and shoddy green clothing plastered with the city's name and emblem were still heavily laden with product in their windows. Their doors shut in one last effort to keep profits from being cut by theft. They were the last salable items left in the city.

Nix left the old training center and moved through the main commercial district toward a place that he'd heard the higher ranking Orangeshirts talk about. Normally at this hour the streets would have been bustling with tourists and shoppers. Everyone was gone, driven to the sea's edge to die by some urge they could never comprehend. For the first time,

Nix's view of his importance in the world was matched by its reality.

He found his desired destination down a side street. The battered sign above the broken awning of the shop said "Bruxelles," but long ago some one had broken and painted the letters to read "Bruces" instead. Bruces was where the upper classes got their favorite drugs. Bruce was the dealer. The fact that he had three floors dedicated to selling and using his wares didn't seem to impress anyone despite the fact that according to the rule of law, his underground market was completely illegal.

Laws were only for the poor like Dunne. Those with the financial wherewithal were allowed to do whatever they willed for a fee called a "fine." The underground economy of money and privilege kept the lawful economy working, and the illusion of the lawful economy kept the workers numb and subservient. The lawful economy existed completely in debt, but the underground traded in dirty dollars — the only credit that held any value outside the rare earth metals.

Nix didn't have any dollars either, but he didn't need them to get the things he wanted from Bruces now. His debit was always good, but now there was no one to scan his chip. Nix didn't know that they knew his father very well there, and that part of their ability to exist as a black market business in the commercial district was linked to his patronage. Nix could have used his father's name to gain access any time he wanted, but his father had never trusted him enough to share his privilege with him.

The two lower lairs of Bruces were always filled with users and abusers, people who spent their debits or cash on feel-good escapes. Nix didn't care about any of them. This afternoon, the lair was empty and the door hinge was bent and broken at the top. It was stuck open, its corner smashed into the cracked pavement.

Nix forced it fully open and shuffled inside, dragging his feet across the sill. The throbbing in his skull had diminished, but it was more than enough to drive him to angrily jump over the bar and pry open the cabinets behind the counter. He'd seen drug tenders pull different bags and bottles of all manner of brightly colored pills and powders from those same sorts of hideaways on the telescreen documentaries. All he found were large bottles of brightly colored liquors and drinks for legal consumption. Then in his foggy throbbing mind, he realized that he could go downstairs to get to the bars with the cabinets with the drugs that he actually wanted. Bruces had three floors, and each floor was designated for a different product. The street floor catered to the tourist crowd that was too much in love with an ideal vision of the city to ever wrap their minds around the truth of the underground black markets.

The lower level had the stims and "dregs," the drugs that were illegal but were accepted as necessary for most people to make it through the day. The "dregs" were the downers, the suppressants that dulled the senses and dulled the user into a deep stupor. The dregs made it easier for the lowest class workers to cope with the conditions of their lives.

The very basement was referred to colloquially as the "Loser's Lounge." That was where the junkies and the bottom feeders bought their socially unacceptable drugs, and where the seats were filled with people passed out or otherwise experiencing the worst of their effects. Nix had heard the rumors that the most addictive drugs were sold and used in the "underground."

After he got his stims to make his headache go away, he was going to explore the rest of Bruces and carry out some of the stronger abandoned supplies. Those drugs were worth credit or cash from the addicts. If the drug stashes were still there and unprotected, it was a chance for him to make some easy money of his own — an easy path to power. Provided he could find buyers, of course. He still imagined that there were others he would find or who would find him.

That was another complex matter. He did the calculations in his head. He could break into the unguarded spaces and take as much as he could carry, but how far would he have to carry it? He hadn't seen any other living people, much less anyone who looked as though they would buy the drugs that he could offer them. No, much better to simply take what he could carry and use himself, to mark where the rest of it was and potentially come back to Bruces if he found someone to buy from him.

Everything in the lowest level seemed as though the vendors and the customers expected to return. Pills and powders sat measured in trays and scales, ready to be doled out for whatever value they could be traded for. Nix thought that he could fill the gap left open by the Bruces abandonment.

He paced the empty spaces of the lower bars, then settled on some blue pills that he thought he vaguely recognized. He explored the space further as the drugs slowly took hold of him, decreasing the pressure in his skull.

With his head now cleared from the reverberation of drinking himself nearly to death, Nix returned to the street to look around the commercial district. The city was more dead than he had ever imagined. Never had his eyes beheld the city anything less than jammed with diesel burning engines, peat burning chimneys, coal burning factories, and humans moving in every which direction.

Somewhere there had to be some others who were still alive. Somewhere there were people he could take advantage of. He thought about the local churches he'd seen on the telescreen. If there were yet people, they'd be sheltering there. People always sheltered in churches in times of great suffering and need. The next best place for comfort after the drug den was the old Paddy's Cathedral. He wedged the door of Bruces shut and headed west.

Nix took a winding and circuitous path. All of the tourist souvenir dens and chippers' shops were closed up and locked down. Without the drunks and the tourists, the city was quiet. To him, it felt like a victim sitting with its knees drawn up to its chest, trying to shield itself from worse blows. All the noise of the city was absent, but under the spell of the drugs he'd swallowed to lessen his aching head, he barely noticed the ghostly pall of the fog draped over the quiet streets. The drugs exacerbated his dullness to the world around him. It was as if the quietness allowed the clouds to sink into the city and wrap around its buildings, up and down the streets like a sinuous snake. He walked on in a haze as the chemicals slowly filtered out of his system, aware of his course only because of familiarity with the city he'd lived in his whole life.

The church front was on the other side of the street from him now. Another less imposing brick building and an alley filled with shopping trolleys lay between him and the church. Plastic shopping bags caught on the trolley's broken wheels and wires and waved like flags in the stiffened breeze. He watched the flock of plastic rags flutter for a moment. There was a dark beauty in it. A plastic flag freed from its post drifted past him and rolled down the street like a tumbleweed from an old cowboy movie. Two more came rolling on the breeze and snagged in the mountain of broken trolleys. It was the only movement that caught his eye.

As he stood there in the silence, he realized that the church was empty too. There were no sounds of people. The city was quiet. The absence of usual sounds struck him. It was uncomfortable — almost unholy. Only the wind wound its way through the streets. He wondered to himself if that wind had pushed the people from the city, wiped them away. The thought fled quickly. He turned and walked the empty road back to his barracks. His head now felt full of sand.

The drugs replaced the church in his questioning mind. He would find nothing there, and there was no more reason to push further or to climb that mountain of discarded shopping trolleys to crawl to the other side. The drugs in Bruces were all his now. There was no one to contest ownership with.

Everything was his.

"...uneducated citizens were fed propaganda from birth to death. As the internet rose in the early twenty-first century, the interactivity of the World Wide Web meant that constant surveillance and interactive manipulation were cheaply and profitably carried out..."
Neo-liberalism Supreme
Emerson Niles III

XI

Dunne surveyed the area, filthy and coated with garbage. The Wellington monument towered over the remnants of the park and the flooded river. Without the polluting clouds from the factories, the powerful sun threatened to redden his exposed face in the denuded former nature preserve. The only shade was under the stone monument.

In the dampness of the shade, short, fleshy fungi were growing from the cracks in the stone and concrete and through the suspicious smelling garbage piled around the base of the towering obelisk. Their luminous blue tones played through the rubbish that threatened to bury them even as it supported their growth.

Dunne couldn't smell them at first over the rot that surrounded him, but a sense of them had taken root in his head. The shade was cool and beckoning. He moved in closer taking respite at the foot of the monument, pondering its height in the shade from the sun. He leaned against the base at first, but then sat leaning against the cold stone to consider his next direction.

At first, the earthy odor was repellent, but the longer he remained in the shade, the less repellent it seemed This change was far too quick to be a natural acclimation. There was something stronger at play manipulating Dunne's senses. In only a few minutes, the smell became irresistibly delicious and attractive to him. He didn't want to leave it. He sat a few minutes more, resting and drinking in both the shade and the scent. He couldn't stop looking at the mushrooms. They were beautiful.

Then the smell started making his mouth water. He hadn't eaten in a while, but he was accustomed to long periods of fasting forced by a weak desire to rebel against the status quo that he fulfilled by not eating himself further into debt. Food had been difficult to find since civilization collapsed on the island, and his wanderings hadn't uncovered many more sources. His mouth watered, and he had to swallow to keep it from escaping his lips and dripping down his chin. The scent of the mushrooms was too much to bear. He could almost taste them already simply from the scent alone. He reached down to take a fleshy growth from its rooting. It felt flabby and fibrous, like a tumor overgrown. He broke the stem and the smell became even more pungent. It was intoxicating. He lifted the mushroom higher to his nose to revel in its odor. He closed his eyes and drifted on the wave of scent.

He bit into one. It was foamy textured against his tongue. He chewed. It was unsatisfying: the taste was not at all like the smell. It was a spoiled fleshy flavor, like the undercooked pasta left in the dirt for a day that he had found and consumed once outside a large house in Sallynog. There was grit on the first one that made him more careful as he chose a second cap to taste in order to attempt to assuage the hunger that the peculiar odor evoked.

He plucked it and brushed it much more carefully than the first, inspecting it closely, even as the drive to put it directly into his mouth felt impossible to resist. The taste was exactly the same, except less gritty. Still disappointing. He hunched over the remaining sprouting caps on the ground and inhaled deeply, moving to his hands and knees as he did so. The smell alone felt like a presage to more, an invitation to indulge in a taste that would surely appear when he consumed enough. He tugged on the remaining fungi that looked ripe enough to eat, collecting and brushing all of them carefully clean, basking in their ripe odor as he held them in the cup of his hands.

He wolfed them down this time, swallowing them almost whole, not taking time to chew their rubbery texture for fear of the feeling of disappointment it would create. Now that all the flowering bodies had been consumed, the smell quickly dissipated on the wind. Dunne leaned against the base of the monument and closed his eyes. He wanted to savor the scent before it faded away. He played the tones of the scent over and over in his mind like a melody, the pungent notes creating a rhythmic pulse that seemed like a memory. Then he realized that rhythmic pulse was the sound of his own heartbeat, his pulse coming through his own ears. He could hear his own heart beat for the first time that he could recall.

It was a regular pulsing tone, reminiscent of the marching videos that the Orangeshirts played on the telescreens on their holidays. He closed his eyes to listen, to focus on the relaxing sound of his own heart. As he did so, he realized a drowsiness settling in. His eyelids felt heavy. His mind was free associating now; he could see the marching feet in his mind's eye, moving to the pace of his heartbeat. Thousands of marching feet in colorful unison, flashing luminous colors of the rainbow with each beat on the ground.

The footfalls of the marching feet got louder and heavier. They felt like they were shaking his head now. He could feel the rumble down through his head into his chest like a bass drum. Then the lights were coming through his eyelids from the outside, flashes here and there of color that dwarfed anything he saw when he rubbed his eyes. He opened them and blinked with the pulses of his heartbeat. The light was steady outside his head. There were no flashes, but it moved and flowed like the waters of the sea. He felt light-headed; his brain seemed to float weightlessly above his neck, tethered only by a ribbon that carried the beat of his heart. He closed his eyes again. The swimming feeling drifted away, but his awareness of self was three inches in front of him. His perception had shifted a bit forward, and it stayed there when he moved his head on his shoulders. The world had turned on its axis again, but he lagged behind just a touch or sped ahead — he couldn't tell much. It didn't move anymore than that, but seemed to stay there no matter which way he turned or how he moved his head while sitting in the shade of towering monument.

He closed his eyes again and relaxed. He could feel the mushrooms in his belly. They sat heavily in a ball, rocking back and forth with each breath. No, not a ball — a giant fruiting cap and stem that swayed to and fro with his breathing. As he focused more on the sensation, he could feel the movement in his breathing being one with the mushrooms, and then as if the movement came from the mushrooms, as if they were making him breathe through them. His breath went into his belly instead of his lungs, or the mushrooms grew roots that reached through the tissues of his digestive tract and snaked their way up into his lungs and were drawing air from him as they continued growing inside his belly. The living mushrooms he had eaten were his lungs now.

He felt more alive with the mushrooms growing inside of him. It struck him briefly that mushrooms only grew on dead things, and therefore they could not possibly be growing inside him, even though he could feel them growing there, because he was not dead. But then he couldn't remember what it was that made him feel alive before he had eaten the mushrooms, so he wasn't sure if he wasn't dead already anyway — perhaps from the mushrooms. But then he woke up from being dead, or from being as near to dead as he was capable of imagining, and he had pinched himself and walked for kilometers. Or he didn't. Perhaps, he thought, perhaps he was a ghost. But no, that couldn't be. He'd once been spoken to by real men, and real men had heard him speak. And the moving colors that surrounded him like a sea. Those were real. Everything was alive, including him. He lifted his hand to his view and studied it. The colors beat through it and with it, ebbing and flowing like water through his fingers becoming one with the air and all that he could see around him. The rhythm of it all remained the same as the one he could hear in his ears, meaning that it came from him — that it all emanated from his heart. This was his blood and the whole world was alive with it.

Then a thought came to him from somewhere he couldn't imagine. Maybe he was dead, he thought again, even though he felt more alive. Maybe to be truly alive, he'd have to be dead. He didn't know what it felt like to be dead, so he didn't have an experience to compare it to. But he had been alive though, or at least mostly alive. He felt pain and fatigue from walking, or at least he had until he had sat down and eaten the mushrooms. He thought about being dead again, if he was dead before, and what that would feel like. He imagined that it would feel much the same as he felt before he was born, except he could not imagine what it felt like before he was born. Before he was born, he had no sense of anything at all. He couldn't even remember most of his early childhood, let alone a time before he was born. He did decide though, that the afterlife would be very much like the beforelife, and since he had no awareness of the one, then he would have also no awareness of the other. But he understood that much. Therefore, he was not dead. Or he had always existed, and this was just a moment caught in time like a specimen on a slide under a microscope.

All of those things came to him in the span of a heartbeat. Either his had slowed down, impacted by the mushrooms he had ingested, or his thoughts had raced by as quickly as the space between the muscular contractions of his heart. Which it was no longer mattered. He knew now that his eyes were closed again and, he could see the same things regardless of whether his eyes were open or closed.

He left his eyes closed, or at least he thought he did, but the colors he saw began to resolve themselves into more crystalline shapes that flowed distinctly against a background of the same flowing colors as the crystalline shapes themselves. Dunne knew that he was awake, but these images were dreamlike in a way — unreal and nonsensical, but they had autonomy and started to fashion themselves into shapes before his very mind's eye. Distant shapes became distinct, their colors brighter and sharper at the same time. One took a humanoid shape in the distance underneath his eyelid. It was as if a little man formed hundreds of meters away and then ambled over the flowing colors and shapes under his eyes that corresponded to the landscape of both the river city and no city that could ever be. The new being moved toward him steadily with intent. As it approached, it resolved more clearly from simply moving like a human to being a human-shape with two arms and two legs and a head that guided its steps with agency and meaning.

The being remained flowingly multi-colored, its bright tones indescribable to Dunne, as he had never imagined colors like these. They had earthy tones, but more energetic, as if imbued with all the light of the sun on a day that the clouds had been blown away. As the being drew nearer and resolved itself more clearly to Dunne, he saw that it was both tall and short, male and female, stocky and lean, muscular and flaccid. It shimmered and rippled, both in part and as a whole with the rhythm that came from Dunne's own heart. The creature shone brightly, but Dunne did not need to squint, as his eyes were already closed.

The being of light was beautiful, even without words or ideas to conceptualize what beauty meant. Dunne knew the word abstractly, and the being projected the meaning of the word through and into him. It filled him with its beauty and that beauty became his own. Then it was nearly upon him all at once or or in the depth of the uncountable hours that he sat at the base of the monument. The face it wore shimmered and shifted; it was all things at once, a mask and a genuine radiant glimpse of the soul it housed. It was both square-jawed and manly, like the plastic surgery models on the telescreen, and high-cheeked and willowy with thick pursed lips like their female counterparts. It shimmered between female and male in color and shape and reflected Dunne's own face at him as well in the moments between each radiating pulse. It blinked at him, its eyes at once large and baleful, filled with some of the sorrow that Dunne felt at being alone again, but also joyous at being free from the social construct of stress, and then again free from all things known and unknown. It was everything at once; it was even Dunne himself.

It was now less than an arm's length from him, gazing at, into, and through him. It spoke to him — its lips unmoving and moving all at once as colors oscillated and throbbed gently from its lips. It said nothing and said everything. Its words were both unintelligible and intelligible, heavy and weightless. Its hands and arms moved as it spoke, and they did not move at all. Dunne understood everything it conveyed as if they were his own thoughts. It loved him and it hated him, but everything that came from it felt perfectly suited for those moments between them.

Dunne did not have time to think questions, but he knew questions, and the being before him answered them before he thought about either. It gave him answers that he could never understand and yet always understood all at once. The voice that didn't belong to Dunne came through his own thoughts, nonetheless.

*"I am a being **you** that transcends all realities, an evolution of creatures who were once like you **beings**, once limited in four dimensions, but I have left those ways **stages** behind. I **you** am conscious and unconscious combined into one **all**. I am desire and realization, energy given more perfect form without a shambling body **you** to weigh me down. I can see all possibilities within you **us** too. My **Our** vision is not limited to seeing you as you are **were**, I **we** can see all things that you **we** could be, will be, won't be, should be, and shouldn't be. What we **I** see in you are probabilities and possibilities. I see your death **life** and I see your life **death**. I see that you **we** already died **lived** a million times, I can see you rot on the ground, food for worms and returning carrion birds, and I can see you **us** becoming like me **we**. I **we** see everything, and in your eyes I see me **us**, I see my **our** reflection in you, as you, behind you and in front of you, beside you and around you **always us**. I know what you could have been and what you still could be, and those things were very limited until you **we** went to the sea. You were caught between, on course laid out long before you **we** had been imagined by the generations that cracked and broke. I **We** can see strings and no strings above you, puppeteers and no puppeteer. You are an agent of something that I **we** can't see either, and this is a surprise because before I **we** saw you,*

*everything was in our view. You are **me** something new and*
something old, something made before long ago in the ages
*before matter came forth and yet you **we** are something*
entirely new and undreamed of, even by me. How can you be
***me** in the past, and be **us** the future?"*

The being's face came into crystalline focus to Dunne merely for a moment, and that face was an amalgam of confusion. It was a bewilderment without the weight of good or evil — simply the look of unimagined discovery. Dunne had never seen it before, but he knew what it was. The creature reached out its hands to him and held them at its sides and lifted them up over its head as if in supplication to something larger than both of them. Dunne took its extended hands in his and held them. They vibrated with warmth as the colored emanations of his heart synched fully between them.

"We have always been here. Your kind simply stopped being
able to see us…"

He squeezed the hands gently and they squeezed his back in response. The being smiled at him, through him and into him, and then he awoke with a start. He was under that same monument, facing the same direction from which the impossible being had come. He was alone. The world was again heavy and grey.

He hands felt cold, as if they had held something that drew the warmth from them. He drew his knees up to his chest beneath the woven cloak and slipped his fingers under his knees. He breathed deeply and sighed. The sun was in a different place, the shadows around him looked pregnant in a way, as if they held possibilities that they hadn't before. The mushrooms no longer filled his belly, but he felt less hungry than before as if an appetite had been sated. The world looked different to him. Things were changed from before and held the potential for even more change. Not only did he see the way that things were on the island, but he also saw more of how they could be. The world had indeed shifted on its axis. The greens and browns of the world before him had moved up an octave and sounded brighter in the fading light. The balance between the two colors shifted as well, and the green looked stronger than it had before.

Dunne felt a sense of contentment that had escaped him to this moment in his life. It was a feeling that he could not have imagined when he was working in the factory. Up to the moment he awoke, there were so many things that he had never before considered. He could understand that his senses were a filter that had been honed through an unimaginable evolutionary process, a way for mankind to focus on the things in his world that represented a danger to him. These figures had become invisible to a world of man that neither benefitted from them nor represented a danger to them. Now he understood that there was more to the world than he had known. There was *possibility*.

His head felt like it sat in front of where it actually did, just an inch or so forward of its actual position. The mushrooms had a powerful impact on him. Everything felt different and new. Despite the richness of the moment, he also felt a loss in that there was no one to share it with.

What did it matter if he found knowledge and hope but had no one with whom to share those things? Now after ingesting the mushrooms, he felt like he was a part of something larger and more significant, but he couldn't know what that would be with no one to share his new knowledge and experience with.

He had to leave the island.

Polite liberal pundits in the west couldn't
bring themselves to publicly state what they
knew: if the media were controlled by only
a handful of wealthy individuals, then it
would only advance an agenda that created
easy profit from the majority's ignorance
and their passion for violence and hatred.
The Rise of the New Kings
Dr. Isiah D. Malthus IV

XII

Nix had walked through the mists looking for his familiar haunts until he found himself in an old church by the sunken city center. Somehow, he'd taken a wrong turn. He hated this church, but he had always wanted to see the golden monument of his leader in person. Just not enough to pay for the honor. There was no one there to collect his debit now.

He was depressed again. The drugs only did so much for so long. The auto-programming on the telescreen grew monotonous or flickered on and off, and he craved new stimulation. He wandered through the city kicking in doors and exploring the commercial spaces they enclosed. He didn't find anything worth stealing, but breaking into spaces where he didn't belong felt good. It was a relief to feel like he was hurting someone again.

Now that he was inside the old church and there was no one about to prevent him from doing as he wished, he was going to satisfy his own curiosity about the golden idol he'd seen on screen so much. It stood before him in all of its shining glory as the sunlight streamed through a set of shattered windows in the vaulted ceiling which reflected from the statue a metallic light. If Nix could have conceived of it, he'd have imagined the yellow-lit walls of the church as rot — a mustardy, feculent mold growing into every nook and cranny of the old church. Instead, to him everything looked golden and thus more valuable.

The statue of his hero towered over him. He knocked down the velvet ropes that blocked it and stood toe to toe, gazing up into the golden eyes and the confident smirk. He did his best to mimic the statue's pose, imagining it as a reflection of himself. He was the "President for Life" of the island now, but it wasn't enough to have this whole kingdom to himself if it had no people for him to control. He felt the desire to travel to the national capital in the west across the ocean. To show those people the mettle of a man of the 51st state — the last man in the 51st state who survived the plague that ruined the population.

He looked at the gold statue and pondered his own future. He didn't know how to sail. Sailing was for the rich. There were no boats that he could charter a ride on with his debit. No planes had flown overhead to or from the airport. He had seen only sensorships moving through the sea since everyone had died or left. They moved automatically from port to port guided by GPS transmitters and carried no available consumables or crew quarters. He probably wouldn't survive the voyage across the ocean if he got aboard one of them. He had to find another way.

The golden idol seemed to be looking down at him, judging him. He wanted to please it, wanted for its smirk to be sign of affirmation for his actions. What would the President for Life do in his position?

Nix imagined himself to look like his role model. The golden hair, the healthy glow of his face. In the gilded statue towering before him, he saw a reflection of who he could be. He could be a leader of men now on this island state. There was no one there to deny him, to rule over him and dictate his actions. He could determine his own fate and the fates of everyone else. All that he had to do was stay on the island and wait for people to come back. He would be seen as a hero, as the last man standing, as the only one strong enough to beat the plague. Then, obviously as the man most fit to lead.

Now that he had a plan, he just had to find enough food and drugs to make it last until the people came back. He was still sure they would come back. He had no skills at making food or drink. He simply purchased processed consumables on credit like everyone else. Now here in the weeks or days that had passed since everyone else disappeared, he was already running out of easily taken food. There under the shadow of his idol in the church, Nix plotted a winding new path through the city to return to his barracks — one that he had not fully explored before. He would circle down through Balls Bridge and back to his home base.

He'd avoided it until now because he was worried about the security measures in those wealthy homes located there, figuring that the security systems were still online in homes that might offer little in the way of recoverable drugs. Now his curiosity was winning him over, and he wanted to see what the wealthy people of the city kept locked away in their homes. He'd heard stories being passed around among the

Orangeshirts about the riches hidden away by the wealthy, and now he felt safe enough to find out for himself.

He left the old, crumbling church and headed southeast. He had a better sense of where he was going now that the city was empty of other people. Knowing that he no longer had to do anything he didn't feel like doing was liberating. He strolled down the street with an exaggerated strut like he'd seen his heroes doing on the telescreen: leaned back, legs akimbo and arms jutting out the side from the shoulders as if his pudgy musculature demanded more space. He strutted over broken asphalt and past crumbling buildings until coming to an older and more resiliently built part of the city.

Here, the buildings were repaired with actual stone in an homage to the money they represented. Some of the wealthiest natives of the city lived here in gated and walled mansions. The grey and white stones, though weathered and gathering a thicker coat of grime each day, presented a deep contrast to the face of the city where Nix had worked and toed the "Orange line" for his masters. The Victorian style facades held no fascination or beauty for him. He wondered if there was a way to guess what was in each one to steal without breaking in to all of them. He looked up and down the street at all of the sooty buildings with their weathered and disintegrating details. There was one with a light green door that stood out to him.

He walked to the entrance up a short flight of steps, a simple stone facade over a brightly painted unripe apple green door. None of the other buildings had such a brightly colored entrance. He instantly concluded that someone important had once occupied the premises. Dangerous things were often brightly colored. The color reminded him of some poisonous satanic serpents being driven out of the island state by the President for Life when he'd made the former republic into the newest state of the union. That was one of his favorite animations. Nix touched the door gingerly, tapping lightly, waiting for a trap to spring or an alarm to go off. There was nothing. It didn't occur to him that the power might have already gone out in this part of the city.

Nix stopped and listened, tilting his head and watching for a flashing light to go off above the door. Then he kicked the bright green door, scuffing the paint and denting the metal panel. There was no response. He grinned and kicked it again, harder. The dent deepened. The green paint was scratched off. It felt good to kick something hard again. He kicked again and again, his smile deepening with each impact.

He directed his kicks at the side of the door near the latch. The door was bending and buckling inward with each impact. The paint chips dropped rusty brown bits on the step. The door had been corroding under the paint and was almost open. He paused to inspect the handle: bent and ready to snap. One last kick and he was in.

The foyer was as opulent as he expected. There was a large framed portrait of the President for Life on the wall opposite the entrance, in a gilded frame. He noticed as his footfall sounded on the marble floor that his boot had split at the seam between the toe and the sole. Now he would need to find a pair of boots to replace them, lest he wander the city with a bare foot.

He approached the painting to ascertain if the frame was true gold. He used his thumbnail to scratch it and found it was only covered with a thick layer of gold-colored latex paint. Still, it looked impressive from the opposite doorway. The ornately decorated living quarters had definitely belonged to someone very wealthy. The gilt didn't just encompass the painting of the president, it coated everything on the second floor.

Nix explored the space, taking note of how the private water closet had a water fountain with a golden handle next to the toilet with a golden seat. And all the water fixtures were gold as well, even as they now leaked noisy drips of water into golden drains. It was nothing like the common water room in the barracks. The golden tiled shower with thirty-five independent golden jets stood out to him. He wondered if the water was clean and hot as it sprayed out. The barracks' common shower water was brackish and tasted like mud when it got in his mouth.

Another floor upward were the bedrooms. One of the smaller bedrooms held a collection of sex dollies the likes of which Nix could not have imagined outside of the store on Graffon Street where the dolls were sold. These were almost entirely the expensive ones that Nix had only ever seen on adverts. Their sizes and shapes ranged from the pre-pubescent bodies hidden in the corner to the giantess two meter doll that was laid on the bed from corner to corner touching each bedpost. Normally Nix would have been impressed by the money represented in this one room, but now these objects of wealth and desire had lost their luster.

Their flexible plastic flesh looked dry and cold. The lifelessness of each one in its lacy finery no longer appealed to him. He couldn't imagine the pleasure each one promised without the programs from the telescreen to encourage his passions. He abandoned the sex doll storage bedroom to search for things that still held his interest. Back to the winding staircase and one floor up, was another level of bedrooms, each one larger than the room dedicated to storage of the sex dollies. If there were drugs to be found in this rich person's home, they'd likely be here as far as Nix imagined.

There were three bedrooms on the floor, each a door away through the sitting room. The first was an ornate and overstuffed room, filled with gold woven fabrics and overstuffed furniture that towered in the space. Nix looked under the bed and found nothing but dust. The wardrobe was packed with leather outfits of all shapes and sizes. They couldn't possibly have all been meant to be worn by the same person. Nothing he wanted was hidden there. He walked back through the sitting room to the second door and opened it into an opulent green room filled with what he immediately recognized as old, authentic wood.

This wasn't a bedroom, it was a storage room filled with old wood furniture, finished pieces that showed a real wood grain the like of which he'd never seen anywhere but on the telescreen. He knew that wealthy Orangeshirts collected real pieces of wood, but his father had mocked the practice as a waste of time and money. Real wood burned the same as the pressed wood used for manufacturing and home goods and lacked the pleasing odor from the fire that turf provided. Whoever lived here had a wood horde that was worth tens of thousands of dollars in the old world. To Nix, it looked absolutely worthless now. It would look pretty burning, but that felt like too much work. Nix exited the wood room and went back to the sitting room.

He didn't notice it until just then, but on the wall facing him was yet another painted portrait of the President for Life. This one was different than the one in the foyer. This was the famous smirking pose that citizens loved so much to use in memes that mocked their enemies. Just for a moment, Nix felt like the man on the wall was mocking him, mocking his lack of success in coming here and infiltrating these spaces meant for people who were closer to God, and thus closer to the President For Life than he was. He felt a brief flash of anger before being overcome by feelings of love and admiration as he stared at the man who had inspired his whole life. It was Nix's duty to honor and elevate him, not to allow these feelings of weakness to overcome him. Anger and hatred were reserved for the people below him, not his idol. He turned and roughly opened the door to the third room.

He could still feel his anger rising. He decided it was because he was bored, not because of the man he wanted to emulate. His patience in this place had worn thin quickly. It felt like too much work for far too little reward. He kicked the last remaining door open with his good boot.

The third room was decorated as a dungeon. The paint was black, and the window had evidently been heavily curtained until the supporting rod, which was now lying in a pile of heavy cloth on the floor, had broken. Plastic chains, fraying straps, and harnesses hung from the ceiling like light fixtures. Nix certainly didn't know if it was a house of torture, but he could imagine. Thinking about torture made him feel giddy. He assumed there was some kind of sexual element to it, but such devices and measures were still illegal in the fifty-first state. On a table by the window lay some empty liquor bottles, and among them were tubes of lubricants and jellies. Nothing he could use to escape the misery of the world around him. He sighed and turned to descend the stairs. He was impatient and done with searching. Little did he know that there was a large stash of stimulants in the upstairs bathroom. He was too impatient to search further.

He went back to the sex dolly room and took the one closest to the door by its arm and dragged it out and through the foyer. On the way down the steps it banged heavily as the plastic body tore and the metal frame inside gave way. Its legs caught on the stair rail and the arm came off in his hand. Nix pondered it for moment, imagined it was a real arm torn from one of the factory workers he oversaw, then tossed it over his back behind him as he turned to the streets to seek another cache of drugs.

*"There are few things more insidious to
the successful business than the employee
who insists that his employer is responsible
for his physical or mental health.
Such workers should be excised like
the cancerous tumors they are."*
How to Run your Corporation and be One
Chumly Macpie, III

XIII

Clouds moved in from the east. Heavy clouds, dark grey in color and luminously backlit, giving them an illusion of fullness. They stretched from the watery horizon across the sky leaving no opening for light. Dunne was going to get wet.

The clouds rolled in a wall that ran from the water on the coast thousands of feet upwards, meeting one mottled gray with another. The rain fell hard, rippling on top of the distant waves, driven towards the shore by the rumbling sky like stampeding wild horses. Thunder echoed deeply, reverberating across the landscape like a drum. Dunne remembered hearing stories that the thunder and lightning were once very uncommon on the island due to the cool winds and water currents of the past ages that had been washed away by the changing climate.

He remembered his own experiences of thunder and lightning crashing right outside the very hive where he lived and worked. It greatly frightened some of the others there who still told stories about a vengeful god that would strike down those who did not display the proper attitude of obsequiousness to the Orangeshirts and to the very mention of the President for Life who ruled over the island with the wisdom of Solomon the Old Testament.

The thunder cracked above him in clouds that flashed with electricity. The lightning danced through the gray banks, illuminating them like a host of blinking warning lights on a control panel. Dunne imagined that there were figures in the differing densities of the clouds, as if he were a child in an era long past lying on his back watching them roll overhead. Then lightning flashed again, and Dunne found himself uncertain that he had imagined the figures in the clouds. The same atmospheric bodies were still there moving forward in the roilng clouds, illuminated in the flashes of lightning, striding towards him and the mountain that he stood upon.

He squinted into the approaching bank of clouds seeking clarity. When he blinked, he lost the figures, but each flash of lighting brought their shapes back into his vision. There were giants striding through the sky towards him. Each flash, each stroke of thunder brought them closer. The line of rain advanced quickly and with accelerating pace from the edge of the water, over the ruined landscape and toward the mountain. The thunder rumbled with it, emanating from the lightning-filled clouds. The rumbling formed waves in the falling rain that seemed to match waves moving across the sea. The sound moved on him from every direction.

There was a loud thunder clap that started in the sky and rumbled down to Dunne, shaking the very earth where he stood. The rain was fully upon him then. The rugged green-brown weave that he was left wearing when he was spat back upon the surface of the earth darkened and shed the water like a second skin. A sigh went through the earth next to him and he turned to look. Not ten meters away standing on the same earth as Dunne was a giant.

At first he saw only the outsized foot, steam rising off it as if it had just fallen hot from the forge into the cool air. Then rising up through the mist was the rest of the leg, the hips and then the low-hanging torso whose chest was lost in the high mists that were still moving up the side of the hill and merging with the clouds of the sky.

The foot shifted to settle more surely onto the rocks, and then he saw the other foot glide straight down from the sky to rest on the ground opposite him. The fullness of hip and the taper to the waist implied a woman, but the further clues were cloud-hidden. Then hands dropped down and resolved themselves, seeming to be formed first from the very clouds before firming into fingers. The giant's skin was fair, the wrists and fingers delicately shaped. Dunne had seen hands like these before, but rarely. Those women never lasted long at the rending factory, taken away to satisfy the whims of one Orangeshirt or another and then actively disappeared.

Dunne looked up to where the feet indicated the rest of their owner was posed above the clouds. The sky continued to roil and pulse with thunder and lightning. If the sound and fury was the herald of the giant, then there were more to come. Dunne felt no fear. Not in his strangest dreams would he have imagined such a figure could be standing before him, but then not even his wildest dreams allowed him to picture being on top of this mountain looking out over the dead city into the ocean that lapped at the boundaries of man. He would never have had this opportunity had the world not changed so quickly.

The loud rumble of the thunder came from near him now, as if the storm center was upon him. The rumble resolved itself into a voice, a profound voice that emanated from the clouds above him. The giant was speaking. It was low and slow at first, as if trying to stretch vocal cords long dormant, just like his own. The words hung together at first, a thunderous murmur, then became more distinct. He heard the voice float higher and lighter than the thunder. It was beautiful. She was singing.

As the words resolved themselves to Dunne's ears, the sound of her voice became more distinctly beautiful.

...the ocean's murmuring tune,
Speaks to my bosom of a time,
When life was as a harvest moon,
Or warbling of a sylvan rhyme.

There was a deep pause and the winds swirled around Dunne. The giant was drawing a deep breath. The rain stopped falling and the sounds of nature organized themselves into the tune that the giantess was bringing to the hills. Her words soothed Dunne. He was transfixed by the way that nature was heralding and then swirling around this looming figure that had descended from the mists. He found that he was mindlessly humming along with the tune without meaning to, as if he were under a spell.

An old grey home upon the beach
A gentle face that blessed the door,

Whose eyes like a saint's from sculptured niche,
Look into mine forevermore
Full voices 'mid the garden flowers,
To soothe and sanctify the day,
These once were mine but frozen hours,
Have stolen them all to debts away.

One after one they glided past,
Borne on the stream that mocks at time,
On dusty thorny pathways cast,
'Mid poisoned cares I lived my prime,
But still the breath of early buds
Remained to scent the cross I bore,
To give me strength to breast the floods,
That break on life's enclouded shore.

Snow, chilly snow fell on my way,
And cast sharp icy thrills around.
But gentle voices day by day,
With hopeful tones my faint heart grew fond,
Soft stars looked through the dark browned skies,
And poured a pulsing light on mine,
I felt they were the radiant eyes,
That lit my youth beside the sea rime.

Back memory! close thy faded leaves,
And let me ope the page to come,
'Tis not with thee my soul now grieves;
I pine for rest; I thirst for home!
I want to see beloved forms,
I want to clasp soft hands again,
To hear no more the roaring storms,
To feel no more the aching pain.

The song ended, and the rain began to fall once again. It left an odd and unmistakably salty tang on his face. He licked his lips dry. It tasted like the sea. The drops felt like lightning on his tongue, electricity in his chapped lips. Then it struck him as he stood at her feet. They were tears.

Then the clouds sank to the ground as the unseasonably chill winds lifted. He was so accustomed to warm breezes of his world, the one formed after the seas rose and the climate changed. This chill was unsettling. He thought about the lines between those who made the world he came of age in and those who would make themselves in the ruins of that world that he now walked through. Everything was changing.

The mist intensified and Dunne lost his bearings. He could see his hands when he held them before his face, but the feet and the body of the giantess had now completely vanished. He wanted to walk to where she had been, to reach out to her and feel for the solidity that he was sure was still there in the mist — to touch that beauty that he had only been able to glimpse — but he did not.

The air once again felt dense, as though the lightness that the song brought to the air had melted in the resurgent rain. He could sense the water in the air being drawn down to earth by weight, mass, and gravity. He closed his eyes and bathed in the mist holding his hand out to the sky to catch the increasing raindrops on his outstretched fingers. The rain felt lightly electric again, as if the fall from the sky had given it a measurable static charge. The hair on his arms stood on end. He could have been struck by lightning in those moments and he would not have cared. He had never felt more alive, and life was filling him more with each passing minute in the rain.

Lightning crashed near enough to shake the earth he stood upon. Its afterimage dotted his vision and he blinked his eyes repeatedly to wash the spots from his retinas. Then the clouds sank further and their weight was fully upon him. He brought his own hand up before his face and it was invisible to him again. Cotton batting obscured everything.

He was lost.

XIV

Dunne was walking toward the hills of the island after the fog had abated, the mountains as the locals could call them, seeking the high ground. It was his most clear course of action when he didn't know where else to go. The landscape rose to meet him and became more bare as he walked. The sun became hotter and the clouds thinned. It shined more directly on him. The air felt heavy.

Dunne felt unsettled and couldn't reason why, but then he realized that he was being watched. He neared the crest of the hill. Plasti-trash fluttered in the wind, blown and sometimes caught between the rocks. Wrapping papers and cups from foodstuffs and drinks littered the ground like paving stones. And at the top, a giant man.

He was seated on the stones and bent over nearly double with his head down. He was not hiding his eyes from what there was to see though, he was protecting Dunne from seeing his eyes.

The giant's voice pierced the otherwise still silence. "Be you a man or a woman? I can hear your feet on the stones, and I can hear your breath." Near him on the rocks lay the complete skeleton of a cow. It looked merely dog-sized compared to the man. Dunne had never seen such a thing before in his life. The giant adjusted his posture, but kept his eyes covered with his hands. He paused as if he could see Dunne staring at the bones. "This is my cow. I stole it. I paid a heavy price though. If not for the cow, I'd have lived forever; I'd have ruled this isle through the age of man, instead of being in interminable darkness until man passed away." The giant rolled his shoulders and groaned wearily. "I've waited for my time to return, just as I waited my time to come, long, long ago. I bided in the depths of the sea for ages, I dwelt in the darkness and the pressure for more days than you could conceive." He shifted uneasily as he spoke. "This was once all ours, you know. We were here first. The others came later... well after the rocks had cooled and the first sedge took root. When my ancient kin landed, we left footprints in the cooling magma. Our footprints became the first flowerbeds. We left the foundation for all of the invaders to come after — even you, man of the hidden spaces. I can see you, even though I hide my eyes, and I see in you that you are as many generations of this island as I am, though I was here ages ago and I am here now." Dunne wondered at the meaning of his statement but stared unmoving.

The giant stood up from his place on the rocks, but kept his arm over his face. "This land has changed so very much from when I last walked upon it. I died here on this mountaintop, killed by my own grandson in a fit of righteous patricide." His head bowed toward the ground, his eye still blocked by his forearm. "That is the way of the world, the young succeed where the old fail, they grow through them, like flowers through cracks in stones, to become more than what their ancestors were. The cycle of death and rebirth is constant. It is always from the ruined remains of the ages past that new ages emerge. Sometimes they come from the sea, sometimes they come from cracks deep in the earth. But they are ever changing." He gestured over the landscape with his free arm. "And now I have returned from the darkness that moves over everything. I have returned from eons lost, from a space where there was no sun or stars to mark the seasons, no greens to fade to browns, nothing to wither and die, nothing to grow. Time did not move for me, but it was interminable. It was forever and and not-ever all at once. It was waiting. Forever waiting for time to fail or time to move. And then I was here. The darkness faded into light and I came back to this very space that I had walked my last steps in, saw my last sunlight. I sat here to ponder this, and then you appeared." He knelt down and stroked the skull of the dead bovine as if to pet its worried brow.

Dunne didn't know what to say. If he had, he would still not have spoken. Some spaces called for his silence. He had much more to learn by listening than by demanding his voice be heard.

"I see you though, a listener though you be," said the giant as he sat back on the natural stone cairn. "I see that you are both things, that you are both dead and reborn, that you are both father and son, that you have sprung up from your own remains in a death and become something new. You are both the past and the future, reborn in your own skin, new and old, greater than the sum of both. You are material and immaterial, and your spirit hovers in the air like a light that threatens to blind even my all-seeing, burning eyes." The man paused again, considering Dunne through the arm that blocked his vision. "You don't know a thing yet. But if you listen more than you speak, if you look more than you act, if you can be more than you do, you might find the things you seek."

Dunne nodded like a child affirming a father's admonition. He sighed and took a deep breath of the air around him which felt cool and clean despite the heat of the sun. He blinked slowly feeling the weight of the giant's words to find that the giant and his cow were gone when he opened his eyes. Dunne was learning not to fear the unexpected.

He looked down the refuse-strewn hill to the boggy lowlands that stretched back toward Sallynog and Blackstone and then back out to the misty sea to the lonely and ruinous crags of the isle of Hooth. Between the sea and his position stretched a walled space, large flat grounds used by the wealthy to play golf and target shoot. The green plasticized turf stretched out like a brilliant emerald patch between the bruised, beaten landscapes on either side. The yet well manicured green spaces still held clean water traps and raked sand pits. The Orangeshirts could trade debt to play on the course, but this one was most favored by tourists from across the ocean because it held the President for Life's personal branding.

The mists from the high moor that bathed Dunne seemed to magnify the views into the surreally tailored landscape. The water traps nearest the seas looked to have misshapen human forms in them, but they reflected a luminosity from the pools they sat in. He wondered if they were merely statues that had been used for target practice by the Orangeshirts or the tourists, but the pool's light couldn't be explained as reflections of the sun.

Dunne's curiosity and his quest for answers drove him down into the artificial greens through a broken gate. The transformation from the browns, grays, and blacks of trash and mud into the plasti-turfed power greens of the golf course/shooting range was shocking to his senses. The mists drifted down into and over the high walls that kept the island's unwanted masses from this dedicated leisure property of the wealthy.

Through the lines of mist in this artificially twisted moor, Dunne could see that the grey shapes were statues in the pools, posed as if emerging from the water. As he approached through the unnatural greens, he saw that they were relics of misshapen monsters, the sorts of creatures relegated to the cartoons on the telescreens made to entertain youth. There was a creature with a single giant eye, his one oversized arm sprouting from mid-chest, a creature with one oversized leg, poised as if to hop to life from the pool. Others trailed from the iridescent pools, each more nightmarish than another. Among them a squat, fat-haunched goblin; a flabby dog-headed man, and an upright body of a fish on two outsized fin-shaped man legs.

Dunne paused to consider these monstrosities, surprised that the Orangeshirts didn't reduce them to so much rubble with their firearms. He paused and looked to his left. He felt eyes upon him, but the greens were clear. He turned back to the statutes. He sensed the fish creature was looking at him through its one stony eye. Then its voice spoke to him.

"You are a man. You walk and live. Every other man is sinking to the bottom of the sea, where we have been waiting for our time to come again."

Dunne was shocked. None of the statues moved or looked more capable of movement than anything chiseled out of island stone. Every other statue in the strange group continued looking forward, gazing upward into the center of the lands that spread out before them. Dunne followed their eyes and saw that the hills beyond the walls seemed greener than when he walked down — as if the artificial green had bled out of the place through his entrance and merged with the muddied, trashed browns of the island. The figures in the water hazard remained as still as ever, not moving or looking at Dunne. He stood still, looking at them as well, a statue of a man staring at statues of not men, considering them as they considered the land before them.

The voice emanating from the man-fish spoke to him again. "We have conversed with each other and cannot ascertain why you walk upon these shores and greening fields. Your kind are dead upon this isle, and yet you remain whole and hale." The voice paused. Dunne waited, holding his breath as if an errant exhalation would leave the creatures before him bereft of their voice that seemed to come from the space within the center of the fish creature before him. "That which is you is more than you were. You are not like us, but you are more than us. You are not like a man, either. We cannot understand what you are, except that it confounds our sight."

Dunne examined the statues' impassive stone stares. The fish-man was quiet. Another voice spoke from the group. It was low, rough, and sounded like a growl coming from the chest of the dog-headed man. "We warn you, man-thing. This island will be ours. The *Tuatha Dé Danaan* will have no say. Their time is past too. It was they who laid the island bare for the men who followed, your kind. They drove us from these shores, took our lands from us, though we were here long before them. Now the order is reversed, and the first kings of the sea, the bottom dwellers have come back. Make way, man. Make way."

Dunne looked for the beings in front of him to move, to make gestures or threats that he was so familiar with coming from his experiences with the Orangeshirts, but there were none. These creatures, as fearsome as they were, were just as still as the statues that they were indistinguishable from. It was as if they had simply stood in this refined and built-upon spot on the old bog forever — as if the landholders built their course up around them. There were as ghosts given physical form. Dunne wanted to reach out, to touch them and see if they were as real as the voice sounded, but he did not. It was not fear keeping his hands from them. Perhaps it was wonder that kept him from wanting to feel their stony flesh, if flesh it was. If he touched them, it might solve a mystery he wanted to allow to exist. He stood there a while longer, listening to the waves and waiting, but they did not speak to him again. They did not move. He looked up the hill. He had to keep on moving. It was the only thing to do.

XV

From the base of the mountain to the city center, Dunne found that his direction was finally clear before him. He had wandered and meandered much than he had intended on his walk to find answers, but the countryside had a way of pushing and pulling him about in directions that did not necessarily make straight lines. Now he looked for the tallest building in the west part of the city and walked through the winding streets to its base, keeping its heights in his sight as much as he could.

As he moved down from the elevation of the old lodge, Dunne could see the rows upon rows of houses and tall buildings rising up before him in the multi-gated and walled compound. Many of the lower levels of buildings near the old river had been consumed and covered by the rising water levels and the large and expansive industrial manufacturing plant was now just a stone's throw from the tidal flood delta. Beer had been made there for hundreds of years and would have been made there for hundreds more, given that the land was owned by a multi-national conglomerate with the unequaled foresight to obtain a seven thousand year lease on the property.

Some things had changed since the lease was signed. As the sea levels rose and the weather got warmer, the conglomerate sought to enhance its short-term profit margins on that property by inserting itself into the lucrative local real estate market. They built upwards on top of the brewing facility after convincing the local boards and committees that their enterprise would improve the community. The additions above the manufacturing and bottling plant became substandard and over-priced hive-style housing with built-in merchant kiosks for workers and their families. The company used the same investment-enriching concept (that was one step removed from slavery) that other companies had used when seeking to maximize investment return: employees were given the opportunity to live on site in indentured servitude with rent deducted from their earnings.

Employees like Dunne traded convenience for constantly-declining living conditions. The workmanship was slapdash, committed by the lowest bidder, who pocketed the majority of the finances dedicated to the materials and substituted substandard materials and labor. The walls were cheap fiberboard, pressed and glued from the only tree allowed to grow on the island, the Shitpine. It wasn't native, but grew quickly in the climate and terrain to be harvested for building materials. It allowed the landowners of the forests that had once been national parks to make a consistent profit on a twenty-year rotating schedule of plant and harvest.

The beer brewed on the lower floors took on the same quality as the buildings the workers lived in. As the climate swiftly shifted toward a warmer but much more erratic one, the materials traditionally used to brew the beer became more scarce and expensive. In order to increase profits, the multi-national beverage conglomerate changed ingredients gradually one scarce input after the other until the product became unrecognizable from its original form. Quality declined, but it stayed relatively cheap, so people drank it — a lot of it. People got sick. A handful died. More and more people were dying in those days, so very few people blamed the beer. And so it went. Whispered rumor in Dunne's hive had it that the beer's latest incarnation was brewed with sawdust and filtered through rags that were also used to clean the machinery of the brewery. It all happened behind closed doors, and the truth was as closely guarded a secret as the brew's original formula.

The brewery was now quiet. He searched the maze of streets around its base for the one that would allow him to gain access to the tower. He found a narrow street between two of the tallest walls in the compound and followed it. On the south side of the wall was a portal that had been used as an entrance for the public relations portion of the building. There, the owners sold tours to gawking foreigners who fetishized the beer's advertising.

Dunne found himself in a carpeted lobby with its velvet ropes and aluminum poles tossed and torn. The turnstiles and gates were broken as well. There were signs of violences affected against the material aspect of the place, but no signs of violence against people. Nor were there any people. The building was just as empty as the streets. It was as though people had gone into hiding or simply disappeared after breaking all that they could. He descended down a hall and then up again into a large atrium area with many steps and levels visible above him. There were more signs of violence on his left. Merchandise shelves and displays had been set upon and smashed. A few emblematic rags torn and strewn here and there. Broken glasses — many, many shattered and broken drinking glasses.

Dunne wanted to climb to the top to look around, to find answers as to what happened to the people of the city. He thought perhaps there would be a bomb crater, or something similar. Seeing the empty city center from ground level frightened him. He could feel a broad new sense of loneliness creeping into his awareness and wanted to find someone who could break those dark feelings that were easing into him.

Before, there were always busy people around him, scurrying like mice from light when the door opened. Now, he was a solitary creature wandering hill and dale alone. He'd always been lonely, but this was a deeper, stronger intensity of those emotions. He had at least been around other living people at the rending factory. Now, he'd gone days without seeing anyone except the mysterious, unreal visions of mythological creatures in the mists. His stomach rumbled with hunger, but a deeper pain grew at his core.

He climbed up step after step, turning at each landing and winding farther up. He found himself at the top soon enough. The serving bar on the highest level was deserted, and the taps were broken and twisted, but the windows overlooking the city were still whole and undamaged. The city was on display from the top of the tower; down below he could see much of the sprawling labyrinthine streets and the dark pool of the city's origin on display.

Years earlier, the tidal river had been trained to new boundaries by a Dutch company which built high seawalls to restrain the river at high tide. The former famous Templar Bar area had washed out and collapsed though, as the underlying River Poddle had also grown due to the increased rain from the highlands and the tidal flow into the basin from the rising seas. The former Sex, Woody, and Wellie Quays had all been lost to the rising waters and falling foundations which had reformed the old "Dark Pool" in a new area at the confluence of the two rivers, both the old one that ran under the city and the newer one that ran through it. It was, as it had been in the past, an open sewer filled with refuse. The wind blew a crawling mist over the oily film-covered pool that was a run-off collection basin for the local injection fracking machines. Enough polluted sediment had collected in the dark pool that the ongoing chemical reactions kept the mist bubbling up from the depths.

Dunne was fortunate that there were no open flames near the continuing flow of the river. Large chemical holding tanks and sluice pits that had been long on the edge of dissolution were now dissolving under the lack of ongoing maintenance. The chemical run-off all went to the pool in the city center regardless, but the rate was accelerating. The winds blew a constant stream of fumes off the pools that still gathered and festered in the lowlands. If he had been down below on the streets of the city when the winds were still, his lungs would have burned under the weight of the chemicals.

Standing now in the tower and peering out over the pool and the city gave Dunne a new perspective. He could see the city, but even at its peak, people would not have been visible. It was always the works of man that changed the world and showed large. They left scars upon the landscape and those marks lingered for thousands of years after men were gone.

Dunne didn't know it, but the island had once been well-forested. It was covered over with a wind-rippled, flowing green ocean of trees. It was also filled with all manner of beings that were lost to the record of history, because they did not shift and change the movements of the very winds as men did. The absent ones did not do as generations of men had done when they found an island teeming with plants they could sell and animals that they could consume. Those extinct beings that came before existed as part of the planet rather than in defiance of it. It was always and only man that viewed the natural order as an obstacle to be broken and dominated.

These strange images forced themselves upon Dunne now in the high tower. His eyes throbbed and his ears rang. Dunne could see and know these things now; they simply showed themselves in his mind's eye as he looked out the windows onto the city. They blurred and shifted in and out from his normal vision. He could see the past and the present shifting into the future, briefly showing through the fourth dimension. He saw the long-gone forests and the natural flow of the clean river unimpeded. He saw these things at the same time he saw the modern city. His head swam with images both present and past. He sat down on the debris covered floor and rubbed his head until it cleared. The sights from the tower had provided him with perspective, but not the perspective he had imagined. He knew more than he had before. Now, to figure out what to do with it.

Dunne was illuminated from the outside, but not illumined from within. He had seen the city in a way that only rich tourists and landowners could, but the vista brought him nothing that he was looking for. He was still a student looking for answers, not prepared yet to teach himself. His meetings with the strange visitors along his journey had changed him, and the sight of the city through the dark pool seemed to be the catalyst that brought a shift in his ability to see the world and to solve problems. There was that demarcating line of mastery that he had a hunger to transcend, but then again he wasn't ready to cross it.

He had never felt any hunger so profound before when he was living in the hive and eking out his existence in the factory. It was hammered out of him, just like it was hammered out of everyone at the mills and factories. The humans involved on the bottom levels were the metal. The tasks appropriated to them were the hammer; their machines and the buildings that they labored in were the anvils. People were simply raw material. Dunne walked down the steps of the tower and wound back to the lower levels.

As he neared the second floor, he heard the sounds of movement rising up from below. Someone or something else was alive. On that floor, near the discarded and torn memorabilia hawking the stout beverage once produced there, was a man and a large boiling pot. They were not present when he had passed through earlier.

The fire for the boiling and the pot itself was laid over the floor where just minutes before Dunne had seen the replica of the signed land lease laid under glass on the floor of the expansive room. He stopped on the bottom step to gawk at the man and his doings.

The man was of average height and build, grey haired and clean shaven. He had a long aquiline nose that seemed to dip over his mouth and lips which were tightly pursed with concentration. His clothes were grayish black, like charred coal, and a high white collar separated his head from his body making it appear to drift above his frame. As Dunne watched, the man's edges seemed to flicker.

Dunne had seen something similar on the hot summer days in Sallynog, as the heat from the sun's eye baked the dark, asphalt surfaces in the hot, rainless summers. The edges of things in the distance shimmered. Rippling waves formed over the roads. Boundaries blurred, and Dunne's sense of lines diminished.

The edges of this man and his work wavered, as if he were generating or reflecting tremendous amounts of heat. He lifted and poured a burlap sack of what appeared to be barley into the boiling mix before him. It reminded Dunne of a tale he'd once seen played across the telescreen on Halloween, or what he'd heard old people mutter and call Samhain. Something with dark human shapes hovering over a boiling cauldron, witches making a dark brew — something to beguile and transform unwitting subjects.

Dunne stepped down to the floor from the stairs and moved slowly toward the shimmering image of a man at work.

The being took no notice of him, but stirred the barley into the boiling mix intently, looking closely into the mix for a sign. Dunne cautiously circled the man, looking to be certain that the image before him was not a simple projection from a telescreen as he had seen so many times before. The man continued to shimmer and flicker at the edges, but resolved to firmness in the center just as he should have. He existed in the same world that Dunne moved through.

Dunne stepped closer, moving into what should have been the man's line of sight, but still the brewer took no notice of the cowled figure creeping toward him. Dunne had been moving slowly so as not to alarm or frighten the man. He moved easily once within the man's range of vision but the man did not respond.

The busy figure paid him no heed. Dunne stepped again toward the boiling cauldron, leaned in its direction, and felt the heat of the fire emanating through the pot of water and barley. He could smell the rich scent now. It made his mouth water. His tongue felt dry. He desired to sample the contents of the cauldron when the man was done.

Closer now to the man before him, he saw the figure's unreality more clearly. He was nearly on top of the vision, could feel the heat from it, could sense the space that it filled as if he were aware of the gravity well that the cauldron created, but he dared not reach out to grasp it. He could smell it all easily, could hear the crackle of the oxygen within the wood grain pop as it was ignited under the cauldron, but could not will himself to reach out. He sensed somehow that to try to touch the man who worked, oblivious to his intrusion, would transgress against some immutable law. Dunne simply watched.

The man now moved on to another step in his process. His cauldron rested over the fire on a tripod, and he grasped a large handle with a rag to tip the giant bubbling cauldron into another lower similary sized container at the side of it. He stretched a large piece of muslin over the mouth to strain out the barley to allow the concoction in the pot to cool. He then measured heaping scoops of malt out of another burlap sack to drop into the cauldron of water. The scent that rose now from his work redoubled its impact on Dunne's senses. He was so thirsty.

Dunne backed away from the man and his work, found a broken turned-over shelf to sit upon, and gave himself over to marvel at the sight before him while trying not to think about his dry throat. The man was brewing a beer, but not the swill that Dunne had been drinking on credit at his hive. That beer was oily, left a plasticine taste on his lips and made his stomach ache profoundly before exiting his body uncomfortably all at once some hours later. This was something cleaner, fresher, more lively, something from out of time.

Dunne understood now, as he sat absorbing the sights before him. It was not a man that Dunne saw before him, but a memory. A cultural memory, a three-dimensional hologram of the past locked in a physical place and given an energy that was pushed through four-dimensional time to become visible to a world in which it was long lost. The mushrooms had given him insights into the characters he'd met since he was reborn.

Dunne felt it was time to move on from this scene. He had borne witness to this myth — this more modern cultural memory — and now he felt a compulsion to move on. He turned his back on the scene to leave, but he felt a light tug on his coat — so light that it was merely a hint of a suggestion to remain. He turned back to the scene. It was the brewer. He held an unbroken pint glass before him filled with a reddish black liquid with a thick whitish layer of foam at the top. The vision looked directly into Dunne's eyes with his head angled impishly, the smile on his thin lips imploring Dunne to take the glass.

He took it from the outstretched hand and inhaled deeply over the glass. It smelled overwhelmingly rich and heady. He raised the glass to toast the brewer who now stood away from him, watching him with his hands clasped at his belly. Dunne tipped the foamy drink into his mouth and drank. He found it to be the most satisfying thing he had ever tasted. His eyes closed and he savored it. He licked the foam from his upper lip and opened his eyes again.

The man who had passed him the pint was gone. The cauldron and the fire were gone. Even the heat which had radiated from it all had disappeared as quickly as the vision of the man. All that remained was the half-full glass now clasped in Dunne's hand, as cold and refreshing as anything he could ever remember tasting in his measured existence. It was invigorating. He savored the taste. He wanted to treasure it, to save the remaining half pint and take it with him wherever he went, but he knew in his heart that this moment was already going away. He tipped the remaining stout into his mouth and drank it as slowly as he could. Two more draughts, and the glass was empty save the residue of foam on the sides of the glass.

His eyes fluttered and he lifted the empty glass to his eye to inspect and found that the glass itself had changed in the blink of an eye. It was now not only empty, but cracked, and dry — as if it had never held anything at all but dust.

Had he imagined the whole experience? No. His belly, once yawning, felt full. He could still taste the drink on his tongue. He had not imagined that. To imagine something such as that means that the imaginer must have at one point experienced that which he imagines. No man can imagine such pleasures that are so completely foreign to his experience as to be a total fabrication of mind.

But strange things were entering into Dunne's experience since he had awoken in the grotto. He was vexed by strange feelings that he was experiencing things again, or even that he was seeing things before they happened. The strangest feelings that vexed him were the ones that made him feel as if he remembered things that had never happened or that could never happen. If they couldn't happen, how could he remember them? Especially if he couldn't remember anything before a certain point in his life, as if he had sprung fully formed from the earth as a large child with the mind of an adult. He couldn't remember things that he was aware that he should have remembered, so how could his mind be telling him things that could not objectively happen?

His thoughts were assailed by deep feelings of presque vu. Something was coming. It was going to happen. He was going to remember something or experience something, or perhaps remember something without experiencing it. That would be some sort of inverse jamais vu. In the back of his mind, he was already questioning whether or not all of this was something that had already happened to him that he could not for some reason remember, and that was why it all seemed fresh and new. But how could he be certain of anything at all when everything felt so uncertain? If only there were someone that he could ask who might know. But there wasn't. As far as he knew, everyone was dead. He didn't know for certain that everyone was dead, but there was a well-defined feeling that he couldn't escape. It came from the pit of his stomach, or from the base of his spine, or from the middle back of his head, well above the spine, but below and interior to the bony plates of his skull. Or perhaps from all of them at once. It was the feeling that he was all alone.

Dunne looked back to the broken debris and the glass floor that still held the aged facsimile of a contract that was legally binding for thousands of years. There had not been a fire on top of it. There had been no man brewing there to hand him a fresh drink. He was alone in the great hall and the signs that he had been the only person there for several days were quite obvious. Dunne walked out through the disordered chaos.

The world kept turning.

*The worst kept secret in the world was that
one man must be miserable for another man
to make a profit. The only question was how
much would a man pay to escape his misery?*
Mastery of Economics in Practice
Som Dumkopf

XVI

Dunne could not know it, but his forebearers on the
island had a proud tradition of building things to last. That
custom faded quickly in the mid twenty-first century as Neo-
feudalism spread from America and took hold in the former
liberal democracies of Europe. Corporate persons took
ownership of everything. Highly profitable practices utilizing
disposable and temporary building materials became the norm
shortly thereafter, as they offered the best short-term rewards.
Investors demanded immediate profits be wrung like the last
drops of filthy water from a publican's rag.

As Dunne walked through the city, he noticed things
that before would have escaped his attention. His ability to
understand the world he lived in had increased since his
emergence from the underground. He had time to think about
his place in the world when he didn't have to devote his
waking mind to survival in a system meant to destroy him for
profit. He often found his mind wandering as he sought
information in the ruined countryside and empty city. Parts of
the city were in ruins, but they had always been in some state
of ruin. He looked up at the buildings and then back down to
the road he walked on. One seemed like an extension of the
other. If the roads were built just well enough to last under the
weight of traffic for a year or two before crumbling to gravel,

then the construction companies that were contracted to do the work on them had a constant stream of business from government contracts. Once the business owners realized the constant stream of money to be made from roads, it became elementary to apply that same model to the buildings that lined them. However, like much of the transportation infrastructure that went far too long without repair and reconstruction and collapsed on or under pedestrians now and again, the buildings sometimes crumbled and fell down onto and under the people who lived and worked in them.

Dunne walked and thought about how the the people in power had the right to do whatever they could get away with, particularly after they had changed the laws to cement their own superiority. Nothing was denied to the wealthy man. The average man had no ability or desire to read or understand the laws that were made for him any more than a trained animal at the circus had a desire to understand the bars of his cage. He also had enough distractions to keep him from thinking about the problems that he faced. If he had, he would have realized that the problems that he found to be endemic in the system were arbitrary constructions built to keep him and his ilk buried below the broad foundations upon which the rule makers exercised their oligarchic superiority.

Besides, if they could read or understand it, what could they do? They had no power. There was no one and nothing to represent people like them in the matters of governance. The business of government was business, and the interests of people who had only debt were not profitable. Dunne could see that now that he wasn't fighting every minute of every day to survive.

The street ended and Dunne came upon an old walled park. The dark, unlit sign over the gated entrance read "St.Evens Green," given that spacing and punctuation on signage had long ago been disposed of in the aim of simplicity. He looked into the city park at the green-less browns and grays of mud and garbage. It had not been green for some time, if ever.

"Green" was a word that had a singular meaning to Dunne. Green was once synonymous with nature, but as the green of nature was lost, the "green" became "money" even as the green of money was replaced first by plastic cards and then finally the implanted chips. Wages had ceased being physical tender that passed from hand to hand and had become transient "value" that was added or subtracted from sub-dermal metal and plastic. If "green" meant anything at all, it meant that space had monetary value that could be wrung from it. This was the St.Evens Green that Dunne saw.

The ducks, pigeons, geese, and seagulls that had once made stopovers in the pond had been poached long ago to feed the poor folk who couldn't afford their debt meat. The open space in the middle of all of the shops was small, as the outer edges had been sold off bit by bit for small merchant stands. Then those small stands had been bought by the large corporate conglomerate that sought to incentivize investment in the city center.

As Dunne looked upon all the different advertising signage, he could not know they were all owned by the same corporation that hawked candy confections of multiple "competing" brands. All of them flowed forth from the same factories across the ocean where convicted criminals and children slaved in their production.

St.Evens Green was brown. The pit near the center was filled with muddy garbage instead of water. Dunne could smell rot, but it wasn't the ordinary rot of the garbage produced by human waste or garbage cast-offs. It was the distinct smell that he associated with the rending pits by the factory: The smell of death that Dunne knew too well: the body left to wither and dissolve in its own juices and dry before being scraped up to be buried. Then a few months later exhumed when the mineral value could be more easily extracted from the corpse.

It was a profitable industry for some. A dry corpse held value because of all the things the body absorbed in the gut. A living body could have organs harvested and sold, but a dead body held a different kind of capital. The truth was not lost on Dunne even if the significance was. The human body had to be dried out for the raw materials to be extracted. A wet, rotting corpse smelled horrid, but far beyond the smell of rot was the odor of the chemicals stored in the lipid cells and organs of the bodies. The body was a penultimate repository for all of the soluble chemicals produced for consumption.

In life, bowels and bladders became cancerous, tongues grew lesions, cells festered and multiplied out of control, forming tumors that could be excised by a surgeon for the right amount of debt. But a body that no longer grew and festered could be legally harvested. There was nothing left to make a man worth more than his raw materials. Every bit of value had to be extracted from him, living or dead. It didn't matter to the people in control. The lives of the working class were simply capital they could expend in the chase for more wealth.

Dunne sometimes wondered if his own stomach pains after eating the mysterious meat on offer at his hive were a result of the tumors in the meat invading his cells and creating a beachhead for a cancerous growth. He'd seen tumors grow on the skin and swell in the bellies of his co-workers. They started as pimples, then became scabs, then became pustulous swellings that rapidly took on lives of their own — seeming to steal their growth from the bodies that hosted them like an inverse pregnancy that aborted its host.

As the tumors grew, the people shrank. If the worker could afford the debt to have them carved out, then they'd miss a day of work and come back painfully hunched and stuporific from the addictive opiate painkillers they were given. If they didn't have the proper debt profile, they couldn't get the surgery. They were doomed either way. They rarely lasted more than a few months after the diagnosis. The tumor killed them or the treatment did. Patients couldn't afford the best drugs available to the ruling class, but they could afford to go into debt for the unregulated free market alternatives that could kill them. Either way the drugs were painkillers.

Dunne walked along the wall, looking at all the obnoxiously bright food adverts. They were all things that he had wished he had the debit to buy just a few short days ago. There were the Jammirodgers, the Tallywhakkers, the

Willypockets, the Orange Smashers, and the Dolly Robbers. All of those corn syrup products that were so sweet and addictive.

Dunne loved the Orange Smashers. They were the official Orange treat of the Orangeshirts. It was an orange corn syrup drop with a gummy liquid center. It had an oil aftertaste, blunted by overwhelming sweetness. Once he'd found one that someone else had dropped to the floor in the common kitchen area of the hive and Dunne secreted it away back to his own cubby where he unwrapped and devoured it.

His palate, so often dulled by regular doses of overwhelming sweetness, was awakened just long enough to catch the aftertaste. That week he'd gone without eating for two days because he was too deep in his debt account. The Orange Smasher on the floor was an unexpected bonus.

That was the moment that he learned the deceptive truth of life: Things that are most strongly promoted on the telescreen are often actually the very worst. It was always short-term pleasure to be traded for long-term grief. There were so many ways to get short-term pleasure for debt. He just had to keep debting over and again after each short-lived pleasure diminished to nothing. The Orange Smasher made his stomach hurt that day, and he never wanted one again. Still, the bright advertising on the sign made him long for the imagined sweet pleasure even as he remembered the rotten-gut feeling that followed.

Many of the telescreens in this part of the city had ceased functioning. The handful that were left flickered on frozen images. The flat screens themselves were in disrepair.

Like everything else, they were constructed with the cheapest materials available. They broke down and had to be repaired constantly. They often malfunctioned, but they were usually replaced regularly by their own dedicated private repair industry. Telescreens had been important to the rulers of the world. Until now.

If Dunne needed further proof beyond the time clocks in his factory that all of the human structures on the island were breaking down, this was it. The automated screens normally operated on continuous loops, broadcasting signals beamed down from satellites and transmitted through cables from across the ocean — but their end failsafes were humans, and those failsafes had failed.

The petrofiberboard facades on the opposite side of the streets from the telescreen wall were also crumbling quickly in the absence of human maintenance. Dunne kept to the middle of the road, stepping over the rails that guided the people movers to and fro under normal circumstances. The tracks were eerily silent, not at all like the constant click and clack that he could hear even at the hive in Sallynog when his shift ended.

The gray fog was strengthening around him again. The mists ebbed and flowed without reason and played tricks on his eyes as landmarks swept in and out of his vision regardless of distance or speed. He kept on the tracks for the people mover because they were easy to follow even as the buildings faded into grey.

He walked through the city until he became tired again. Then he settled under a stone portico on a crumbling building to take a restive nap. He drew his earthy green cloak around him, gathered the extra length underneath him to insulate his body from the cold concrete and fell swiftly asleep.

XVII

The tall edifice was covered with signs on the outside
advertising everything that Dunne could imagine. The steeple
had collapsed upon itself and the remnant, including a lately
restored cross on top, now stood beside the entryway adorned
with an orange sign that advertised the "Presidents Favorite
Fish and Chips!" in glittering gold lettering. Just inside, the
gift shop was broken and left in shambles. It had been looted
recently, but most of the gewgaws and knickknacks were
simply smashed to bits on the floor instead of stolen, as if the
perpetrators knew how worthless they were and left the
shattered pieces on the floor in protest.

A bust identified by a sign below as "Johnathan Swift"
looked down on Dunne condescendingly in the entryway as
though he were a fool to come seeking anything meaningful.
The pews were overturned and empty. There were no spirits in
the old cathedral, not even any lost souls flittering about
between the monuments to the dead sponsors whose wealth
could not save them from the darkness of eternal non-
existence.

The walkways delineated with velvet ropes
crisscrossed the interior, keeping the dirty feet of the pilgrims
from the brightly colored floor that had been preserved for
centuries. The pilgrims and tourists paid for the upkeep of the

building by paying to see it, which allowed the owners to continue building capital on the property. Wealthy investors bought signs to place in and on the altars bearing their family names and legacies. They invested in spaces under the floor to be interred until Jesus would come again to raise them up. The lower classes of economically insolvent debtors could only pay to see those things that the wealthy could easily claim as private property in the church.

Dunne looked around at the interior space that he could never have afforded to see if the world had continued on its previous course. Near the front altar was a well-lit golden effigy of the great President for Life of the western hemisphere. It was much trimmer than the original gold plated model it had replaced which had rested inside the church for decades previous. That one had been built to life scale, demonstrating the paunch of a plus sized man of his eighth decade. This newer one was much more idealized: much leaner, much more muscular in how the artistically licensed creator had depicted the actual man. The figure resembled the truth only as much as an advertisement for a fast food hamburger resembled the salted, spoiled, masticated mass on a cellulose bun that a customer received for his debt chip transaction.

Where the original golden effigy had gone, Dunne could only guess. It may not have been pleasing, but it was more accurate to life than the current one. This version of the glorified President for Life was more inspired by his comic book and animated exploits than his real world dimensions. The arms, flexed and holding the hips, held elbows thrust outward at exaggerated angles; the unimaginably large biceps bulging at the viewer in a mockery of humanity: a glorious falsehood that no man could ever achieve. The exaggerated V taper of the torso, rippled with tens of extra muscles, made the hips look small and child-like. The oversized, perpetually-flexed pectoral muscles were forward-thrusting melons mounted on collar bones. The skinny legs hung precariously below the mass of muscles in the torso. Muscles sprang through every clothing surface texture as if they were wrapped in skin-tight spandex rendered in computer animated splendor on the telescreen.

The image ruled over the interior of the building much as the figure it emulated ruled over the church and the political realm in the world that Dunne lived in. The cathedral had been a mockery of a church, even during the days of Dunne's ancestors, displaying advertising for businesses and families who had paid substantially more than the ten percent tithe to buy advertising space on the walls between the Stations of the Cross and the stained glass windows. It was a glory to the rich families who invested in its construction, who believed that their money would buy them a better place in the afterlife. Even now the building remained a powerful status symbol to demonstrate their closeness to God and his avatar on earth.

The cathedral that Dunne stood in was simply an object to attest to the power and wealth of the President for Life and all of his gilded, golden glory. Now, like the man it represented, it was hollow because all of those for whom it held meaning were gone. Dunne was looking for truth and meaning now that he was freed from his bonds of labor to do so. He was exploring all of the mysteries that had long been denied to him. Except there were no mysteries here. It was just a building — an old building that had existed for a long time in a world that was built to be disposable. Its mysteries had been sold a long time before, and it had outlived its utility even before the plague that swept all the people away.

Full of symbols but devoid of symbolism to Dunne, the decorations and their accompanying artwork simply looked garish. There was no beauty found there now, if there ever had been. It had been sold several times over — every single part of it, sectioned off and sold. Dunne stood staring up at the light coming in through a high window when he heard a sound that he had not heard in days.

"You look like someone that I should be talking to."

It came from behind Dunne. He turned to face this strange human sound that felt vaguely threatening due to the lengthy absence of kind words spoken to him in his life. In the dust-filtered light streaming from the high windows was a tall, robust man, dressed in shades of dark green. He was cleaner and more sharply dressed than anyone that Dunne had ever seen in person. He wore what seemed to be a suit coat with an overcoat layered on top — too many layers for the heat of the island. The skin of his face and hands was almost a creamy white, whiter and more artificial looking than anyone Dunne had ever met. This man who stood before him was eminently out of place in more ways than one. Dunne looked at the odd man dispassionately, hiding his alarm, and said nothing.

"Yes, yes. Well, I'll do the talking. You look like you don't have much to say." The green man was correct. Dunne kept his questions to himself but sensed that this talkative man would say much without prompting. He was content to listen.

"I saw you when you blundered past the Green and through the beer factory. You know, you use every minute to get anywhere. This city is a mess, but you meander like a cock-eyed drunk. Are you pissed?" The green man leaned toward Dunne as though trying to catch an odor of spirits. Dunne continued silently looking at him, not knowing yet what to make of the man. He was so well accustomed to trusting men who spoke with authority before the fall, and the green man exuded authority.

"Well, you came in here like I owed you something. Who are you, the TV License inspector? Are you going to fine me?" The question was nonsensical, and Dunne found it odd. It was confusing enough to be approached by this strange man. He didn't know that "teevee" was an archaic phrase for the telescreen. There was no need for workers to know the alphabet or how to read. He didn't know what a license was either, because it was not germane to his existence at the lowest level of the working class. He didn't own anything. He knew what an inspector was: an inspector was an Orangeshirt who looked over your work at the factory and made certain that it was up to snuff. An inspector could beat or kill someone like him without much in the way of reason or provocation.

"Well are you?" The green man looked him over again. "Cat got your tongue?" The man stepped in even closer, peering deeply into Dunne's eyes, then stepping back sharply. "Oh, I see you been sick lately. You got the look about you, deep in those eyes of yours—" The green man looked him up and down. "Even if the rest of you don't match. You're straighter. You're breathing well." He leaned back and stroked his chin in thought. "I daresay you went in one side of it and came out the other, didn't you?" He squinted at Dunne, but again he didn't hesitate. "You have seen some things too, I wager."

Dunne didn't nod, just continued watching the man speak animatedly to him and through him as if his answers were written behind him on the floor. "I'd say more than a cat got your tongue, but the look in your eyes tells me the answers I'm looking for — more or less anyway. That's fine. You just listen for a bit. Save your words up for now. You'll need them later." He looked around the surroundings as if to evaluate them, then looked back to Dunne.

Dunne appreciated the permission to remain silent. His throat had not hurt from the sickness in days, but he couldn't remember a time when he had needed words to issue forth from his own lips in the old days. Even at the factory, everything in his life that he could recall had been a flow of simple expectation that he met wordlessly. The green man was just a new stage in the same existence, one that demonstrated a heretofore unexperienced level of respect offered to Dunne as a being of some importance. Dunne had never been the last man. The green man turned away from him and beckoned for him to follow.

"Walk with me lad, walk with me. Keep up as best you can in both ways. I'll narrate for you and I'll get you up to speed."

Dunne followed because he was told to. That part of his programming would take a while to overcome. The man in green led Dunne out of the cathedral through the open doors and into the street. He gestured to another smaller building to their left.

"This place, my place, was known as the Mars Library. Well before the land around us became a marsh, yes, back in the days it was dry land up here, well away from the river and hidden by this old cathedral that has seen some better days." The green man shuffled his shoes on the stone path. "You know, the cathedral was named after the patron saint of the island long before the new god of patronage and his scheming fans took over." He paused to smirk and showily gestured with a broad sweep of his arm to the east.

The green man cleared his throat and went on as he walked. "Did you know that he was the turning point? The first man world famous before winning the presidency? The first true celebrity leader! A trailblazer who successfully blended the world of entertainment and politics! He was elected by throngs of uneducated and apathetic countrymen and those who abstained from voting! They said that he was elected by people who saw themselves in him, but the truth was that he was elected by people who were absolutely filled to the brim with apathy and ennui and cared nothing for the direction the world around them took. But that was just the start, back in those days every citizen over the age of 18 could vote, whether or not they owned a business. Then things changed — because that's what things do." The green man straightened his tie as if talking had made it askew and continued his soliloquy. "When people from over there got a bit of power here, they moved to take much more as quickly as they could. First, it was by restricting the vote to property owners because they were the only ones with enough of a stake to make choices in the best interests of the republic. Once they won that, they decided it wasn't enough. A few years later they revised the rules to include people who owned businesses, even if the business held no property. This was the way that citizenship as a guarantee of voting rights was eroded." He wagged his finger at Dunne. "Then, the more property or business you owned, the more votes you got. Then they changed things again, because that's what they always do. Nothing stays the same. Not even this land." He gestured with his hand to the area around him.

Dunne looked at the buildings across the street with their crumbling facades and cracked windows. He hadn't imagined that this part of the city would be so dilapidated. Everything he had seen on the telescreen looked so new. There was no gut sense telling Dunne to be cautious, so well conditioned was he to listening to authority that he simply moved where the green man told him to go. The green man's voice was comforting and compelling to Dunne. It felt natural to follow his instructions and he went along unquestioningly.

While continuing his history lesson, the green man led him slowly through a broken churchyard filled with refuse. "Before long, voting became a simply symbolic gesture. It happened very quickly while people were distracted," he raised a single finger between them to emphasize his point, "and I certainly didn't see it all with my own two eyes, but I read it. You see, I'm the caretaker here, and I take care of the books and many other good things that the republic has forgotten about. The river got bigger and the water got deeper, then that all turned to swamp as the old underground rivers washed out the city. Papers and books from all over were moved here. I take care of it now."

The green man paused again as a new thought entered his head. "Do you know your name..? You probably don't know your surname." He smirked at his own joke. "Most folks don't know what a surname is. There's no need, right?" He looked back at Dunne again and nodded for him. Dunne didn't know why it would have even mattered. He couldn't remember a name besides "Dunne."

"It's all right, lad. Your eyes speak volumes. I would wager that you have some stories yourself, don't you? In due time, in due time. Here we are." He had led Dunne to a tall black iron gate. There were three giant padlocks fastening it shut. He pulled out a device that looked for all the world like large knife with blades hidden in the handle, but instead of threatening Dunne with it, he simply flipped out a large key and inserted it into the first lock. "We had to lock them up well, you see. Paper is what I have here and paper burns. Some of our paper here that I protect is old, ages old, and even though most would say it's only important enough to burn, I say it's important for more than that. It contains ideas and information that some folks would rather be forgotten. I'm in the business of remembering though, remembering for lots of people who don't know what has been forgotten, even yourself, I think." He nodded knowingly at Dunne. "I think you've forgotten more than you now know, but we'll talk about that later, or perhaps I'll talk and you'll listen." He chuckled to himself again. "Perhaps that tongue will be freed yet. We'll see, won't we?" He flipped the first key back into the handle after putting the lock on the door loop and flipped out a second key, never breaking into the flow of words that spilled from his mouth.

"I think I sound like I haven't had anyone to talk to in ages, don't I? I think you might sound the same when it all comes out of you, won't you? Once you've got someone to listen, I mean — when it's time for you to talk." He reached out and patted Dunne's arm. It was a gesture meant to create familiarity, and it made Dunne feel more comfortable with the green man. "Oh I can see it in your eyes already, there's a light there that wasn't there when I found you. Your eyes were dull a few minutes ago. Not dull like an animal mind you, dull like gem stones that hadn't been polished in ages, like the old crown jewels of this island lost and hidden — but I can see that there's a bit of sparkle hidden that has been looking for safety! Yes, that's what I see."

He flipped the second key down and hung the lock and flipped the third key out to unlock the door all in one smooth motion, just as smoothly as the words continued flowing from his lips. "Yes sir, the gift of gab you'll have, just like me, and neither of us has ever kissed any of the Blarney Stones! Though I can see by that scar on your lower lip that you've kissed something rather hard perhaps, a stone or two maybe, but surely not the Blarney Stones! You know, there used to be just one, just one until people figured out that more stones meant that there was more money to be made."

Dunne felt the scar under his lip. He'd never thought about it before, but now he remember running and falling as a child. Falling and landing hard on his face, losing two of his baby teeth before the adult ones came in to take their place.

The green man drew the third lock from its place on the heavy wrought iron gate and swung it open for both of them. "Follow me in here lad! Lots to see and hear and the sooner we start, the sooner you can start. There's questions that you didn't know you had and answers that you'll get here that will just give you more questions and answers, and soon your head will be all swollen up with things you'll remember that you didn't have an idea that you'd forgotten."

The green man stepped lighter now, closing the gate behind both of them. "Oh yes, I believe that I am your white rabbit even though I look and sound like your Mad Hatter, and I reckon that makes you a bit of an Alice, eh? Have you heard of Alice?" He leaned in and smirked at Dunne, "I wager not though I'm sure you're thinking in that inner monologue what she said in the pages of that book right now, eh?" The green man chuckled at himself again. It made Dunne feel more relaxed in his company. "'Curiouser and Curiouser, cried Alice' — who had perhaps forgotten how to speak proper English, just like you?" The green man winked at him.

It was another question with an answer that didn't matter to the green man, but it mattered to Dunne. He began to think even as he mechanically followed the little man along the cobblestoned path through the garbage-strewn courtyard.

Did he know proper English? His thoughts were short before he was interrupted again.

"The litter you see, this looks like a giant bin emptied out… I know, but it's good camouflage, right? No reason to break in, to climb the wrought iron and take a peek in the old library if there's nothing but refuse to be seen — just guarding refuse I am! No need for guns here! No, those are for the Orangeshirts only, and this is no Orangeshirt business that we keep here, no nothing of the sort to bring this to anyone's attention! No need to be drawing the attention of those who could find offense here in the history we keep…" He turned to face Dunne again and winked at him with theatrical flair. "That's what history is, you see? There is a truth in history that some folk take offense to — an offense to facts, because when you need facts to paint a prettier picture than what your eyes tell you, you need to control and change those facts." He moved his hand to his chin as if in thought. "What did he say back at the start, something about what you are seeing or what you are reading is not what's happening? Boyo, he sure set the lines down there, eh? Lots of folks climbed on that bandwagon. Lots of people wanted to believe that they were too smart to believe what they were told, but believing that is just believing what someone else tells you to think. You'd need a pretty dim lot to believe that, wouldn't you? 'Don't believe anyone, but believe me.'?" He chuckled lightly, "I could see in your eyes that you're not that thick, I can see the clouds clearing for you as we walked from the church. If I didn't, you wouldn't be here within these gates, no you wouldn't be here at all. But when people don't want to see the truth, you got to hide it in something or else they'll destroy it, yes they will, and after they destroy the truth all that's left is what they tell you. What they tell you is the same sort of poison as what they feed you, it's what profits them, not what is good for you. And if those two things should accidentally have some overlap, it's not by design."

He stopped in front of steps that led to a large ornate door into the dirty brick building that stood before both of them now. The door was as green as he was. "Are you with me, lad?" Dunne's face felt strange, like muscles that hadn't been used in many weeks were getting pulled and prodded. "I can see you are." This time, the green man took out a large single key from his green breast pocket. He inserted it into the door and winked at Dunne as he turned it in the lock. There was an audible clunk from the door and he smiled and pushed.

It was dark beyond the green door, but it was a darkness that beckoned — not at all like the darkness that had almost consumed Dunne days ago when his death should have been certain if not for the mysterious intervention of a stranger. The same bovinity that had allowed Dunne to follow the green man through the first gate now compelled him to enter through the door into an unknown space at the behest of this stranger.

Dunne stepped into the darkness and the green man closed the door behind both of them. There was a loud "thunk" as the lock was put back into place. He was now locked in the darkness with the mad hatter.

There was a shuffling from the darkness in the direction of the green man behind him. Then a loud but different thunk, as if the sound of metal on metal, a spring released, then a low hum rose from the quiet. As the hum built, a glow from thousands of dim incandescent lights strung across a high ceiling began to illuminate the space in a dream-like fashion. As the light slowly built and Dunne's eyes grew accustomed to it, he could see that the space he was in was large and filled with irregularly shaped stacks of objects. As the lights came up, shelves upon shelves packed full of books became visible. There were books everywhere. Dunne had never imagined so many books.

The green man was watching him intently through the darkness and Dunne met his eyes. "What do you think, laddie? Have you ever seen such a sight? Of course you haven't! You live in a boil on the back of a donkey's arse!" He laughed without malice, but his comment clearly amused him. There's a lot here in my library that you've never seen, I'll wager, but I'm not a betting man, and even if I were, I'd not bet that you have led a sheltered life out there on the barren garbage dump that is this island." The light was strong now, and the glowing filaments illumined a whole room that turned a corner into another room full of more of the same.

"I've got all the books I could save here, my boy. Some ancient ones that were meaningless to keep, some that were worthwhile, and some of the more recent ones from the last modern age before man gave up print for the screen and traded thinking about the world around him for passively watching it turn to a wet gob of dog shite smeared on everyone's shoes." He grinned and winked at Dunne. "The thing about the dog mess, though, is that anyone worth a fart would wipe it off, but the world went on tracking it around all over and got it on everything nice! Before you knew it, there was nothing nice! It was covered with the stuff! Then it was just normal, because no one left could remember a time when everything wasn't stained brown and covered with it." He cocked his head, "That's how it works you know; things go to pieces when no one is paying attention, and someone is getting rich by making sure you're distracted, then they're getting rich again by wiping their arse on your shoes, and then again when they get you to give them money for new clod-hoppers just before they fall apart! You got nothing but the garbage on you and you've paid for it yourself three ways!" He laughed, but didn't stop talking. Dunne just looked on at this one-man vaudeville show delivering his monologue to a now captive listener. The green man slowly walked down an aisle through the books and Dunne followed him, transfixed as he was by the vision of this green showman and his cavern filled with books.

Dunne looked around in wonder at the high shelves packed so solidly every which way with bound paper that each shelf appeared as a wall and only low light filtered through the stacks. The whole of the dimly lit chamber had the gritty look of a charcoal sketch. The margins were a dirty white, and the rows of books stood like letters in rows that he couldn't possibly read.

"I have a bit of everything here: a bit of everything and then also a bit of everything else that may not have been present when the shelves were first filled. This is a bit of a repository — a bit of a bit — as it were really, just a thin slice of a library of what man had learned and tried to save on paper." The green man kept leading him on slowly into the building, weaving a narrative as he went down his woven path. "You know what the thing about paper is?" he went on rhetorically. "It lasts forever if you keep it well. Not forever-forever, but forever to men. Did you know that men were still uncovering paper texts hidden in caves in the arid Middle East two thousand years after someone first daubed it with primitive ink? Marvelous, isn't it!" The man kept walking and turning, surveying the books and the building and then moving on with his story in one continuous interwoven movement, like a ballet that was recited and danced simultaneously. Each step took them deeper into the building, and deeper into his narrative.

"Those images on the telescreens are all fleeting, lad. You must realize that and treat them as such. Of course, you may not need to think about them anymore, but we can agree that the old world is getting washed away and that things will be different as we go forward." He spun again and walked deeper into the vault of books, checking his place on the floor as they walked down the narrow path between the stacks. "If things had gone on as they were going, those screens and cables and the things that power and connect them would have become obsolete and gone to trash inevitably. The information on them will become irretrievable. They will be lost. Do you think that those power supplies, those screens and cables and connections will still be here in two thousand years? No lad, they are as fleeting and as meaningless as a peasant's life! And all lost to time just the same!"

He twirled his finger in the air at Dunne to direct him to once more look around the room filled to the ceiling with more books than he had ever imagined, and then he led Dunne through the room and around another corner to the back of the space while continuing to talk.

"You see these books? Some from England, God save the Queen! Some from the Americas, whose culture overwhelmed us all, and some from this very island itself. Can you believe that some of the ancestors of the folk that you know fancied themselves as writers? Can you even imagine the people of this island with a literary tradition?" The green man laughed with incredulity at the notion, but Dunne could imagine it easily. Surrounded by books for the first time in his life, he imagined himself able to read them, to absorb all their stories and ideas. They seemed at once so much more meaningful than all of the programs and commercials from the telescreen.

"This is my library now, but it's so much more than just a library. It's a collection of evidence of how the world once was. I've an odd notion in me that you're different, and it's not just the manner of your lack of speaking. There is something in you that I've not seen before in all my years on this isle." He paused again as if to consider something important. "You should protect yourself better, boy — there's a host of parasites looking to make your weakness their profit. Be careful lad." The green man smiled protectively. Dunne thought about his words momentarily and yawned.

The day was long and he had only eaten sporadically since he awoke. The green man took notice. "You can stay here with us for a night or two. I don't believe you've had good night of sleep in days, judging by the look of you."

Dunne simply gave him a look of assent. He didn't nod or smile. His softened eyes gave affirmation enough. The man in green had drawn Dunne deeper into the building, but Dunne could see now how small this building was. There was a window at the back, just past the bend in the cleared path. Most of the windows were blocked by the stacks of books, allowing no light from the sun to enter, but an uncovered window through a canyon of stacked books allowed a narrow view of the outside. It opened upon a narrow alleyway behind the cathedral that was filled with piles of abandoned shopping trolleys. Dozens of stolen trolleys were dumped there, all of them festooned with dirty white plastic shopping bags caught in their wires and blowing in the wind.

The green man turned to face him in front of the window. He tilted his head and adopted a more serious tone that had been lacking as he had gone on and on about other things as they'd made the short walk from the empty cathedral to the packed library.

"You know, things became ugly when people began getting ill. I watched it all on the telly. I stayed here in the library. I felt strongly that if I stayed here that I would be fine no matter what happened on the island, and I was absolutely correct." He turned to face Dunne before leading him farther into the building. They were both standing just beyond the fading light streaming from the shopping trolley vista. Dunne felt vulnerable in the edge of the glow, as if someone might

180

drift by on one of the plastic shopping bags caught in the wind and see him.

The green man took on an even more grave tone, serious and lower, as if telling a secret. "This wasn't the first time that I've hidden. You see, it's not just the books and myself that I hide from all possible danger, it is these books and my fair girl, my Erui. I keep my girl safe." He slowly turned back to face another dark turn in the library and began walking more slowly.

Dunne felt wonder at this news. A girl was alive too. In one fell swoop, he had discovered two other survivors. Still there was something about this green man that felt off-putting. Something now felt wrong — it was almost unnoticeably small, but nevertheless it discomforted him like a bit of sand in his stocking. He sensed that if he had met this man in his old life, the green man would have turned his nose up at him and ignored him. Now, finding out that there was a girl hidden back in the darkness of this hoard of books troubled Dunne.

He wanted to trust the green man because he seemed so respectable and upstanding. He was dressed well and spoke so fluently, both things that Dunne had been conditioned to trust without question. He also spoke so authoritatively that Dunne was swept along by everything that he said. But why was the girl not allowed to go out like the green man?

A set of steps leading downward was visible underneath a slim, shallow light around another corner of the stacks of books in the library. The green man led him down the stairs that were at the back of the L-shaped building as he continued to talk. Despite the misgivings that were beginning to form in Dunnes's mind, he still followed without question.

"This is where I sleep, myself and my Erui. After all that was said and done and the Orangeshirts and the rest of the new trouble that came, I knew that I had to keep her tucked away and hidden because she's got such a mouth on her that something would have happened to her without a doubt, and I didn't want to lose her." The man trailed off and he stopped at the bottom of the steps, his head bowed in the shadow. The green man was lost in his memory, silent and adrift in a sea of old troubles. He drew in a deep sigh and slowly started telling a story.

"You see, not that it matters to you, not that you'd understand what it was like after the fascists came to power here — but just like everywhere else, just like Portugal and Spain, Italy and Germany, they drove anyone who wasn't like them out or underground. Sometimes literally underground..." He swept his hand around the dim light in front of himself and Dunne. As he spoke now, he continued walking slowly down and into the dimly lit and book-crowded space.

"Do you know what it's like to be in love when you're young? Do you know what it's like to be in love at all?" Dunne didn't think he did. Love was an abstract form, like a mathematical proof drawn on clouds. He'd seen people speak of it on the telescreen, but he didn't believe that what they spoke of was love in any meaningful way. It felt more like a product being advertised when they talked about it on screen.

"It's better when you're young, you know... That incredible rush of anything that happens to you for the first time. It's exhilarating, like the first ride on the carousel, except you feel it in your nethers instead of just in your loins. Do you know that? Can you imagine that?" He paused ever so briefly, as if to allow Dunne to imagine that, but Dunne couldn't imagine either side of the analogy.

The green man went on. "I'd spoken to girls, I loved the girls, I felt like I had more in common with the girls than the boys, and I would follow my older sister around like a lost puppy. Do you know that I'd let her paint my nails just so I could be around her and her friends? I even allowed her to do my makeup and dress me in her old clothes one year on All Hallow's Eve for a costume lark! Back then, it was comedy, mind you, a man dressing as a woman! I knew later when I was older that the comedy came from a juxtaposition of the manly characteristics and the womanly costume, but when I was just a little slip of a lad, I didn't care. I pulled those stockings on and I felt as free as I ever felt my whole life! Oh, the Scotsmen know that there's something to it all right, the kilts they wore! The freedom of the wind blowing on your bare skin!" The green man seemed lost in reverie, but he didn't stop talking. He never seemed to stop talking. He turned to face Dunne, and looked deep into his eyes. Dunne could only stop in his tracks and peer back at him wide-eyed, waiting for him to continue the story.

The green man seemed satisfied with what he found in Dunne's response, and turned back to finish walking down the steps as he continued his story. "You can't imagine how it was back then. Back in those days, when it was just becoming free enough to be who you were here on the island, here in the

republic… It was so different before the fascists took over."
He nodded and went on. "But it didn't last. It never lasts, eh?
Nothing good, but nothing bad either. If you're around long
enough, if you can stick through the bad times, then you find
out they're not forever. Nothing is. Nothing ever is." He
trailed off, seemingly lost in memory.

The basement of the library was also filled with
shelves and racks and stacks of books, all piled on top of each
other, in neat, orderly stacks. Dunne gazed around the space in
the dim, incandescent light. The green man caught his
wonderment and addressed it. "Yes, yes, there are rooms here,
filled with books and things I've saved from the Orangeshirts,
and other things too. My girl is here, safe. Safe from
everything and everyone. Safe from you, safe from whatever it
is that took away all of those threats that were out and about in
the city and the countryside." The green man sighed and
seemed to shrink as he drew his breath, but his energy
redoubled almost immediately. He became serious once more.

"I saved her. I saved these books. I've saved
everything that I could before it was destroyed in the name of
their golden idol. Here, look at these…" The green man
reached over to a cache of books and pulled two of them to
show to Dunne.

"I had to save books, but I couldn't just save the great
ones, otherwise all we'd have left is Joyce and Stoker, eh? No,
no, no. There are books up above, the main collection of the
library, but down here too, I kept all the books I could find
once the burnings started - once the peat logs ran out and
books, oh those sooty, sooty books found a thousand hearth

fires to burn in. People went out and ransacked the shops, the antique shops that held the old books, they burned them down, after they emptied them out. I saved books from the second-hand and charity shops, got a lot I did, whatever I could find that had trickled down through the years. It wasn't easy though. I didn't pick and choose those, no I didn't - I just took what I could get. Sure, there's some good ones probably, but some bad ones too."

Dunne took the two from his hand. There was a dusty dampness about them, something that approached mustiness, but didn't cross the threshold into irretrievably damaged territory. Dunne had never held a book in his hand that he could remember, but somehow the texture and feel of the glossy cover paper gave him an undeniable sense of deja vu. Somehow, there was a memory seething below his consciousness that felt as uncomfortable as it felt comforting. The books were oddly familiar to him. The green man continued to drone on about the great service he was doing mankind by sheltering these books, but Dunne's attention was absorbed by the paper he held in his hand.

Dunne returned the first to the stack. Its cover was a simple line sketch that looked like a pencil drawing of a jungle and boys walking through it. Dunne held the second, feeling its weight and balance. It lay heavy, almost magnetic in his hand. On its cover, a simple illustration in red, white, and blue — the colors of the country that had taken over the whole world with its culture of commodification and greed. The red, a rich bloody sort of red, was a figure of a man who appeared to be dancing a jig of sorts on the field of blue, like the kind of jig that flashed on the tele-screens when the celebrity hosts wanted to make fun of the people who lived on the island.

"Paddies" they called them in their mocking tones, stiff simpletons who danced not with their arms and heads, but mostly with their legs. The hosts made fun of them, directed "shillelagh men" to come from the sides of the stages and beat them with knobbed cudgels for the amusement of the audience. He flipped through it, marveling at the symbols on the pages, tens of thousands of words, representing ideas that could start fires or enkindle hearts. He couldn't read them, but he could appreciate the power that they must have held because it was a power so long denied to him and the others of his working class.

At the back of the book, on the final page before the cover, he felt a texture. It was pressed mostly flat, but the book had been stamped. He could read the letters that sat in a circle around the symbol of a book: "*From the library of Joseph Niles*" it said. Then he gently placed the book back on the stack and **read** the cover. At that moment he realized that he could read. He stopped dead in shock.

He did not know that he could read. He had never read anything before. He'd never seen a book. He knew what the symbols on some signs meant because someone had told him, but he had never had anything to read or a reason to. He dropped the book back to its stack and stood motionless.

His memory was a lie. He could always read.

The green man saw his shock. "You saw something in that book, did you?" The green man craned his neck to peer at the book. Why would you recognize that? The dancing

186

figure?" He waited for a response from Dunne for the first time after asking him a question. "What did you see in that book?" He reached in front of Dunne and seized the book from the stack to flip through it from front to back. "There is nothing in a book like this for you, young man." He harrumphed. "I should be more cautious about what I allow you to touch." The green man looked at Dunne now suspiciously. His tone changed. Dunne didn't know how to respond. He had no words for the confusion that enveloped him.

The green man's cadence slowed, and he directed each word at Dunne with a metaphorical weight that Dunne could feel push him down. "You should simply listen. I have no idea why I asked. I know that you cannot read. There is no reason for you to be able to read. Whatever you think you saw is meaningless. You do not have the intellect to understand anything in any of these books. Not the words. Not the ideas. Nothing." His words cut. They cut deeply and threatened to cut deeper. Dunne had heard the Orangeshirts speak with blunt force time and again, but never did he hear a tone that cleaved into and threatened to split him as the green man's did now. "Be a good listener, boy. Be a good citizen of this new world and learn from me. I have such sights to show you." The green man stared into Dunne's eyes looking for acquiescence and found them close enough to satisfy his need for power over the silent, dirty stranger.

Dunne maintained an emotionless composure when confronted with this new hostility from the green man. He was well accustomed to pretending that he was calm when situations drove him in the opposite direction toward panic. Working with Orangeshirts had made that a practiced skill. The green man now felt dangerous to him, more like a loaded gun in the hands of one of the smarter Orangeshirts. He had become a threat of violence. Dunne should have been more cautious. He'd allowed the green man to lead him into the basement of a dark building and to lock the door behind him. He was so taken by the green man's confidence and verbosity that he forgot that in all his life, he could only recall dimly a handful of people who weren't out to hurt him.

Dunne looked more closely at his guide as he attempted to evaluate the threat that stood with him in the library basement. In the dim underground light, the green man's skin matched his clothes. His pupils, dilated to the size of his iris, gave him the appearance of something inhuman wearing a man's body. Dunne said nothing. He focused on keeping his face blank to cloak his growing alarm.

The green man's face softened slowly. He stared at Dunne without blinking, without speaking. Then he suddenly looked away from Dunne. The angry chill melted from the room. The green man looked to the floor between them, and Dunne half expected a trapdoor to open and a chasm to swallow him. The green man looked back at Dunne and continued speaking, his voice softened with a condescension that Dunne could feel in his bones. "I would expect more but I should expect less. You haven't been around other humans in a long while, I suspect - and even when you were, I don't believe that those who were around you were very human at all. You're of the same ilk as the rest of the islanders here though, and I must remember that. Even if you haven't been drunk or drugged and subject to the dominance of your own superstitions, then you're the child of such base exemplars of real men and women. You achieved your current state of adulthood bathed in those horrid values."

The green man harrumphed, wrinkled his nose and continued. "I need you to understand the truths that I believe that you only have a vague sense of in a way that likely outstrips your personal intellectual abilities. You know that you are likely the last man of your people left on this island. I've seen you wandering around this city enough to be sure that even the most base degenerate — if that be you — understands that truth. The other truth that I ask you to understand is the confidence I have taken you into in order to share the possibility of a greater future for you. Like all of the representatives of the queen from the past, I hold the key to betterment for the men of this isle. I offer the opportunity to become more than you are." He shuffled his feet awkwardly, as to shake off mud or something else stuck to his soles, then moved deeper into the lower level.

Dunne forgot his alarm of only moments before and passively followed again; such was the sway that the green man held over him in combination with his years of socialization. Dunne was accustomed to blind obedience of authority. Moreso if he felt threatened.

"Down here there are more books than on the ground floor, though it's a sad bit tougher to keep them like those scrolls in the desert caves. This island's always been wet, particularly closer to the rivers that still run from the headlands down to the harbors."

The basement air was damp, holding a certain scent that Dunne couldn't quite place yet. It was beyond the smell of paper — there was a hint of something deeper and darker. A hint of something sickly sweet, like sugary offal. The man in green interrupted his thoughts. "I must remind you that you and I are not alone here. As I said before, I have another here. Another person that I cherish. My girl is here, safe and sound, protected as the treasure that she truly is." His body straightened as he spoke now, he tilted his head up as to speak down to Dunne. "She, like you, needs a firm hand to guide her to control her more base urges, to drive her toward the higher self… to help her serve her better angels, as it were." He turned to look again at Dunne. "Like you. Or else I wouldn't have pulled you in from the street."

They had moved around two corners now and the path that Dunne had walked in following the green man was now lost behind him in the dozens of narrow paths between towering stacks of books. "My daughter stays down here where it is safe. No peeping Toms in the windows to put her at risk! Why they'd rape her if they could, take her from me if they had a chance. Those fanatics are a danger to everyone!" His voice held a dangerous edge, a pitch and a timber that gave Dunne goosepimples. He didn't doubt the green man's words. He'd seen it happen often. Women were property; their bodies simply objects to serve men.

The green man went on. "I expect that you'll sleep down here tonight where it is safe." He led Dunne forward into the dimly lit lower level that was illuminated only by a few dangling incandescent bulbs. The odor lost its sweetness and thickened as they moved forward into the depths of the interior. "I've a room down here for you. One that I've kept as well as I've kept the others. No books in this one yet, but only because the island ran out of books to save before I ran out of space to fill." He winked at Dunne. The wink made Dunne shudder inside just a bit.

The green man smiled and went on: "I once had many children. All round the globe they came from, all of them gathered to the metropole, the motherland of the kingdom to the east of us. They gathered round me there for opportunities and learning. Oh they were all colors, all shades of the equator where savagery ran unchecked until my strong hand brought them all together. I taught them that English was the right way to speak, and that the Protestant God was the right god to worship.

One by one, they all left me after I had lifted them up though, one by one they all argued for independence. When they became too much trouble, I let them go. All of them for a time… until they started coming back." He stopped there, holding the round head of a bannister partially hidden by a stack of softcover books that diminished in size as they rose toward the ceiling. "I have one though who never truly left. She stayed nearby and kept our relationship mostly intact even as I allowed her to call herself independent. Here on this island Eiru and I have stayed. We live here together, maintaining this collection of books and keeping them safe…".

The lights on strings flickered dimly, almost imperceptibly. Dunne felt fear, but pushed through it. The green man's near obsession with his "daughter" made him feel ill to his stomach. It felt threatening to both the girl and Dunne. He wanted to find this "daughter" and to rescue her from the green man.

Critics of the modern world would always
say that the death of public libraries was a "canary
in the coal mine" type of incident for free
speech, but the truth was that the free market
had spoken and public libraries had no place in
the modern world of value and commodity.
Reflections on the Modern World
-E.L. Wang

XVIII

Death on the island was always wet. The bodies on the rending pile swelled and split, spilling their moist contents over the older remnants of others gone before. It was a horrid, dank odor, redolent of the sickening fungus that sprouted on the dead parts, breaking apart the components of each body and consuming the toxic remains that not even the roaches would scavenge.

Dunne paused. As they approached a door on the right through a trail walled with books, the odor's intensity caused him to stop in his tracks. Suddenly he was assailed by the certainty that there was something dead in the room behind the door. His hungry stomach rolled in confusion and disgust. His heart started pounding in his chest and a lightness in his head made it swirl enough for him to clutch a stack of books for support.

The green man seemed not to notice either the odor or Dunne's sudden discomfort. "That is my daughter's room. I'll keep you separate for now until I know that you are safe for her to be around... That is, if we decide to allow you to stay."

Ahead of them through the dim light in the subterranean library was a branching path through the cavernous stacks of books. One path, almost directly in front of them led to a tall heavy-looking door set in the stone wall. The other wound around a dark corridor between more books before trailing off into the darkness. The door set in stone looked too dark to be real compared to the stacks of books and the stones of the wall. It was painted with the very blackest paint, a shade of darkness that pulled the light from all else around and swallowed it like a star in its death throes, shredding and swallowing all light that entered into its strange gravity. As Dunne looked at the door, he sensed the waves of rot emanating from the spaces under and above the hinged monstrosity that promised to make him regret following the green man into the library.

The green man recaptured his attention by continuing to talk about the other person that shared their space. Dunne was concerned about the girl. "My girl is the hope of this island, but only with the proper guidance — only if she allows me to continue to make decisions for her, to lead her to better places and to her better self. Like I will with you... Yes, it is the most fortunate event of your new life to have come here, for me to have found you. The fact that you are still alive while so many others are not is important."

Dunne felt the reflexive urge to shudder, but he suppressed it as he was holding back every manifestation of his emotional state from the green man. Hiding emotions like fear or anger was a matter of survival at the factory, and here in the basement of the library with the green man, he feared it would be tested again. The darkness was advancing against the light in the underground space.

The smell emanating from behind the locked door was nauseating. It was worse than he remembered similar scents being when he worked in the sea-side factory. Out there, the strong winds could often blow the odors from the tall piled refuse out to sea, and the sun and the rain would hasten decomposition. In the dank basement, the esthesis was trapped and allowed to redouble and redouble again upon itself. The green man kept talking as if nothing had changed as he walked through the subterranean space and showed no recognizance of the rising tide of putrid air. Dunne was having a difficult time hiding his disgust.

He lost the sound of the green man's voice in his ears. It blended perfectly into the smell of death, became lost in the background essence that demanded attention and resolved to allow for nothing other than what felt like a new and immediate obsession. The darkness of this underground space threatened to overwhelm him and his head started to swim, but he never looked away from the green man. He knew that his life depended on it.

Dunne wanted to speak and he did not want to speak. To speak meant that he would use muscles that had not been used in years, that his diaphragm would push air over his vocal cords to make a sound that he might not even recognize, a sound that the did not want to hear. For as long as he could remember, his voice was something that no one wanted to hear, not even himself. His voice reminded him of weakness. It reminded him of loss, but what was there left to lose now? The world was gone, all that was left was this green man and his daughter, and maybe not even either of them. What if the green man was a ghost, or a ghoul, a fantasy made flesh? What if Dunne had never made it off that shore, if everything since then was nothing more than a fever dream of a dying brain, a moment stretched out to a near infinite place by a collapsing mind? Hearing his own voice, having some agency, taking action in the world that he was standing in would end the dream or at least collapse the unbelievable dream into an ugly reality, one potentially even uglier than the reality that existed before he swooned in a fever.

But he had to know.

His voice cracked. It was broken, but the pieces of it were rising out of the depths of his chest.

"What is in that room, the one that smells?"

The green man recoiled. "You speak!" he shouted. "Now you say something? What have you been waiting for? I already told you. My girl is there, safe and sound and safe. Always and forever, safe."

Dunne croaked again, his voice growing clearer with each slow, careful word, though still ragged. "She's not safe in there... That smell... That's not safe. Whatever is in there is sick, green man."

"She..," he stomped his foot. "Is..," he stomped again for emphasis "Safe..!" and he moved a step closer to Dunne. Dunne held his feet in place, even though he wanted to run.

Even though his confidence had dropped, Dunne's voice was stronger and didn't betray him. "If she's in there, she needs help..."

"Who are you?" The green man tone was tense and dismissive. "Who are you?" he asked again, more loudly, not allowing Dunne an answer. He swelled up in his green clothes and filled them 'till the buttons seemed ready to burst. "Aren't you simply a man that I found wandering the dead streets? A native savage of this isle? Did I not just save you from whatever it is that took everyone else away?" His voice escalated in volume with each rhetorical question. "Don't you owe me, don't you think that you should stop asking me questions and just listen to me like the nice young man that you were until just a few minutes ago? Not saying anything at all? I liked that young man. I brought that young man into my house because he was a listener. Because I thought that I could teach him something!"

The green man was speaking faster and faster, his voice growing incrementally louder with each word. "Where did you come from again? I saw you come out of the east, but where from on the far shore? From the south, I wager was your start, although I certainly couldn't guess for sure given how much I saw you meander through the city as I watched you from the church tower."

Dunne held his composure even as a wave threatened to crest inside him. His reply came out with a cough. "I came from a factory in Sallynog. We collected plastic from the sea for manufacturing."

The green man seemed to calm with Dunne's response. The opportunity to press the newly conversant Dunne for information pulled him away from his anger at being questioned. "So you worked for fourth baron, the one who was the most environmentally conscious of any of his family?"

Dunne felt the wave dissipating within himself. Calmness flowed back into him. "I don't know. I worked for the Orangeshirts."

"You contributed to the darkening of these skies! All of those factories pumped out thick black smoke from oil burning engines for no other reason than the fact that they could. You were a party to that!"

Dunne paused only slightly. "There was nothing else for me to do."

"Your ilk always says that! The ignorant poor borne on the backs of the capitalist elite, the ones who made your world go round. 'Just following orders' to the very end, eh?"

"I was born there. I don't remember anyone except the Orangeshirts. No one taught me anything different."

The green man was taken aback. He allowed quiet in his presence for the first time since he had made Dunne's acquaintance. He didn't consider that this mis-formed man out of the wastes had no mother or father to protect him from the notoriously awful Orangeshirts.

"Still, you should have learned. You should have become aware enough to choose a different path. You should have been different." His voice was slower and quieter. Dunne mistook the change in tone for compassion.

"Who could have taught me?"

The green man answered Dunne's question with questions of his own. "Why are you here? Why are you alive? The Orangeshirts wouldn't have taught you how to read, yet you know how to read. No one learns to read without a teacher. Who taught you how to read?"

"I do not know. I didn't know that I knew how to read until you showed me books. I had forgotten that I knew how to speak until you heard me." Dunne was panicked inside, though he hid it. He was trying to tell the green man what he imagined he would want to hear.

"How does a man spend his existence voiceless? Surely you are a liar expecting me even for a moment to believe that you are so clueless about your own abilities as that? Do you think me a fool?"

Dunne, who didn't know the benefit of a lie for his new-found voice could only reply honestly. "You might be."

"Well, damn you, you rascal. Someone should have taught you to know your betters as well." The green man sniggered at his own reply.

Dunne simply looked at the green man impassively, hiding his fear. The green man was becoming increasingly more unlikeable by the minute, and there was still the matter of the girl. She was locked in a room emanating a horrid smell, and if the odor didn't make her ill, then whatever was causing it would have. An anger toward the green man over her imprisonment was rising, replacing the fear and anxiety that held him speechless before.

The green man went on, never allowing a real pause for Dunne to think deeply. Then his tone shifted again, he became very avuncular. His lips turned up in a smile, but his eyes remained cold, calculating. He stepped toward Dunne as if to block him from the path to the room where he claimed his "daughter" was. Dunne stepped back and allowed the green man's presence to push him farther back in a different direction, toward a different path through the labyrinthine tunnels of books. "You simply must stay with me for a few days, and while you're here, you can plan where you are going to go next. I would suggest that you leave the island. There is nothing here now, not that there ever was. All that anyone has said about this island for years is that to truly become something meaningful in this world, one must leave it."

The green man stood straighter. His posture relaxed. Dunne felt secure again. The green man continued his history lecture. "Did you know that our diaspora is the largest in the world, that more people have left this place than have left any other? That truly says something about the island, doesn't it? At least fifty million people have left this god-forsaken place, but probably more if anyone had ever bothered to count them. The thing is that these people don't matter, the things they do don't matter. They never mattered. They were never anything more than a a people to be colonized, to be subjugated to a higher purpose by a higher power. For hundreds of years, that power was the King — God save the King!" The green man looked up for God in the ceiling to emphasize his words. "I'll never forget that Windsor lineage, that blood that flows in my veins too, you know! I was a descendant of those God-chosen nobles, those finest of the English lot! Oh, we had land, and we had titles too, real ones! Not pawned false titles like so many pretenders!"

Here he paused for a thoughtful moment as something had occurred to him and he wanted to address it immediately before it fled from his mind like rats from the light. "You lad, what's your name again?"

The green man had talked so much that Dunne couldn't remember if he had asked his name. It didn't seem to matter until just now. He thought back to his earliest memories, to the days when someone had called him by a meaningful name, but he couldn't remember being meaningful. By the green man's description of his island home, he certainly belonged here.

Dunne drifted through his returning memories as if in a fog. What was the name that he was called so long ago? It was lost behind a forest of hatred and disrespect. Lost and buried beneath the hatred that the Orangeshirts had heaped upon him and all others like him for the generations since the despotic President for Life had ascended to his office.

But it was coming back. His head was clearing. His thinking was growing sharper, sharper than he could ever remember it being. It was as if he was learning how to learn from the world around him now, every bit of information that was coming in from all of his senses had significance and depth, it all held meaning in the grander scheme, even if that grander bit of the world hadn't been revealed to him yet. He could feel it building.

His life was no longer a monotonous daily routine of pain and seeking to escape that pain through whatever means was provided to him. The dim fog of existence was growing brighter ever since he had emerged from the woman's cave reborn and healed. It had taken another step toward light on that day under the monument with the meal of mushrooms.

It came to him in the same way that the words in the text had come to him when he held the book. The knowledge flowed in from outside of him. "My name is Dunne. It was given to me by my mother." He thought about the name, the last time it had been spoken to him, the odd way that it rolled off the tongue of the face that he now recognized as "mother." Finally, he could see her face in his memory. "She loved me." He knew it as he said it and the saying of it made it real, made it meaningful, made it more true than anything that anyone else had said to him in the years since.

He was shaken from his reverie by the green man's laugh.

"What a ridiculous name! Done? That's not English! That's not even of this island's backwards native tongue! That's made up! A perfect mock up name for a perfect mock up of a man! If I didn't know better, I'd accuse you of making that up, but I can see by the look on your face that you are serious! By the crown, your mam was setting you up for a lifetime of failure, wasn't she!" The green man's chest heaved with laughter, and he doubled over to hold his knees for support. "You're Done!" Clearly, the green man found Dunne to be a joke.

Dunne didn't react. The green man's mockery was meaningless: he'd been subjected to much worse for much less by the Orangeshirts for much longer. Hatred had given him a callus.

"Well, you can stay here for a night or two. I don't expect that there is much else place to go, eh? Only death and darkness out there. No, I expect that you'll be best off staying here, though it's worth nothing to me. I've got rooms here, a place for you to put your head down at least for the night, and then on the morrow we'll figure out what's best for you." The green man paused and laughed at himself. "A factory rat named 'Done' has his days mapped out entirely for him. I'm sure that you're not accustomed to thinking about such things as what to do and where to go. After all, I watched you stumble around the ruins of the city long enough. We'll figure it out though."

Dunne didn't answer him. He felt ever more strongly that sometimes he needed to wander in order to find the right path. His walk from Sallynog through the heart of the city had shown him things he needed to know. The green man's condescension was meant to be a bludgeon, but Dunne shrugged it off. There was little the man could say to hurt him. Instead of weakening him or taking away his resolve, the things that the green man said instead felt like something to push off from. It was a force to resist.

Dunne had felt force pushing against him before, but he never had the wherewithal to push back instead of allowing it to run him down. There were many things that were in the process of changing about him. This was a major shift in his thinking, in his ability to think.

Inside, he felt warm.

*"To control a man, tell him you hate
the same people he does and then
pretend you have the power
to hurt them more than he can."*
The Wealth of Human Nature
Tatte Spong

XIX

"So, your name is 'Done' then? That's as odd a name as I've heard, and I've heard some odd names. It reminds me of something though, there's a book here, a book about airplanes. I've read part of it, but it's American — Jewish-American, I believe, so I didn't dedicate much time to it at all." He paused and made a distasteful shape with his mouth, as if he'd eaten a spoiled walnut. "Jews controlled the world once, you know? If there is one good thing to perhaps come of this die-off, its that the inferior races must have been wiped away by it. Surely the English are still here, just as I am." He paused again, uncertainty returned to his expression, but then his mocking smile returned and he continued. Dunne understood racism was played for a joke by the upper classes in the media. He didn't smirk, only looked on impassively.

The green man looked Dunne up and down again, this time more critically. "Well, you're dirty, but not brown. You don't look Jewish at all. But you don't look English either. Perhaps there's a bit of noble blood mixed into your mongrel appearance..." He stroked his beard. Dust and crumbs tumbled out of it to the floor. "So many gentried landowners took mistresses of lesser blood. Perhaps there was some of the Englishness in you that spared you as it spared me. I can't for the life of me see a better explanation for the fact that you are standing here in front of me." He continued leading the way forward through high stacks of books as he walked slowly, constantly turning to look Dunne in the eye as he moved inexorably deeper into the bowels of the underground library.

Dunne simply nodded and followed. His own well-trained tendency to follow made it feel simple and natural. This man held a charismatic and controlling authority over him as he moved quickly with purpose in the direction of his goal. There was nothing else Dunne could do but follow.

"You know, if I had your surname, I could tell you more, but perhaps your Christian name is good enough for that, as odd as it seems to be. He gestured to a red-spined book that sat atop a pile of other similar paperback artifacts. "I kept these books down here. It's a bit damp. It seemed to suit them better. Hardcover books I kept upstairs with the English books, away from the damp. Their authorship demanded it."

He pulled the top book from the stack and tossed it to Dunne. He caught it with little effort and looked over the cover. It had the parts of an airplane on it. They looked like plastic toy pieces. The upper part of the cover showing the title was torn off. The author's surname on the spine was "Heller." Dunne felt the slightly musty paper between his fingers. It was a satisfying sensation. Before he could discover any inner truths, the green man interrupted his thoughts by resuming his monologue.

"You know that all of the records of births, deaths, and immigrations were moved from the regional GROs and put in the National Archive as the government started consolidating services in the twenty-first century. They're nearby. I have access to them. If you want to know more about who you are, I can take you there in the morning." He spun around to look down his nose at Dunne. "I sense that you are a man without a history. Don't you find that a bit troublesome? I do." The green man furrowed his brow. "I brought you here into my castle and gave you refuge, but how do I know that you're not some kind of degenerate? How do I know that you won't kill or poison me or my precious daughter with whatever it was that wiped the degenerates off the face of the island? Let us find out your name. With a name like 'Done' you should be easy to track down in the birth records. We know where you're from too, because no one ever goes very far away from where they were born anymore, or at least if you did, you'd be the exception… And you, lad, are clearly not an exception."

Dunne looked up at the green man. It occurred to him then that the green man seemed to change in size according to his manner and demeanor toward him. As his anger toward Dunne faded, his size diminished. Did the Orangeshirts do the same? He couldn't remember. Then the green man interrupted his processing again.

"I have a room for you. A place for you where you can actually spend a night indoors." The green man stopped and gestured to a door covered with paper signs.

Dunne looked at it and paused. There was something odd and off-putting about it. Then he stepped forward and put his hand to the door to open it. In the dim light, he saw a lone lightbulb hanging from a long, thin wire over a single small cot. He stepped in to look farther into the darkness and the door slammed shut behind him.

XX

Almost half a shift had passed by in Dunne's estimation since the green man disappeared on the other side of the door. The room was little more than a large utility closet, but the cot was more comfortable than Dunne's blanketed mat at the hive in Sallynog. He felt like it was all that he could have asked for given his circumstances. Dunne thought that as long as he respected the green man's rules, that things would be fine.

The green man had tried to lock the door behind him as he left Dunne in this room, but couldn't get the mechanism to work. Dunne heard him fumble with the knob for what felt like an eternity, but the old man gave up, leaving the door barely latched. Dunne saw no reason to struggle with the door given his own well-learned habits of subordination. He was tired and lay down on the cot. Sleep would not take him though.

He allowed himself to relax and ponder the books. He did know how to read after all! How could he have forgotten that until just this very day? Someone had taught him how to read a very long time ago, so long ago that he could not remember it. Until today, he could not remember being around books. He couldn't remember who would have shared books with him, except for his faint, cloudy memories of a mam. There was a kindness in those memories, perhaps even a smile born of love, but he wasn't certain. The more he thought about it, the more he associated books with his mother. That must have been the person who taught him to read. Now he wanted to read some of those books hidden by the green man before he left this library if he had a chance — if the green man would allow him to.

The noises of the green man had ceased a while ago. Dunne pulled the overhead string on the dim dangling light bulb and lay in the darkness pondering his next move. It was a restful place. His weariness fled even though he did not sleep. He was still far too accustomed to the mind-numbing work of the factory. The labor was exhausting. His wanderings through the island nation's capital city were much less exhausting than that, and even less tiring than simply being bored in front of the telescreen. He pondered both the darkness of his room and the greenness of the green man. There was much less to his story and also much more to it than there should have been. Dunne wondered how much of it was a lie and how much of it was truth. The more he thought about his green host, the more certain he became that the man might be deceiving him. There was only one way to know with any certainty. He had to find the green man's "daughter," Eriu, and ask her.

He hadn't yet considered rescuing her though he lay in the dark in an unsecured room. It didn't even occur to him that he himself might need to be rescued. The unsecured door made him feel less frightened of the green man's motivations.

There were so many contradictions to ponder in this whole situation.

He did think that perhaps the girl needed to be rescued, but how could he rescue someone unless she herself knew that she was in dire peril? What peril was she in? Perhaps she was safe and simply accustomed to the scent of rot in the basement. The more he thought about her, the more he questioned his fears about her safety. Dunne had been trained his whole life to second guess his own thoughts and feelings, and his rebirth hadn't changed that foundational aspect of his personality.

He recognized that he himself had narrowly avoided the successful completion of his own death sentence on the rubbish-strewn shores of Sallynog. Perhaps being outside in the mists and hazy sunlit days was more dangerous than being where she was. Wasn't his own saving predicated upon being under the earth in a tomb-like chamber of darkness and dirt? Is this how the green man saved her?

He didn't understand the gulf between life and death, or how one navigated those shallow waters, even though he had drifted there for days. He had much to learn. Perhaps he could learn some of it from the green man's daughter. Certainly, her connection to the green man would answer some of his more recent questions.

Asking questions of the green man was akin to interacting with a very early basic computer program. It seemed as if he could only respond along a pre-programmed track, or as if perhaps all of his answers were scripted by some madman behind a dictaphone. Dunne decided that since sleep eluded him, he would try to access the daughter's chamber — simply to talk. He wanted to hear someone's voice besides the green man's. She would know some things that he didn't.

He slowly felt his way up from his cot and along the wall of the room, moving very quietly. He felt that silence and darkness were in order at this moment if he were to achieve his goal of meeting the green man's daughter. He didn't want to risk drawing attention. He found the door and lightly, ever so slowly twisted the handle. The metal parts in the mechanism made only the barest of noises as they shifted against each other. He angled his body and slipped through the opening just barely bigger than his frame and into the hallway where he had last seen the green man.

The green man had left the string of lights lit down the lines of the library basement. The barely luminous narrow book-lined passages stood between Dunne and the girl's room. He crept among the stacks and carefully made his way back to the chamber, navigating as much by scent and touch as by sight through the dim illumination.

He suspected that if she were well, then she would be more active at night — given that her father's eyes would be turned inward and that he would not monitoring her as closely. Dunne did not even know where the green man was, but he assumed that he slept in some room that he had not shown him during the library tour.

Dunne moved quietly through the stacks of books and the overcrowded shelves. He found her room in a different place than he expected. It was as if the layout of the space had changed. Still, he knew he was in the correct place due to the strong odor. Each of the switch or toggle locks on the door were accessible from the outside. He counted five locks. No keys were necessary. All that Dunne had to do was silently turn the locks in succession to gain entrance to the room and to win access to the girl inside.

He started at the top lock, near the limit of his own reach. He twisted the handle slowly and listened cautiously as the metal lock slid against its place in the door frame and landed tightly back in the door with an audible "tok" sound. In the bare still air of the dark space, it felt much louder than it was. The stacks of books absorbed the sound and kept it confined.

The second lock down was a chain and lever mechanism. He pulled down the ratchet apparatus and the chain went slack. He caught it with his left hand, but the links rattled against each other ever so slightly. He paused and listened for the sounds of stirring elsewhere in the building. There came a regular sound, like the low stomping of feet overhead! He held his breath and listened. How close was the green man to the stair? He panicked for a moment and almost bolted back to his room, but then noticed the sounds weren't advancing. It was the sound of his own heart beating in his ears. He breathed again.

The third was a latch with a revolving three digit combination. He looked at each digit visible on each of the nine digit barrels. Some of the numbers were more worn than others — more grimy with use and less with age. He flipped the first digit to the most worn of the nine numbers, then followed suit with the second, and then the third. At the last twist of the third, he heard a satisfying click as the barrel dropped away from the latch. He caught it gently with his free hand and laid the lock on a stack of books beside the door.

The last and lowest was a sliding bolt at ankle level. It slid roughly back into the housing. It made more noise than the rest, possibly because the weight of the heavy door partially rested on it.

Dunne tugged slightly on the heavy door using the latch clasp. It did not move. Then he cautiously lifted the door by the clasp and moved it slowly open. The room was dark. A thin block of light penetrated to the center of the room from the doorway that he held open with his body.

The girl was there. He could see her in the beam of dim light. She was there but not there. He wondered how long had she been gone, but it was a statement of expectation, not a question. There was no way for Dunne to know except to ask the green man, and the green man would never tell him. Dunne doubted if the green man knew the truth of the world around him. His stories may have all been lies.

She was sitting on a chair in the center of the room surrounded by a puddle of ichor that seemed to be source of the odor he found. Some of the water that circulated under the streets of the capital city had seethed through the cracks in the floor, as if in angry response to mankind's efforts to pave over it. This room felt more deeply abused by the green man and all that he embodied than the rest of the basement space that he'd seemed to care for so determinedly.

If there was any meaning to be found in the room, it was the meaning of decay. All that was visited upon the island since Dunne had become ill was visited upon the green man and all who were like him. Sickness of some form or another was upon the whole of the island and those who remained there. He had been ill as well and wondered if he were dreaming now.

Dunne gasped in disbelief. At first glance, she wasn't breathing. As his eyes adjusted further to the light, Dunne knew that there was no way that she could breathe. Her life had long ago stopped depending on breathing. She was a mummified remnant of a human being. The sour stench emanating from that location in the basement didn't come from her. She was desiccated beyond rot. He leaned in to look at her features and found that her mummified corpse actually smelled faintly sweet. Her aroma overwhelmed the stink of the room in close proximity. Her body rested silently in the chair — stiff, unmoving.

Dunne moved closer. Upon inspection, the corpse started to glow as if emitting a light of its own — even though his vision earlier indicated that she had a problem for which Dunne had no solution. The body in the chair glowed and as the light increased, her desiccated wrinkles filled out and the grey fled from her complexion. Dunne couldn't believe what he was seeing. He stepped back from the human form at the center of the room and cautiously brushed his fingertips on the wall near where he had entered through the door. He found a switch on the stone wall. A line of plastic conduit ran from a switch box toward the ceiling. He pushed the rocker switch carefully, covering the switch box with his palm to muffle the click of the circuit being connected, fearing a noise that would alert the green man to his trespass. A trio of thin filament bulbs pushed the darkness aside from above.

As the light trickled down, he saw that her hair was now as rich an auburn as any jewel he had ever imagined. It sparkled like sunlight on the Irish Sea. He could see her skin had become a pale white now, not grey — almost porcelain in the dim light, and the illumination seemed yet to emanate from within her even with the dim bulbs above. Her lips were a tightly drawn pale pink bow. No breath moved through her and she remained perfectly still, but she seemed more alive than anything that Dunne had ever seen. She was dressed in earthly green garments, woven of threads in a pattern that looked like leaves of hawthorn, bound together finely with a red thread that almost matched the hair on her head. Her hands rested quietly in her lap, folded in repose, almost as if she were patiently awaiting a scene change in a play.

Dunne was breathless; otherwise, he would have noticed that the pestilent funk that permeated some of this below-ground level was now completely absent in her presence. She repelled the odor just as she repelled the darkness. He was enraptured by her beauty, losing his sense of self momentarily in her company. He could not help himself. His hands rose to touch her but instead floated over her arm and shoulder as if he were gathering warmth from a fire.

Dunne had felt hungry and thirsty from biding his time sleeplessly in the green man's burrow, but his human needs lessened greatly in the company of this woman. It was as if her presence filled him up. He was warmed inside and out in her company. As he lifted his hands to feel in front of her nose for breath, her penetrating grayish-blue eyes opened slowly. He drew his hand back to his breast as her eyes opened to look at him. He felt vulnerable in her gaze, as if she could see deeply into and through him all at once. Dunne was caught by her eyes like a deer in headlamps.

She opened her lips and breathed in deeply, filling her lungs as if to speak for days. "You're here." Her voice was a rhythmic melody that touched on all the natural sounds of the sea and the island. She paused, waiting for his response, though not for him to speak. "I've been waiting for you." Dunne blushed and felt instantly contrite. He didn't mean to make her wait.

She spoke slowly and rhythmically, her voice remaining sonorous. "Fret not, I've not waited long, not long to me — though perhaps long to you. For me, the wait has been entirely right. You had to come through an experience, the world had to change. I've not been in a hurry myself. I am timeless. Each of my breaths is a million of yours and I exist in a time that you could not understand if you had to." Dunne was awestruck and speechless, but she didn't need him to have a voice, not yet.

"I am Ériu," she said thoughtfully, "I recognize that name the best, although it hasn't been used in ages. I have been called Éire more recently, and Erin even more recently than that. Those are my favorite names." She looked wistful and smiled, as if remembering all those and many others kindly.

"I have been alone for a time, but not lonely. I remember my people, long past, but not lost. The Tuatha Dé

Danann we were called. My sisters too, forgotten by the men of your age, though we are ageless. They are elsewhere." She turned her head to listen. "I can hear them now… Do you hear the sounds of my sisters' strings on the wind?" Dunne heard only the music of her voice, but as he turned his head to the direction that matched hers, he believed that he heard a faint sound — as if of a harp swelling on a breeze that he could not feel.

"I hear them too," slipped from his lips almost before he knew it. His senses compelled him to speak in response even if his mind did not.

"Of course you can. You couldn't hear until now, because you weren't ready. But now you are. You can hear them, and you will hear the other voices now, increasing in volume and mass. You are changing, just as the world around you has changed. More change will come. You are a part of a new world. It will be for you and others like you. Not the ones who were washed away." Dunne felt like he was in a dream.

She stood from her chair in the chamber and pulled a woven woolen shawl from the seat and wrapped it around her shoulders. She clasped it with a pin that was a five-lobed hawthorn leaf. "Let us go from this place." She motioned toward the exit and swept past the still dazed Dunne through the doorway. He followed her without considering where she was going. He would have felt fulfilled to follow her anywhere for the rest of his life, so strong was his behavioral programming. She smelled of heather and moss, of fields of lavender, and of the clean salty sea. These were all scents that Dunne had never experienced in his life, but as he smelled them, he knew them immediately. The scents themselves imprinted past experiences that he'd never had into his receptive brain.

She led him past the piles of mouldering books and up the stairs to the main floor of the library. As Dunne passed by the stack that he'd examined early under the green man's eye, he took the top three books from the stack and tucked them into the pocketed folds of his cloak. The dawn's sunlight crept through the cracks in the covered windows as shafts of dust swirled through the light in their passing. They turned the corner of the L-shaped building toward the main door and Dunne spotted the green man seated in front of the exit waiting for them.

Dunne was suddenly overwhelmed by feelings of apprehension and guilt. He had explored beyond the limits of the building that was offered to him and broken the green man's trust. Even though he'd had bad feelings about the green man, he felt he had abused the green man's friendly treatment. This being that he had found behind the locked door was not the "girl" that he had expected. This was a woman, and the green man had claimed her as his because he thought that no one would challenge him. The fact that she had appeared dead when he first found her was swept away by her sweetness and her voice.

Ériu slowed as they approached the seated figure who blocked the door — not out of deference or fear, but to allow Dunne to see what the green man was and was not in those moments: his hands folded on his lap, face impassive, though stern and set. His clothing was no longer green. As Ériu approached him, the green tint of his clothes fled his garments like dust being swept by a breeze. His coat was red and his shirt was white. The formerly green man did not rise up to stop them. He was no longer moving and would never move again. The red and white of his costume shifted to gray as they approached. Ériu stepped to the side and Dunne moved past her to see the red and white man more clearly. As he did, the air moved around him in a swirling fashion, swept from Ériu. Then Dunne watched all that the man had been crumble to the floor like sand.

The pile of material that he had become then disappeared into the air, melting away into nothingness. Dunne watched him dissipate into the air on unnoticeable zephyrs. The chair was empty — not even a residue of his passing. The false green man returned to the nothingness from which he had sprung. The door was now unblocked. Dunne turned back to look at Ériu, but she too was gone. Her scent of hawthorn and clean sea salt air remained more strongly than it had when she shared his space, but she was gone.

He unlocked the door and stepped outside of the library to walk into the warming rays of the morning sunlight. Dunne understood that the false green man was gone forever, but that Ériu had merely gone free. He felt that he might see her again, if things moved rightly.

It was good to be alive.

XXI

Dunne closed the library door behind him. He hoped that the books there would survive whatever came next without the green man there to to watch over them but knew that holding out hope for anything positive to come was simply a waste of time and energy. His life to this point had taught him well the folly of positive thinking and hope. He patted the books tucked away in his cloak. They were a start. He would read them, then find more.

Dunne went back to the cathedral where he had fallen under the green man's spell. He expected to find a simple path to get to the north side of the river through the old building. The extra doors on the river side of the church swung open in the breeze. It would have made easy entrance for the rats, except that Dunne hadn't seen any of those lately either. He walked through the doors toward the flowing waters of the river once again. Outside, he looked behind him to take a last look at the no-longer imposing edifice.

The sign over the door at his back read, "St. Patricks Kayak Floats" and advertised a ride on the Liffey that replicated the fabled Saint Patrick's float after he finished driving the serpents out of Ireland. Dunne had seen the story played across the telescreens a half dozen times; every spring

220

when Saint Patrick's Day rolled around ,the animated special was aired. It recounted the classic story revolving around the beer brewed in Dublin for thousands of years and of the religious ritual Saint Patrick created by drinking it until he saw a vision of the reincarnated Christ's second coming. Then the cartoon saint drove around the island capturing all the snakes to cast into the sea before building a golden monument to the coming of the savior who bore a remarkable resemblance to the American President for Life.

Dunne wondered if the church named for the patron saint of the island had always been in the business of offering boat rides along with salvation. Had the masters of the old church taken every opportunity to profit from the building? Certainly the broken gift shop inside was a strong answer. The popular Saint Patrick stories were shared in order to bring tourists to the island to visit specific sites. The commercialized myths were a major driver of the tourist industry that brought money to the corporations that owned everything. Everything, including history, was worth exactly as much as it could be sold for: every location, every event, every holiday.

Dunne thought back to the parades that were shown on the telescreen every year. They traveled through the city center and wound over the bridge on each holiday. The floats and the characters were bedecked in green and gold and danced out the drunken ethnic stereotypes of the island's people that were globally popular. Everyone on the island looked forward to it, as it was the only holiday from the factories that anyone got. Otherwise, it was the ongoing drudgery of work, just as it had been the true luck of the Irish back in the days of their English masters. Little people from all around the island state or the rest of the country overseas were shipped into the city to be dressed as mythical leprechauns and driven around the city as mascots for drunken celebration. They were then tossed and thrown, dunked in tanks, and rolled down hills to celebrate the mythical life of Saint Patrick and his prophecy of the President for Life.

All the boats at the Saint Patrick Cathedral kayak launch were gone. Dunne knew that he wanted to get across the river, but he didn't trust the water enough to swim it and he was still wary of the security devices present on the MacDonald Street Bridge.

He knew that every river on the island was used for dumping waste materials, from raw sewage to run-off from the production factories further upstream of the city. Even if the dumping had ceased when the humans ceased, it would take centuries for water to wash the wastes from the soils and sediments of the river bottom.

Dunne looked up to the sky again as if for an answer to solve his problem. The clouds looked pregnant with rain, making the sky glisten darkly over the gray city. Dunne breathed deeply. He closed his eyes to focus his thoughts. He had been wandering without aim in the city, looking for other people but finding none. The more he walked, the more he concluded that there would be no people and no reason for their disappearance found in the city. His walk had served mostly to distract him from his loneliness.

He'd never been connected to the people around him even through the hours in the factory. They simply kept the spaces around him from being vacuums of emptiness. Without people now, his sense of self in relation to others began to lessen, and he found himself wondering on his walk if he truly existed at all. The green man and the girl didn't make sense. The church man and the giants didn't make sense. Few things he'd seen since leaving the barrow had felt normal at all. He wondered again if he were actually dead and if these strange days were nothing more than his ghost wandering around like he had seen in stories on the telescreen.

He glimpsed another steepled roof down through the tunnel between the tall buildings that kept the street in shadow. Another of the church temples of tourism. The city didn't have the gothic spires of other parts of Europe, but it had pull on the imaginations of the tourists. Dunne was drawn there as well. Things were taking shape in his brain. He was putting things together, solving a mystery, making connections that he could not have just a short time ago.

He was changing, just as the city was changing in the absence of people.

"The red stout was the lifeblood of the island economically, and it was as much of the island as anything else ever was, which meant that it wasn't, as its creator was of and for the queen as much as she was for herself. Nothing on the isle was of its own ethnic, spatial, or racial heritage. This made it a perfect addition to the USA."
Britanica Wiki-pedia

XXII

Down by the ruins of the flooded Christ Church, Dunne found a set of three river kayaks piled into a trash-filled alley. He chose the most river-worthy looking one and flipped it over to clear it of the plasti-trash that filled it. He dragged his new watercraft down over the broken asphalt and concrete into the water and stepped lightly onto the flat topped float. It would hold against the water long enough.

He sat down on the cracked seat and allowed himself to drift with the current for just a moment, enjoying the ride, as he had never been on the river before. He'd seen it advertised for the tourists on the telescreens and it had always looked so fantastic. The river provided a view of the city not often afforded to poor workers from the factories.

Then he turned the boat and paddled against the weak current of the river, but just for a few moments before he gave himself over to riding on the current once again. As he drifted toward the sea, he heard a strong sound growing louder over the rippling of the current. It was a human voice, but it was being broadcast in a way he had never heard before. It sounded like someone singing, but without the computerized attuned inflections that he was accustomed to on the telescreen.

Dunne passed under the MacDonald Bridge. The triple arches of the supporting structure were clearly marked with the corporate symbol from the telescreen ads as he passed below them. He knew the symbol well. It was the biggest and most expensive toll bridge over the river. Dunne could not cross over the road for fear of the automated security measures that might still protect it, but he could pass under it.

The booth where the Orange shirt overseer watched over the road sat empty now, but Dunne could see that the barricades and the tips of the giant tire spikes were still raised to discourage any notion of his to cross it. He knew as well (from watching scenes on the telescreen set to a laugh track) that there were laser sensors and sound weapons typically used for riot control employed at the bridge to stop people from crossing over if they hadn't paid the toll. The targeted weapons were wired to proximity sensors and motion detectors. The bridge overseer was there to simply drag the incapacitated bodies away from the deterrents. If there were too many bodies, the sensors were blocked. The telescreen program was meant to frighten anyone who thought of crossing from one side to the other without paying the toll, but it also served as high comedy when displayed on the telescreen to the people that it was meant to socialize.

Nevertheless, it served to make Dunne deeply wary of crossing over the high bridge, regardless of the current state of humanity. He knew from experience that there were many machines in place that required no human input to respond to environmental stimuli. There was no watchman left to pull his spasming body out of the line of fire. He was glad that he had opted for the leaky kayak instead.

On both sides of the river, the streets were lined with tourist shops that pandered to the marketed image of the inhabitants of the former island nation and fifty-first state. Those souvenir shops sold visitors hundreds of thousands of worthless trinkets at high profit margins. He drifted further down river toward the sea. Then Dunne spied the remnants of the famous Spire monument which had been dismantled and sold for scrap after the island republic became a state. Only the stump remained, then renamed the Doonbag Testimonial after the prestigious brand of golf clubs and resorts that took over sponsorship of so many of the island state's attractions.

Then he realized that he was not yet prepared to attempt paddling in open waters. The thought frightened him, and he wanted more experience paddling and balancing the boat before he took on the uncertain sea. He experimented with steering the boat with his paddle in the current then turned back against the outflow and passed once again under the unsafe bridge. He paddled steadily on against the outward flow and made good time to the west, passing even the old, sunken church where he had put in. The old stone Doonbag Testimonial was now visible against the sky to his right from the risen waters of the river.

Dunne paddled further, using the giant stone monument as a guide. The water splashed coldly from the paddle, and he dragged his hand in the current more than once to bask in how clean it felt compared to the salty ocean water that he had waded into farther south down the coast in his younger days. He'd never been into the city to see this river before. Here, the waters ran down from the highlands.

He could paddle and balance well now. He was getting the hang of the proper depth and angle of the paddle to make headway against the current. The city on both sides of the river was broken down and dirty, devoid of character. The buildings constructed as the nation fell into decline took on a decidedly box-like shape. They lacked the windows and ornamentation that would have marked them as uniquely originating on the island, as opposed to being generic products of their more culturally relevant and much larger neighbor from across the sea.

In this part of the city, high stone channel walls kept the waters from washing away the buildings on the riverside. Dunne was parallel now to the high testimonial in the old park. This was as likely a place as any other for him to disembark and look around at the world on the other side of the river so long denied to him on the north side of the city.

Dunne paddled right to the stone wall that held the river back from the monument. There were still rows of ruined foundations leering from just below the surface of the water, buildings that had been abandoned as the river had risen in response to the higher tides. He could see them clearly under the running waters. Then he looked up and saw another world transposed over the real one that he existed in.

If it was a hallucination, he could not be sure, but the world looked different. If the natural world had been allowed to progress as it would without man's intercession, this would have become a tidal salt marsh, and the mouth of the river would have widened massively, engulfing the area downstream. He could see the world in both ways now, with men conquering it and with nature allowing it to move in its own natural rhythms. As it was, the river was still constrained on both sides by the sunken works of man. Dunne paddled up to a buckled, broken, and submerged section of the wall that opened toward the old monument.

Dunne lodged the kayak there, tucked into the rocks of the broken stone wall that kept the river from washing away more of the muddy field around the monument. New green grass was beginning to come up between the piles of garbage where the increasing amounts of sunlight were able to penetrate to the muddy earth. Dunne found a rutted path that led north. He could see a series of small buildings and enclosures well to the far side of the monument. It was the former city zoo.

His vision clouded and he could see a herd of small roan deer from the past filtering through the present world. They were inbred and stunted, and Dunne could sense that they were not native animals. They had been imported by the island's English overlords to hunt for sport when all of the native animals had been hunted to extinction. Then the vision faded and Dunne knew that even these alien animals were long gone, themselves hunted and poisoned into history.

Dunne walked toward the cluster of buildings beyond the sign marking it as the zoo. He could feel now that there were certain places on the island that he was drawn to, even if he did not yet know why. The zoo was a repository for vanishing species even during its heyday. Then it became a literal boneyard as the animals passed into history. Skeletons of extinct species were warehoused here for their potential monetary value in the future. There was a trade in the powdered bones of dead animals for use as token potions for male sexual enhancement. The animals had little value as tourist attractions while living, so more value was extracted through their deaths when their scarcity increased their value. Nothing was wasted. Nothing except life.

As he walked, Dunne reflected on the lives of those who controlled the island state. They had the means to defy the death that they so often profited from. They had biotech implants, blood transfusions, lab-grown organ replacements, and hormone injections. They didn't hide their advantages in life; they paraded them on the telescreen and promoted their advantages as evidence that they were given their privileges by the creator whose altar they bought ad space on. They not only had everything they needed to prolong life but also every reason. It was a gift that kept on giving over and over in terms of privilege, rights, and advantages. Their lives were enriched by family names with divine right. This granted privilege to them far above those accorded to their fellow men. Their God was a kind and giving god, but only to the correct people. To a fortunate few His love was an extension and evolution of the long-standing covenant from the Book of Isaiah in the Old Testament wherein the earth belonged to the chosen people to do with as they wished.

God's chosen people used everything up, exhausting the most profitable resources first, then moving down the chain of descending financial gain. The death of all undomesticated animal species on earth was a footnote in the history they wrote. They simply moved on to other profit streams. Everything they did was His will. For as long as mankind had pushed toward civilization, he had also pushed wild animals into extinction. Human civilization could not allow for wild animals co-exist. The island was a textbook example of this truth. Not only had the trees been cut down hundreds of years before, but the animals that had depended on them for sustenance or shelter had followed them quickly into extinction. By the early twenty-first century, academics could no longer agree on what the "native species" of the island were. Adaptive foreign species came in on ships as the climate changed, and the local species were driven beyond memory.

Dunne had seen the telescreen programs that sold the island's history to tourists. He knew there was a history of large predators on the island before man. There was a skeletal cave bear on display in a dusty bone and rag shop in the west of the island, until the bear was stolen and ground into pills to help rich men maintain erections. All the living animals left at present were tumor-ridden feral cats and oversized rats, feeding on each other and the wastes left behind by man in his quest for profit. Pundits argued over which was more "native," and the islanders hunted both for meat.

The remaining insects of note were voracious, predatory cockroaches. All other insects had fallen before man's pesticide onslaught. The cockroaches crawled and flew and bit and sucked, taking the place of every other insect through their own evolved adaptive nature. They were the six-legged version of mankind.

The dead zoo that Dunne stood in was a museum of death and the pinnacle of man's relationship with the earth's beasts. It was the fate of every animal to become extinct in man's quest for profit. It was all part of "God's plan," assured the capitalists who profited from extinction. Who could doubt them? After all, God had marked them as his chosen ones by showering them with economic privilege, and they had the money to prove that God loved them. Such was life as Dunne understood. Now he was confronted with fact at "The Dead Zoo."

Its halls and walls were filled with taxidermied corpses and wired skeletons and had been showcased on the telescreen for the tourist market. Dunne had watched the documentaries over and over. The displayed bones had once been real. The history of the museum that he didn't know because it wasn't showcased in media, was that the real pieces had been replaced to be sold or ground into poultices and powders and plasticized into the talismanic pendants for the new Christian rulers from across the sea for whom idolatry was second nature.

Everyone on the island knew about the black market, even the poor workers who couldn't afford the high-end goods sold there. It struck Dunne as an odd dichotomy that while the new Christians of the modern age so strongly believed in publicly expressing "thoughts and prayers" for things that they didn't want to take direct action toward, they still valued the exchange of gold for that which they did value. They were the ones who offered thoughts and prayers through social media when the hurricane force storms struck the west of the island with increasing normalcy, but they also bought the bones of the mammoths, tigers, and the cave bears from each other on the black market. They drank the bone brew, and rubbed the marrow balm made from extinct animals and gold flakes on their skin. Dunne found it odd that thoughts and prayers rarely availed themselves on erections. God had to find other mysterious ways to work on those.

The American god's followers were convinced that he did answer their personal prayers with action as if their god were actually a djinn or genie of myth who responded to wishes of unlimited number. Everything was "blessed" as long as the person asking for favor through prayer performed the right rituals with the right words in the right order. Dunne wondered who had prayed for all the changes he'd seen on the island since he became ill.

He found the back buildings of the zoo all burned. The ruins still reeked of ash and charred plastics blowing downwind. Small eddies of black dust yet swirled among the broken foundations. There was nothing left in the ruins to learn from. Dunne scanned the horizon to the east and north. There was more of the city to explore, though the parts on the north side of the river were less developed than those on the south side.

He felt somewhere deep inside his gut that he had to work his way back south through the city streets closest to the sea since he had covered the cathedrals and the beer factory, as well as the tourist centers nearer to the old green. This would be his last march through the old city. He already knew that each step took him closer to leaving the island.

Dunne took stock of what he had learned on his long, meandering walk through the city and its sprawling wastes. He had seen things he'd only glimpsed through the telescreen before the fall of civilization. He'd seen both the metaphorical and the literal dividing lines between the workers and the corporations who owned their lives. The factories in the heart of the city and the lives of the workers here seemed not so unlike his own. He'd learned that he knew how to read, and that beings sprung from the stories of the old country had somehow come to life at the same time as the people he had known had passed into memory.

He wondered if there was a necessary trade-off in the reality that he lived in before and the one he inhabited now. If one couldn't exist at the same time as the other. If he could, he would ask someone if the things and the people he saw were only possible because of the vacuum created by the millions of lives swept from the island by mysterious causes. Did one cause the other? Was either inevitable?

Dunne thought back to his younger days; how he was often criticized and mocked for always "being too much in his own head" as others put it when he shied away from the telescreen or taking in part in the sport events. Now here he was on the island with little else to do but wander and ponder his own existence. Now the broken homes of the old middle class stretched between him and the seashore.

These crumbling houses were built in the golden days of the island, between two periods of foreign rule when it was an independent nation. Each block house was original built to house two families, one on either side of a central wall. By Dunne's lifetime, each house held several multi-generational families on each side. Cousins and aunts and uncles slept on floors with grandparents, and all scrabbled for the same short food supplies or scant comforts within the deteriorating interiors.

The old homes were crumbling rapidly into their composite materials. Most had been slowly collapsing in on themselves while the people were still living in them. Dunne wondered if this strange death that swept the island was a blessing for some. For many, it brought for many an end to suffering. He was certainly miserable in his own prior life.

As he walked over the pockmarked asphalt through ruined block after ruined block, he felt more sure that the god of material wealth from across the sea had found the island people of the fifty-first state wanting and struck them down in a righteous fury. And what was a god anyway? Were they all just stories? Certainly aspects of them were. Sometimes Dunne thought that they were just men who grew larger than life through stories passed through too many sets of lips.

Ahead of him now was the lower part of the city where some of the DNA miners lived in tenement homes with the dock workers. The familiar tattered red, white, and blue flags hung everywhere, now fading to alternating lines of dirty brown, dusty pink, and weathered purple with the familiar star pattern of the United States. These were buttressed by painted images on the walls of proud, strong, tanned, blonde men defiantly facing the pan-European union with its partner the proud Union Jack of red and white.

For the first time, Dunne wondered about the world beyond the island state. Had this plague set upon the whole world? Could he leave the island and find others, and if he did would he simply be returning to a world of systems built to keep him a victim?

He walked and pondered his own future. The broken, pitted streets were puddled with water from recent rains, and he could smell something undeniably earthy in the air. The buildings here were in a more advanced state of decay than those he had explored in the city center. Dunne wondered if they'd been deserted earlier in the process of the plague or if something else was speeding up the process. He suspected that something was driving all of man's works on the island into ruin much faster than simple environmental degradation, but he couldn't be certain because man never built his products to hold up to the stresses of regular usage.

In front of him lay the old cemetery where some of the republic's historic heroes had been interred during its brief era of independent nationhood. Dunne knew it as the nation's largest DNA mine where old DNA was exhumed to be repurposed in the biological data systems. The work there was boring and dirty, requiring each burial to be exhumed by human hands and carefully sent to the DNA sniffer factory for processing.

After leaving the tenements, he would move south down the coast looking for boats that he could pilot. Something in his head told him to pay his respects to the island's dead before leaving. He would cross through the cemetery to make one last farewell to the people who had made the island great before him. Then he would head south to find a ship to use to escape.

XXIII

Nix walked through the age-old broken cemetery. The wind blew over the dust. The silence of the city annoyed him. He wanted the buzz and the hum of constant machine and human movement. He thirsted for the bustle and the grime it produced everywhere. The rains that had come since everyone had gone away washed the streets too clean for him. He hated this place. In between his drug-induced stupors and sleeps, he hated everything.

Once the telescreens stopped broadcasting, there was little for him to do. He'd emptied the weapons he'd found, firing them at anything that looked remotely like a target. He found more bullets stored away at the barracks. Then he shot those too, saving only a handful in case he found someone to shoot. Some of the guns malfunctioned. One exploded in his hand and took chunks of skin and flesh. He tried crushing some of the pills that he thought were painkillers and rubbing them into the open wounds to ease his pain, but it didn't work. The powder burned and stung first before settling to a strange throbbing swell. Nix found some plastic wound-tape and wrapped the wound. The pain served to make Nix only angrier. He was angry that the gun exploded in his hand, angry that he kept running out of bullets, angry that there were no workers remaining to intimidate.

If everyone was dead, Nix wanted to go to the US where he knew that he would welcomed by the president and the people that he loved and idolized. He'd had the fifty-one starred battle flag tattooed on his chest since he was a child. He was a huge fan of both the United States and its President for Life. He hated being stuck on the island even before everyone else on it died; now that he was the only one left, he hated it even more.

He smashed a few remaining headstones that hadn't been broken already by the corpse miners and urinated on some of the other plots where bodies hadn't yet been exhumed. It was a vicious thrill to do these things, but with no one to share them with, much of the rush was lost. It wasn't as though he could impress himself. He was merely biding his time waiting for something to happen, waiting for some new outside influence to impress itself upon his existence.

His time stayed as slow as ever, but time seemed to be moving ever faster around him. There was nothing for him in the cemetery. The pits left by the DNA miners held nothing now except the mix of the island's dirt and the plasti-trash caught there as the winds continued to sweep the rest of the island clean of human evidence.

The shops here outside the city center were just as desolate. Even the alcohol had gone bad. The last plastic bottles he'd found had been dissolved from the inside by their contents and had then spilled across stained shelves and floors to evaporate. Everything was falling apart much faster than it had up to this point in his memory. All of the foodstuffs imported from overseas on the sensor ships had rotted inside their plastic packaging and oozed into foul-smelling pools of goo on the store shelves. As much as things were made to crumble and decompose, food was usually the opposite. Formerly, he could depend on the usual plasticine-tasting sausages to remain edible indefinitely, but even those manufactured and remanufactured food goods were being attacked by something in the very air that he could not see or understand. The preservative chemicals were failing. He could no longer find anything edible.

He turned to trudge back to his barracks. At least there he still had the remnants of his stash of drugs that he had scoured from the city hideaways. The loneliness was finally starting to wear on him. He felt the pull of the icy cold Irish Sea calling for him to fill his pockets with rocks and wade out far beyond the tide line.

That was weakness, and he recognized it as such. He clenched his fist and chewed on his lip. His faith in God and America would keep him going. They made him strong. He would keep going until he got to where he needed to be and everything would be better.

XXIV

Away from the Doonbag Testimonial and the dead zoo, many other parts of the suburban zone had fallen into profit. The large monument was once a part of a sizable green space that had been long since sectioned and sold off to the corporate interests that had taken over the island nation. At first, there were large mansions and manor estates; then the property was subdivided into smaller and smaller chunks as the propertied gentry fled further and further from the heart of the city after reclaiming this once public green space for their private use.

Dunne traveled over old broken rail lines, unused since the island achieved statehood and dissolved the national service to trade rail transport for trucking in a move that increased profits for the privately owned trucking companies. Until then, they had been shut out of the island by the more economical but less profitable government-owned trains.

He crossed over a mud canal filled from the side to side with heaps of refuse on the border of the cemetery. There were signs all over for the local company which had mined the graveyard for potassium decades ago, then more recently for DNA when it became easier to harvest human DNA from the soil than it was to grow it in the lab for information storage purposes.

240

Dunne paused to take in the local scene. Several of the mining tunnels had collapsed, resulting in a landscape that looked like a garbage strewn battlefield of Verdun, France in early 1917 — with the exception that some of these holes in the ground had been made into burrow-like homes for the workers after the corpse-mining companies retreated.

The wind blew coldly across the broken stones of the old graveyard. Dunne thought he heard voices among the whistling of the wind over cold earth. The sounds grew louder as he drew closer, even as the winds lessened in the field of rubble. Over the sounds of his own footsteps on the hard scrabble plain, a sound of murmured voices became more audible. There were voices in the graveyard clay.

Dunne paused to listen more deeply. There was certainly an unnatural sound, a human sound. It was coming from among the broken stones of the pitted and cratered graveyard. The murmur was irresistible and drew him forward into its source. With each step toward the broken field the murmurs grew louder and more distinct from each other. Dunne found individual voices filtering through the winds and his footsteps. He could hear women's voices, men's voices. The voices of children. He could hear wailing and chatter, laughter and exclamations, odd bits of conversation and things he was never meant to hear. Voices started to emerge from the jumble at his feet.

At first, they weren't talking to him. They took no notice of him and were talking about people — other people long or recently dead. Gossip resolved itself to Dunne's ears. It was the sort of conversation that he was a mute witness to during his own too-long life working in the factory. They were common conversations, salt of the earth conversations.

The nearer voices paused gently, then spoke of him, but not to him.

"Eh, who's this fella up top, pushing down on us now? I can feel his feet, though he's not a large one."

"How d'you know it's a man, Ella?"

"His steps are heavy — heavier than any woman ever stepped, Ara, except maybe you, but I can tell the weight's not his, it's something that he's carrying. He's carrying quite a load. Short steps, ball first and then heel not so deep. This man's got something there."

Dunne stopped and tried to stand more upright. He had hunched over, leaning forward with every step, straining to hear the voices coming up out of the land.

"Who's that steppin' up there? Are you 'nother digger?" came a male voice from the dirt.

"You oughta know yerself!" a voice shouted.

"I thought we was done with them, didn't you, Ella? I hadn't heard nary a hop, skip, or a jump in days! And no shovels and picks either!"

"Don't count your chickens before the shell cracks open from the inside, dearie! Just 'cause they took a break don't mean they broke!"

"Well, where've they all gone? What happened to 'em? There haven't been any new voices comin' from down here either! I ain't heard a new wail in a while. Use'lly we got a few new ones e'rey day all cryin' and moanin' about how cold the dirt is 'til they get used to it, but we've not heard a new voice in a while."

"Yeah, it's high curious, in't? I hadn't paid much notice, but we've not 'ad any new gossip about the above grounders! And you're startin' to right bore me, Ada!"

Dunne spoke, at first in amazement at the voices that originated beneath his very feet, and then in relief at these normal human voices without conceit that he had not heard in far too long. "I can hear you, ladies! I can hear you!"

He was met with silence. Then from the ground came a tentative reply,

"What's this then, my dearies? This sounds like one of them first few that came here to treat us like a quarry! Like one o' the prods who busted up my fine cross for flag stones for his garden and dug into the ground where my bones had been planted like the flowers that should have been growin' above us!"

"Is ee one of them?" came another voice, "Is ee one more of 'em come to take away what'ver is left?"

"What is left to us, just our voices now down here in the graveyard clay, just the bits and bobbles that seeped out the boxes as the roots and the worms worked their ways in? What more can these kinds steal from us?"

Dunne was struck dumbfounded. He sat down in the dirt and held his ear to the ground.

"Do you feel 'im up there? Whuts he doin' now?"

"I'm listening," Dunne answered without thinking. The voices screamed in shock, nearly all at once.

"'Ee can hear us down here!"

"No! He must be talking to another one of them!"

"Another one of who? You know as well as we do there ain't another up there! No one to hear us that we can't hear, to be sure!"

"Sure enough!" came the other voice.

"Try it again," one suggested.

"You up there, are you bless'd or curse'd that you can hear us down here?"

Dunne answered once again. "A bit of both or none at all of the first. I don't know how or why I can hear you. What are you doing down there in the grave mine?"

"This ain't a mine a'tall, lad, t'is simply a garden."

"Mind?" said a voice. "They's minding us again?"

"No, you sad sack, you worm's rump! I said 'mine' not 'mind!'"

Dunne couldn't help but to laugh. The voices from below took umbrage at his finding humor in their conversation.

"Now he's laughing at us!"

"Better than digging us up!"

"Down't be spreading idears if he hadn't taught of it yet, ya arse!"

"I don't want anything from you...," Dunne paused to consider his thoughts, "unless you can tell me what is happening to the world."

The ground was quiet. Dunne kicked at a rock, waiting impatiently for a response.

"We dunno. We been buried..."

Dunne laughed. The frankness of the response surprised him. "Honestly, that makes the most sense of anything I've seen or heard in a few days."

"You mustn't 've heard much then, because nuttin' good'll be coming from those lips, well off the bone as they are!"

"Oh, hush ye scoundrel!" the other voice hissed back. "You don't 've any teeth left to be taking such bitin' liberties wit' me!"

Dunne laughed at the banter. He had not imagined anyone having this kind of conversation, let alone dead people. They were cross, but seemed to be having more fun than he had imagined anyone ever having. Certainly more fun than he had ever had.

"What 'appened?" came the question from below. Dunne thought for a moment before responding.

"Everyone died."

"To be fair, that much is plain, even down here. Are ye a bit of a dim bulb?"

"Why did you ask?" Dunne was still lying on the ground talking into the dirt.

The ground below didn't answer, but instead asked another question."What killed them?"

Another voice from below answered instead. "Life killed them. Life kills. One of two ways — either it kills you to live, or it kills you when you run out of it."

Dunne rolled to his belly and spun his toe in the dirt making a shallow depression in the ground. "That's quite dark, no?" was all he could say.

"Would you rather I lie, lad?"

Dunne couldn't answer. A different voice chimed in from the dirt below.

"You been lying here since you fell down up there, you old sot. Ever since they tossed ye' in a hole in the mud and shoveled more damned mud on top of ye!" came the reply from below.

Dunne chuckled at the thought of being buried after death instead of being burned or left to rot in a pile. What strange personalities he'd met since everyone else on the island had died. He rolled back on his side, with his head on his arm to listen to the voices as they continued to argue below him. The earth felt comforting and soft.

He shifted the books in his cloak. He still wanted to read them, but not tonight. Tonight, he was weary. The disturbed ground had an ease to it that the rest of the island state lacked. His eyes closed in a blink and did not reopen. He fell into a deep and empty sleep.

"Land is the ultimate investment. Land
with a building on it is a better investment.
But, anyone who allows their building to be
occupied is diminishing its investment value.
Land must be developed but not utilized in
order to maximize investment earnings."
Real Investing for Real Morons
D. Cheetum & Ann Howe

XXV

Dunne was stumbling over the soft oil-soaked filth
through what was once a capital city in the long-defunct
European Union. Now it was a hollowed out monument to
man's mastery of the earth. He was tired, but something in him
drove him on toward the south of the city from whence he'd
come. He'd awoken in the cemetery gone quiet. The voices in
the dirt were gone, and he moved on to the south along the
coast.

The boggy ground held little green that was not
shredded petroplast; instead it was a brownish marsh of oily
mud mixed with fecal run-off from the housing hives that
squatted on the high banks of the flood plain. Along his road
were other factories like his, poised on the river banks and the
sea shore to harvest plastic waste from mankind's primary
dump, the ocean. Here, the human waste was even processed
to remove the unabsorbed psychoactive chemicals and
vitamins that many citizens consumed in mass quantities.
Drug residues were collected and recycled into new pills for
other people to swallow down.

Dunne was now among the wharfs where the sensor
ships dropped their cargo, He found another hive and factory
similar to his. He didn't know what they did there, only that it

in some ways resembled the place that he himself labored in until the freeing day of his almost-death. If he had known the history of the place, he'd have known that several decades before, this same set of buildings housed a "school" for young poor boys sent from the Irish countryside to the cities to be civilized. It was a place where those potentially misspent youths of Catholic families were abandoned when their kin could not effectively care for or control them in the eyes of the local constabulary. Here they were taught to be "useful."

The sea waters looked like a pane of glass in the harbor, reflecting the deadness of the air and sky. The environment was eerily silent as he slowly approached the broken walls of this factory. No clouds moved today, just a hot sun that shone down relentlessly and seemed stuck to one spot in the sky. Dunne half expected black smoke to come billowing forth from the makeshift twin smokestacks that hovered a few feet above the sagging roof, but there were no signs of movement within.

Unbeknownst to Dunne, a man was hiding in the barracks side of that ruined factory. His shirt had returned to a brown color — no longer orange. It was stained deeply and tattered from bathing in the local effluent — far from the color that it held on the man's last day of work. He gripped a gun tightly.

Each of the Orangeshirts was issued an automatic carbine on his first day as part of his induction ceremony. It wasn't a carbine and it wasn't fully automatic, but the truth didn't matter as much as the advertising, and the description (although false) carried a great deal of prestige with ownership. Power was a gun and a gun was power.

Nix's day was not off to a good start. A few days ago the lights went out for the last time in this part of the city, and the looping automated programs on the telescreens in his crumbling factory shelter gave out as well. As the hours drifted by in a haze and things didn't start up again, Nix felt his own discomfort increasing. When things were unsettled, people did unsettling things. They killed for fun and not just for profit. Nix enjoyed it because it was fun even if things weren't unsettled. He hated that there was nothing left anywhere to kill.

Today, things didn't feel right at all. He wished that he had conserved more of the ammunition that he had found, but it was too late. He fired it all off, most of it while he was drunk or high. He shot at walls, lights, telescreens... even the far away sensor ships traveling across the sea. Later today he would search farther through the city for more ammunition and more drugs. For now though, he lay on a damp cot and tried to think about his longer term plans.

He wanted to cross the ocean to get to America, but had no idea of how to do it. The easiest thing to do would be to try to stow away on one of the still mobile automatic sensorships that were going back and forth, but then he had no idea which ones were going where or even if any of them were on their way to the other states. He had no idea of how to find the information either. He knew best how to do things that he was told to do. One direction at a time. He had trouble plotting to achieve anything beyond a two step process. He kicked his tattered blankets off and rolled his feet to the floor. His boots were falling apart again. "Godammit," he cursed aloud. On his way out to look for more drugs, he'd have to find a new pair of boots too. The left boot had now split between the sole and the toe as well as breaking open at the flex point between the laces and the toes. He pulled the cracked petroplast boots on and stared at the wall. He was tired.

The days were dragging. His searches for the things he wanted turned up less and less that he could use. He was starting to feel despondent and hopeless without his escapes. His daydreams had shifted from shooting other people to shooting himself. He imagined how cool and cinematic he could make his death scene look. He was disassociating the act of self destruction from suicide. Suicide was weak, but he could kill himself nobly if he was the last man left in the world. "Only the weak commit suicide" he muttered aloud to himself and headed out to look for more bullets and a replacement pair of boots.

Nix had been through many of the local sites over and over again, looking for hidden spots or abandoned drugs or ammunition. He turned toward the coastline again. There were some factories near the water that had been damaged by the storms and sea water that had broken through the retaining walls. It made sense in his head to explore them one last time before they crumbled fully into the sea.

The first one near the mouth of the river was on ground already returning to the sea. Waves lapped at the walls and flooded the building, causing parts of it to collapse. The roof was falling in on the side closest the city and the main entrance was now open to the sea.

He climbed through a broken window on the city side and dropped to the floor. He splashed onto a thin layer of water that overlayed the cracked concrete like plastic film. He'd been in this place before, much earlier after everyone else had disappeared. He remembered that the commander's office was upstairs. That was the place that offered the most opportunity for hidden treasures. He climbed up the stairs two at a time, catching the toe of the crumbling boot on the very last step and tripping. He tried to catch himself on his hands but fell on his face through the open door and directly in front of the commander's desk. Through the thin space between the desk and the floor, he saw an ammunition box hidden beneath the desk that he had missed on his first sweep of the room days ago.

He pushed himself up and moved around the back of the desk, shoved the bent chair out of the way and pulled the box from its hiding spot. The only thing securing the cover was the latch, no lock. Obviously, this commander had trusted the lock on his office door to be enough to protect everything in the room. It may have, if he had closed the door on his last exit. Nix popped the latch and opened the case.

No bullets, only a stash of a green buds in a bag and some mixed "barbies" and "nummers" in another bag. He took both, pocketing the green weed to smoke later and closely examined the pills, holding them to the light coming through the cracked windowpane. They looked good. The moisture in the factory hadn't touched them. He left the office and walked back down the steps, his broken shoe sole slapping on the floor. Then his boot sole fell off in the thin layer of water on the floor as he walked to a back wall where some of the structure had collapsed, leaving the building open to the sky.

An old reclining office chair sat upright where it had fallen from the floor above when the wall and part of a conference room collapsed into the ground floor. Nix rolled the chair into the shade behind the remaining wall and popped three of the pills. They took effect almost immediately, and his head began to drift. He slouched into the chair and nodded off before sliding onto the damp floor and passing out.

When he came back to the world hours later, the sun had moved across the sky to put him directly in its rays and his face and neck felt hot and dry. He rolled over to his side and hid his face in his hands, rubbing his dirty fingers into his eyes. The tide had gone out, leaving only puddles in the low spots in the floor. His head felt congested and unattached from his shoulders. He pushed himself up from the dust and gathered himself. He was sleepy yet; the downers still flooded his bloodstream.

The ongoing degradation of man's works on the island state had accelerated well beyond what was natural due to the processes of weathering and the lack of maintenance. Even Nix could see it now that his head was less clouded. He climbed over the ruined lower portion of the wall and under the partially collapsed roof into the Orangeshirt's sleeping quarters.

He found an abandoned carbine that someone had left behind on a rumpled cot and examined it for damage. It was rusted. The plastic stock was cracked as well. He opened the chamber to find one round left in the weapon. He sighted it in against the wall on the opposite side of the sleeping room, then spun to the gaping hole in the wall to sight in the long distance. The barrel looked warped and the sights didn't line up. It was then that he saw the movement down range. He squinted and looked again. There was a distant shape moving toward him, and it wasn't rubbish being blown in the wind. For the first time in his life, Nix felt panic. He didn't know what it was. His heartbeat sped up and he wanted to vomit. He dropped to his knees to hide behind the ruined half-wall and squinted into the distance, trying to resolve the movement approaching his crumbing personal citadel.

His mind raced. He had been trained on how to control the cowering workers in the factory, but this person coming toward him had mass and moved with a strength he hadn't seen before. It must be a man. Nix knew that women never moved like that. His fear grew. He scrambled behind his covering wall to ready the rusty carbine. He looked around in a panic for more bullets or more weapons but found none. The one bullet remaining was in the chamber.

Nix didn't trust his ability to hit the man from this distance with just one bullet. He had to wait until he came closer. With the man's each step forward, Nix's anxiety and uncertainty grew. He wished there were a squadron of Orangeshirts here to help him, or a commander to tell him to shoot. He crouched low and banged his head twice on the wall out of sight of the interloper. He fought his breathing, the anxious breath wanting to race out of control.

Nix could feel the being coming toward him. Although he was still hidden from the sight of the intruder behind the ruined and partially collapsed wall, it was only a short matter of time before the threat would be on top of him. Nix knew that he had a mission to protect material wealth from outsiders, but his training also taught him that when the mission was lost, the last bullet was for him. He would not live in a world where he would be a loser to the brown skins.

The man only looked brown. Dunne was not an equatorial immigrant. His family had been in the state for generations, very likely prior to the republic becoming a state. He was actually as white as Nix, but he was covered with the filth of the island. The dirt on his face and the unfortunate mottled browns and earthy green shades of his raiment lent him a distinct air of a dangerous immigrant in the eyes of the trembling Orangeshirt.

Looking down at the slowly approaching man, Nix knew he could either use his last bullet against the threat outside, or he could save himself from the shame of losing the conflict to an enemy. One bullet was all he needed. One bullet meant eternal safety, a direct shot to Heaven that awaited all of the faithful: those chosen ones who had heard the President for Life's words and made the correct choice to follow that imperfect vessel of God's will.

Nix was shaking in the remnants of his boots. Each of the figure's meandering steps forward meant that the threat was more definite, and each tremble and increase in Nix's already pounding heart rate meant that he was less likely to make that kill shot that he so desperately needed. He could wait until the threat was almost on top of him, but what if he missed then? He couldn't bear the fear of being tortured and beaten by the drug-crazed immigrant that was moving toward him to engage in what would clearly be a climactic battle of good vs. evil.

Dunne, on the other hand, had no idea that Nix was a mere hundred meters away with a gun. Dunne didn't want to hurt anyone, not even an Orangeshirt, and would have been happily surprised to find anyone else still alive.

Nix was shaking terribly and he fumbled with his weapon, almost dropping it noisily to the ground. He still had the element of surprise against the approaching Dunne, who was moving closer to his position every moment.

Nix had a choice to make and very little time to make it. To him, the deadly threat was imminent. If he took a shot at the approaching man, he risked missing entirely. Then he would be at the mercy of this dirty foreigner. He wished that his commanding Orangeshirt were there to help him, but the commander disappeared along with everyone else that Nix had known.

Dunne paused to look around. The dilapidated city behind him was a stark contrast to the Orangeshirt compound crumbling into the sea before him. The Orangeshirts often commandeered the local Gardai stations, especially as the Gardai had blended and morphed with the Orangeshirts soon after their inception. This barracks near the factory was simply a repurposed school. The church next to it that had been a part of the facility had caught fire some time past and burned down. Only the hollowed out, collapsed shell remained.

Dunne was anxious to explore this last bit of the city before leaving his island home for good.

Nix had to make a choice. The threat was only thirty meters away and closing quickly now. Nix could see the man squarely down the iron sights, and if he fired, he would surely hit the target.

Or would he? He could see now the barrel was slightly bent to the left. He had never had to sight and hit a moving human being with a damaged weapon before. His confidence in his ability to compensate for the barrel's bend was weak. He couldn't draw a solid bead on the slowly approaching man because the shaking in his arms had gotten worse. He shook as if a great wave of cold had washed over him.

Dunne stopped. He could hear something. A rattling or shaking that seemed to come from the dark shadows of the factory-school. Someone or something was moving in there. Was it the wind? He hoped that it was not an Orangeshirt with his weapon loaded. An old fear flashed through his mind. Dunne crouched next to a pile of garbage just for a moment before realizing that hiding was absolutely useless. If it were his fate to die, he might already be gone, like everyone else he knew. Whatever would happen to him was going to happen no matter what he did.

Nix watched as the man crouched down next to a pile of garbage and then stood up again as if he had examined the refuse and found it wanting. The man seemed to sense that Nix was there. The cloaked man paused to listen and then looked directly at where Nix was hiding behind his ruined wall of pressed fiberwood and broken plaster.

Dunne moved more slowly now, but in the direction of the noise he had heard. There was something living here. Another person! The only sounds he'd heard since he'd left the cemetery were the waves of the sea washing against the buildings and the shore. Now he could hear an almost dog-like whine as he cautiously closed the distance to where the sound was coming from.

Nix was shaking even worse. He could not fix the gun sights on the approaching man. He would have to wait until the target was upon him, and then Nix himself would be at tremendous risk. If he missed with his only shot, he was dead for sure! Or even worse, violated by the threatening form that was coming ever closer. Nix realized that his teeth were chattering now. Surely the approaching man heard him and knew exactly where he was!

Dunne moved cautiously closer. He could hear a light chattering sound now. In the sometimes still air that he'd experienced since emerging from the ground, void of the clamor of man, it was very easy to hear most everything. It felt like his senses had become sharper since he had emerged from his underground rebirth, but it was simply his senses adjusting from a lifetime of excessive noise and overly bright telescreens controlling his vision.

The man was within five meters now. If he wanted to, he could easily close the gap and be on top of Nix, tearing out his throat and raping him, just as Nix had been warned for years by nationalist media that foreigners would not hesitate to do. He had one bullet, and two options: kill the man or kill himself. If he missed the man with his single shot, he would surely be tortured and killed in the most painful ways possible. Brown people were horrible sub-human monsters who lived only to cause pain and discomfort to pure-blooded people like Nix. He had to act now. His choice was as clear as the approaching threat.

One or the other.

He raised the barrel and pulled the trigger.

The explosive sound rocked Dunne; he fell forward instinctively. The sound of a gunshot was all too familiar even if he had not heard it in so many days that he could no longer reckon. He took stock of his body, felt his face with his hands and patted down his chest through the dirty cloak. He knew that sometimes the pain of a bullet wound was not immediate. He'd seen enough people be shot outside his own factory. The shock of a bullet ripping into their flesh was sometimes more than the brain could process in those first few seconds even as the blood began to pour forth from the wound.

Dunne was unwounded. No red stains in his clothing, his limbs still complete. No wave of numbness or pain. Perhaps he had misheard the sound, and it was not a gun but instead some sort of pressurized gas tank rupturing after being left too long exposed to the salty, moist air. He looked up. The clouds overhead had gone gray and were sweeping quickly down from the northeast. The high pressure that had kept the sky clear and calm had broken.

Dunne climbed a low broken wall and looked into the space where the sounds that he'd heard earlier had come from. He saw a body slouched forward onto the wall. The corpse's mouth gaped open, and there was another violently engineered opening in the opposite hemisphere of the man's head. The filthy man's brain matter was still sliding down the nearby rubble in ruddy red and purple splotches. Fresh blood soaked the man's shirt and pooled below him.

The corpse had also shat himself, and the odor blended with the scent of the open wound in the back of his head in a way that struck Dunne's belly particularly hard. Perhaps it was that the odor evoked a similar taste to the sausage meat that he had consumed in the hive.

There was nothing else here for him to find but the corpse of the Orangeshirt. He had spent days searching for another living survivor on the island, and had missed this one by mere moments. Dunne chastised himself for not having gotten there even just a few moments sooner to save this man. It didn't occur to Dunne in that moment that the last bullet in the man's carbine would have been used to end Dunne's life instead.

Dunne left the corpse behind. The encroaching sea would take it soon. He gazed out over the sea and reassessed his travel plan. If he could catch a current, he could use the water to travel faster to find a bigger boat.

He set out once again back upriver to find the kayak he'd used days before. He planned now to make his way south on the sea current instead of walking near Sallynogg on his way south along the coast. He didn't want to have to revisit his old life. It was time to move on. If he could find it, a small yacht or sailboat would provide him a quicker path and allow

him to get a feel for being on the sea if his plan to cross the
ocean was to come to fruition.

XXVI

Dunne drifted in his kayak, obeying the tidal pull like so much refuse tossed into the water with no regard for where it would go. Here and there, the towering hulks of abandoned buildings loomed stories over the murky water in what was once the city's waterfront. The tide pulled him out of the drowned city; the ruins caught floating debris from the currents and held it until storms came and stole it. One thing caught, then another, and then so much flotsam and jetsam accumulated, like the plastic garbage that cluttered the water's edge near Sallynog where Dunne had labored for so long. One of the giant Poolbeg stacks from the deserted power plant still stood not far from the mouth of the city's river, leaning precariously a few degrees in the direction of the city as if pointing for the water to go there at high tide.

He looked down the coast and could see the ruins that he knew to be his old home. Sallynog was where he died and was reborn — where he went to the sea in his last fluttering memory and where he awoke in the mound lair of the mysterious *Ben síde* woman to start his second more lonely life.

His questions about what happened in the in-between still haunted him. He had not yet found an awareness to cover that space, whether it was three days in the would-be tomb or more than that. He had no apostles waiting to greet him on the other side, no mother and no aunts looking to bathe his body after days interred. When he passed out in his fever, a world of people were around him, but when he awoke, only he and a handful of other beings remained. And he could not reconcile these odd beings with everything he'd known from the world before.

Now he was out to sea, a kilometer from the shore in a place he had seen but never been. He had never seen the island he lived on from a boat. When he was living his first life, the water was only for people of a higher social class than his, ones who could get on the boats and travel far out to sea where the refuse of the land sank to the bottom or collected in far-away gyres beyond their care or notice. He patted the books in the pocket of his cloak. It was important to keep them dry until he had a chance to properly read them.

The kayak that Dunne took afforded him a path forward and potentially a path through some of the mysteries that vexed him. What had happened to him and where did everyone go? Who was the man in the factory and how had he survived for so long only to take his own life? Could he still succumb to the plague that had killed everyone else? Were there others like that man out there that he had missed by mere moments? Those questions had replaced his questions about his own dreams and memories because he was anxious about what was to come next.

The sea winds still occasionally brought him the stink of human waste and excess, but with each succeeding tide in the absence of man, the materials that generated the smell were being taken by the sea and pulled down to the depths that men never explored. They simply dragged nets over the deep bottom to pull the sunken plastics back to the surface to burn.

The cracked and jagged remnants of the second broken Poolbeg stack captured waste outflow from the river at the shifting of the tides. At high tide, that stack was below water level. It was there, trapped between the Poolbegs and caught on the sharp edges and jutting rebar of that stack that connected the sky and the waters, that Dunne found part of his answer.

Dunne floated and paddled through the low-lying fog coming in from the sea toward the leaning stack. There he found a floating mass of debris. It was a coagulation of human bodies and their assorted detritus caught like a clot in a blood vessel. Like most things that mankind had thrown away, the bodies had been swept into the oceans.

He slumped in the kayak and surveyed the scene. Before him floated hundreds of bloated corpses. They were tangled with each other, forming a mass that covered the water like a heavy tarp. He was fortunate that the wind was blowing out to sea. He paddled backward, lest he be caught in the floating mass. He turned back toward the south.

From where Dunne paddled on the waves, he could see the shallow cliff of Killiknee Hill standing through the fog like a sentinel. He felt a strong inclination to go there. It stood out from the shrouded coast, and the light overhead illuminated it through a hole in the clouds. The whitewashed limestone of a castle mansion on the peak of the hill beckoned to him. He paddled toward the shoreline to catch a parallel current and drove his kayak down the coast and toward the hill. He could feel that water was starting to fill his worn plastic watercraft. The waves were coming over top of it, and he wanted to keep his books that were in his cloak dry.

From his factory, Dunne could see the cliffs of the former Killiknee Hill on most days, but there was no reason at all to look at it. There was a castle on the hill, as there always had been. Dunne didn't know who lived there. There was no reason to. It was simply as immovable and as immutable as the rocks themselves and as unarguable as the wealth that separated him from the water and the hilltops in his past life. If he had guessed, he might have thought that certainly a wealthy person who owned his own factory may have lived there on that mountain which had been a public park.

The castle on the hill rested near one of the well-known "famine follies." The castle and the folly both were built by the private funds of a generous landholder who allowed the starving island folk to build an obelisk monument to him during the historical great famine. He traded the hungry peasants a bit of meagre cash for their hard work in building a folly, because no starving man or woman could be suffered to receive a handout. Those unworthy islanders had to learn to thank their betters over and over again for generations in the same way that the good Catholics of the island had given thanks from their knees to the God whose blessings all too often included their sufferings.

The property had been taken back into private hands when the republic became the fifty-first state. It was that castle on the hill and its courtyard that was Dunne's new destination. From there, he could move forth again south to find a harbor.

Even recently as he had wandered the east side of the island, he awoke from nightmares of working in the factory; there was no respite. Ofttimes, he wanted to linger in older, kinder dreams that he could find no real-world inspiration for in his memories. They were dreams being someplace warm, of being held, of feeling safe and cared for. Those were dreams that he never wanted to leave in the old days, but the conditions of his former life forced him to rise up from his sleeping rags in his cubbyhole quarters to earn back the debt on those rags and that shelter. Now those dreams no longer came to him. He either woke dreamless or with his arms going through the motions of his work in the factory.

There were some things that Dunne could imagine because he could remember having experienced them. He could imagine the days when he could be outside to see the horizon of the sea reflecting the natural light. Those days that the sun would linger longer in the sky rendering some color of rose to his pale, grimy skin. He could remember the days when the meat served by the vendor in his living quarters didn't chip and crunch in his teeth because of the dirt or bone fragments present throughout. He often hoped that the meat would return to those textures, just as he would hope for a reduction in the debt assigned to his account for each bite, which seemed to climb each year as the portions shrank both in size and in sense of satisfaction.

His mind came back to the present where he paddled, swiftly carried on currents that felt purpose-driven for taking him to the hill. Dunne landed his sinking kayak near a ruined church at the foot of the quarried hills of Walkey. Waves now lapped where once men quarried stone for the rail line that ran down the coast. He grounded the kayak and dragged it beyond the tideline. Sea water seeped from small cracks in the hull.

Dunne easily found a path up the hill. Though men had not walked it in some time, and green was growing through the browns of the urban wreckage of mankind, the paving stones still reflected light from their foot-polished surfaces. Near the top of the hill stood high gates and walls that surrounded the castle and its sizable courtyard.

Just for a moment, as he walked the winding, paved path up the hill, Dunne imagined what it might have been like if these views that were now opening up had been available to him all his life. What if he and others had been allowed to see the rest of the land from where the wealthy did? What if they had been allowed to look out over the sea for kilometers from the hills and mountains, to see how far it stretched, to see how wide it swept? Would the world have been the same if they had been allowed to understand that there was more to be had from the world than labor and debt?

A heavy, moist air was blowing up from the easternmost side of the hill now. Dunne could feel a bit of weight from the water added to his cloak from the Ben Side. From this new vantage point, the factories he knew looked small. The capital city that he had wandered through looked underwhelming. All of the houses and ruins looked minuscule and meaningless.

His life had been artificially limited for so many years. Now, that world was broken, and in its brokenness it became larger than he could have conceived of in his limited mind. Without the Orangeshirts or the rest of mankind, the spaces felt both less controlled and more compelling.

Once constant debt became the norm,
wage slavery followed it into the realm
of normalcy shortly thereafter. It was barely
a full generation before no one could
remember what it was like to be debt-free.
The New Work
Harry A. Showers

XXVII

The iron gate swung slowly to and fro, creaking in the stiff winds driving off the sea. To the left and right of the wrought iron monstrosity stood heavy stone walls with a delicately broken rainbow of shards of glass embedded in the cement at the top. Two closed circuit cameras guarded the gate, as much for intimidation as for security purposes. Dunne had no doubt the cameras still beamed their video directly to the screens of whomever had done the security for the estate, but he no longer feared anybody was enforcing the prohibition against trespassing.

He walked through the gate with a sense of impunity that had grown exponentially since finding his voice in the lair of the green man and his discovery that so much of the island was empty. There was no one left to deny him. The only others left that he had found had been inexplicable visions that faded, beings that he couldn't be sure were even real. The man he'd recently found dead of a self-inflicted gunshot wound seemed like just another impossible dream to him, no different from the cleric, or even the giant in some regards.

Dunne moved slowly up the cobblestone drive nonetheless. There were a dozen blue and silver tailed magpies watching him from the ragged and windblown flower gardens. Whoever had maintained the house on the hill had kept swaths of wood anemones and bindweeds of various colors to decorate their garden amidst the stone walls placed in intervals beside the cobbles as if in an odd mockery of the old famine walls that still littered the landscape around the island state.

In front of the stone structure, by the drive that had wound its way to the top, was a statue of the descendant of the President for Life who had a summer home on this formerly green isle. The manse was tall and foreboding. It was angular and sharp, designed to resemble the cliffs of the far west coast in its hard, marbled features: its walls white and narrow. Butterworts decorated the ground around the main house, sheltered from the sea and the sun by its features.

There was another gate inside the first, high and topped with oxidizing and cracked wrought iron that circled a courtyard garden wherein the original folly, built in 1852, had once stood before it was razed to build this new and much more impressive folly. It was always the wealthiest men who demanded that their houses be on the peaks of the highest hills that they could buy on the edge of the sea.

Whatever or whoever was in the house didn't matter to Dunne. It could have been the earl, it could have been some squatters who had survived the culling like Dunne had. The mansion didn't look like it had a played host to anyone in weeks.

The inner gate that circled the very spot where the original folly once stood was unlocked. No one who lived there had ever considered that the outer manor walls would be breached by an intruder. And even if they were, who would seek inside what to outside eyes only looked like an open well with steps trailing down into the depths of the stony hill? Dunne was very curious about what lay in the depths. He felt drawn to hidden spaces now that the island seemed to be sharing its secrets with him.

Dunne stood at the top of a narrow stair where the original folly had been built. Pondering the depth and steepness of the path downward, he felt uneasy. There was something else discomforting about entering the very earth again, even though it had saved him before. He turned away from the path inward and walked over a stone paved path to a broad stone terrace that overlooked the water.

The weather was shifting quickly now. The world seemed to be moving faster with each passing hour. The skies around were clear and bright. In the sunlight, the sea shone like a rolling blanket of diamonds. As the weather and natural forces continued to disperse the pollutants left behind in the wake of the human population, the sea took on a clearer tone of blue that was both less and yet more like the sky that it reflected. It was cleared daily by the winds coming from the major currents that swept eastward. It was darker and richer — the sea being flushed, the heavy metals and petrol-plastics going away from the island to land on other shores or to sink deeply to the seabed to lie in dark wait for sea life or for the buckling and shifting continental crusts to carry it downward to the earth's molten furnace.

Dunne's experiences since the sickness overcame him had given him plenty of time to think in ways that had never been available to him in the past. His new awareness was no longer restricted by financial concerns and economic matters that fluttered far above the heads of his working class brethren. He and his ilk were too often concerned with the basic necessities at the lowest levels of humanity: hunger and safety. People like Dunne were kept easily controlled by enslaving them to their own needs.

If they were forced to struggle each day to meet their basic nutritional needs, if they were kept from getting enough restful sleep to restore their work-worn bodies, if they were continually distracted by sexual imagery on their telescreens —then they would never have the energy to cultivate the self-awareness to rise up against the neo-feudalistic aristocracy that profited from their debt slavery. They would never have the time or the energy to dream of things that were so far beyond their reach when they didn't know where their next meal was going to come from, or if it was going to destroy their teeth that they had no medical recourse to care for if they were broken or damaged. The world he had known had created humans too distracted by the minor pleasures of the telescreens to think about their own enslavement. These things occurred to Dunne as he looked out over the ocean.

Dunne looked back over to his path from the high point to where the cavern led underground. He could see the flooded city to the north from where he stood atop the hill. He was done with that place now. There was nothing else for him there. His immediate path now lay downward: down into the very earth and stone of the island, down into the history and the sweat-stained peat and limestone of the island. Dunne felt that he needed to see what was down there before he left, the need to satisfy his curiosity one last time before he left the island. A new desire for knowledge had opened within him.

The path downward into the island was open to him. It was also open to the sky, admitting any of the rains or fogs that could have entered into the realm below. His hand itched where the old ChipIn was implanted. He scratched it absentmindedly and pondered the depth of the stairwell. It looked like the opening of a natural cave that was originally hidden by the builders of the folly. Dunne cautiously took his first steps down the path into a hole in the ground.

He descended several meters, then paused on a landing where the steps changed direction and looked back up at the entrance. He could see the levels in the build demonstrating horizontal layers in bands like sedimentary rock. It was obvious that the entrance to the cave had been built upon in successive generations. The bands closer to the landing that Dunne looked up from were rough hewn — made of larger, irregular stones. Bands nearer to the portico that Dunne had stepped through at the top held more regular and machined shapes topped by cinder block walls that led up to the rich man's compound that covered the cliff top.

There was a rocker electrical switch and aluminum conduit on the wall at shoulder level. Wedged into a wide crevice next to it was a battery powered torch. Dunne took it. From there, wires snaked out either side, hidden in the crevices between the rocks going both up and down. Dunne felt like he was midway between heaven and hell, like the characters in the video games he'd watched on the telescreen.

Poured concrete steps beckoned him down another ten narrow feet before ending on a boulder. From there, the stones downward were rough hewn and irregular. The overhead lights continued downward like flowers on a long stem leading into darkness. The air was dank and still as Dunne descended further on the irregularly shaped, worn stones. The path below looked ancient, as if it had been extant but forgotten for centuries, as if only spirits of the dead or spirits of the land used it to pass to and fro between the worlds. As he crept slowly downward in the dim light, Dunne thought this was just the place where the spirits he'd met might have crossed from.

Dunne descended deeper and deeper into the mountain, cautiously moving under the impossibly long string of dim bulbs. He was now far below the crest of the hill, below even sea level, and yet his path wound and curled ever downward into darkness. Even though his eyes had adjusted to the loss of sunlight, the lights had grown dimmer in the depth, as if the pressure under the mountain had compressed it into the bulbs that still drew a mysterious power from somewhere above the ground.

As Dunne continued his cautious descent into the underworld, he began to consider that the energy that powered the lights might not be coming from above and flowing down, but could be doing the exact opposite. There were things happening in this new world that had no logic in the world that had ended.

Dunne pressed further and further down the steps, farther down than he could have imagined. By now he must have been deeper down to where the pressure of the rock or water above could have choked and crushed him into non-existence.

Around a switchback in the steps, he found himself now without the conduit or bulbs of the upper path. Somehow, the same pale light washed over the rock that surrounded him. It was as if the very air were luminous. Then a vast underground cavern opened up in front of him. He had entered into a level underground space, one that had every indication of having been worked into the stone with man-made straight lines and angles, but at the same time it felt wholly natural in form to his eyes. It was as if the cavern had carved itself. He lodged his battery torch in a low corner of the passage. He felt certain he would not need it for what was to come.

In the dim luminescence a form began to take shape before his very eyes. It was unlike the mushroom experience. This one was only just a few meters from him. It was from the start the shape of a man — one clothed in brightness. Even the air around him was suffused with his light that increased as his solidity did. He was bearded and clad in earth colored garb, much like Dunne's.

As Dunne curiously approached this shape of a man illuminating the space, he saw that colors were forming in his once earthen robes. The man slowly took on more colors than even the most robust rainbow that Dunne had ever seen in his days living on the island's coast. There were those days when the winds cleared out the clouds of pollution and the rains came through, when late in those passing storms the sky formed the most beautiful rainbows that Dunne had ever seen until now. The man before him was made of this light.

Now only a meter or two away, the man looked down to him and smiled gently, as if taking notice of something inconsequential but warmly amusing; it was a smile filled with all of the warmth that Dunne had only felt in a time long before his memory formed fully. The man spoke to him.

"I've waited a very long time to see you. I know who you are, Dunne. I also know how far you've come, and I know what you've experienced to find yourself here in my company."

"Who are you?" Dunne asked, knowing that this man of many colors was something different than the other beings that he had crossed paths with since he was last under the earth. The man eyed him cautiously, as if he worried that Dunne had an unspoken and ulterior motive for asking his name instead of asking any other question, but the man did not stop smiling at Dunne.

"I've had many names in this land. Most of them long forgotten now. I was known as 'Ecne' when men were needing names to know things. I had three fathers when the women folk were less in number than the men because of the Dubgail raiders from the sea. They took so many of the women away to the lands of ice and stone." He paused thoughtfully before continuing. "Before that, I don't remember a name, just sounds on the wind." He paused again reflectively here, his eyes looking through Dunne into a past that man could not imagine. "You can call me Ecne so you can feel that you know something, which is one of the essences of naming. I know why you are here, as well."

"How do you know these things?" Dunne asked.

"It is my reason to be to know things. That men may know is the cause that makes me be, even now when there are fewer things to know and fewer people to know them. I know all things to know about you too, because you may be all that there is to know about now on this island."

"You know about me? Then you must know what I am looking for..?" Dunne paused again. "...I don't even know what I am looking for. I thought I was looking for answers and other people, but the more I found, the more I understood that I needed something else. Why did I survive and no one else?"

"Yes, I know... I know how she found you, and I know why you were the only one that she pulled into her cave." He paused here to convey the weight of his words. "You were simply fortunate. You were the one she found. She had no idea that hundreds of thousands of others would follow, that all of you would be driven by some unknown urges to the tidal zone where you'd lose consciousness to drown and be washed away like so much else that mankind had cast in the water."

Dunne was perplexed. "Why were we drawn to the water?"

"Much of what drives a man in what he does and where he goes is not him. There are multitudes beyond him, not in the spirit world, but also multitudes within him, things that drive his moods, methods, and motivations. Man is not simply man. He is made of a legion of things that he will never see."

"Are you saying that something within us wanted us to drown?"

"I'm saying that there are many things possible that you can't even imagine. Like a mouse carrying a parasite that infiltrates its brain and manipulates its behavior to make it prey for a cat that the parasite needs to be consumed by in order to reproduce. There are many levels of things that control us, things that work through relationships that man in his small mind and limited experience still could not comprehend, even before catastrophe fell upon you. You were sick, there is no denying that. You had a fever that would have destroyed your body and brain. That's what drove you to the sea, down to the water to cool yourself. The *Leanhaun Shee* pulled you from the shallow water before you could drown and took you back into her mound to save you. She might have saved more, or she might have saved less, but you were in the right spot at the right time. After she made certain that you would not die, she went back out only to find that thousands of others had followed suit and lined the shores of the Irish Sea, passed out — some of them already drowned in the surf. She was overwhelmed, not just by the task she thought that she'd begun, but by the very thought of so much death surrounding her — potentially the death of every living thing on the Isle. She went back to you to care for you, and hid both of you for three days. When she emerged again, satisfied then that she wouldn't somehow die as well, she found the city as empty as you did. She also found the corpses in the surf. She saw the death that she had saved you and herself from. Before you awoke from your death sleep after those three days, she'd been worried that you'd gone too, but the smell of death that bathed you was simply the sweat that streamed out of you in your fever and soaked your rags. She had to take those and cast them into the sea with everything else that was to pass away." Ecne paused here as if to consider the weight of the knowledge he had shared. "I don't know that she would have taken ill as you and everyone else did. The *Shee* lived a life alone, although she was always within your midst. She and hers all live as such. They've been there for ages beyond your ken, and mine too. They are as old as the island itself."

Dunne was confused. How could anyone be that old? "What do you mean by that? I don't understand anything anymore..." He felt overwhelmed by his new knowledge.

"I mean that she is not a she, but that she is something that preceded the "she," a being that is elemental to this part of the world and only this part of the world. She is a "she" because your people could only see her in that way. She is not mortal, but she is also not immortal. She can die, and when she saw what was happening to you and what quickly befell the people of the island, she felt a fear of mortality that she had never imagined before. You were a reminder that her time is not unlimited, and so she saved you — but not because you were special. You were simply the first person she saw succumb. That may have made you special in itself, but I cannot speak to that. If you are more significant than that, I cannot imagine it. You are a man, and the time of men here is over. I know that, even if I cannot tell you what I see coming next. I know that what comes next is not an age for me and those like me. Our time is past too, though we are returned here in these last days of the world of man."

Dunne found Ecne's answers unsatisfying though illuminating. They offered only more questions. "You know much, Ecne. Can you tell me where I am to go next, what I am to do moving forward? I... I feel that I must leave here, but I don't know where to go."

"I know this, but I also know that I am not your guide. I am a light here, but here is where I stay. You will be carried away by currents that you do not know." Ecne smiled softly in his rainbow raiment as if for a joke that Dunne had missed. "It was often said of men of this land, that in order to be whatever it was that were were to be, that they had to leave this island."

"What do you mean? Where else is there to go? Where do I go to become whatever it is that I must be?" Dunne was concerned. He still felt adrift. He had wandered through the city and back again exploring the eastern part of the island on whims, following his weak intuition. He still wanted someone wiser to tell him what to do.

"I cannot tell you that. There are tides that draw and winds that shift and move my own sails which even I do not understand. I simply know that sometimes I myself am a boat that must be steered both for and against forces that are beyond even my keen eyes." He paused here to measure Dunne's worth before continuing. "Like you in that regard. We have more in common than you could imagine, or even dream when your dreams are not your own."

"Can you tell me which direction to turn? I am so lost. I've been wandering since I came up out of the hole, and I think much time has been wasted. I just want to do what it is that I must do."

"Sometimes lad, the waiting and the stumbling and the failing is what you must do to reach the places you must go. Do not rush through. That will only lead to confusion."

As he spoke, Ecne's coat slowly and almost imperceptibly gained in illumination and brilliance by degrees.

His light finally now became blinding, and Dunne had to look away. He covered his face and the brilliance faded quickly, leaving spots of light in Dunne's eyes where moments ago he had looked upon the man in his coat of brilliant colors.

Ecne was gone. The cavern faded once more to the low brilliance that it held when Dunne first entered. No other trace of the man or his bright robe remained.

Dunne stood there for long moments, pondering the importance of the man's appearance and the meanings of the last words that he imparted. The fortunate thing was that in the immediate moment his next steps were self-evident. The cavern surrounding him now looked smaller than it did before, and Dunne could only see one way out. It was the way that he had come in. He resigned himself to retracing what had seemed like an interminable walk downward into the very heart of the hill. It was now time to leave.

The climb up and out moved much more quickly than the cautious walk down. Dunne felt lighter than air, as if there was a force pushing him up and out, back into the open spaces on top of the hill. He walked up the steps and found that the light now seemed to be following him as he moved upward, darkening the hole behind him.

He stepped out of the stairwell and found the mansion at the top to be in a more dilapidated state than when he had descended. Weeds and other greenery had grown over the walls and the rust-reddened wrought-iron black fences as if to reclaim them from the men who had abandoned them. Time moved quicker while he was under the hill.

Looking down now, he could see that the landscape beyond the manse had gone farther to green as far as he could see. Gorse had retaken parts of the hill that were denuded when he walked through them earlier, and young saplings grew among the thick and flowery cover. Dunne couldn't imagine where there would have been trees to provide the seeds, but he knew that they must have come from somewhere. Trees didn't spontaneously generate from barren stone. Yet, there were trees that were several months or years old springing up everywhere he looked. He looked back toward the city, toward the places he had been. It looked smaller and darker than it had before, as if shrinking before a natural onslaught. One last look at it from high atop the hill before he crested it and trekked southward down the coast to find a boat that he hoped would carry him to wherever he must go.

Behind him, the old city was enveloped in a dark cloud, existing through it as if a transparent plastic overlay was put over a still photo built from a milky, degenerated negative. He squinted and rubbed his eyes. Nothing that he had seen in his long, winding journey had been similar to this vision. His pulse quickened and he got a sense of the darkness emanating from a particular spot down near the flooded river on the coast. Something down there was different than anything else he had encountered yet. It was something new, like him. Just then he remembered the other man he had found, the suicide.

There was a movement in the darkness of the city, a swirling point, a vortex of sorts in the three dimensional world that was still unfolding down below him and across the way.

He felt his consciousness drifting, as if he were falling asleep, then he snapped back into awareness and saw that the landscape before him had cleared. The darkness had disappeared and the horizon looked as clean as it had before the vision came over him. Something was down there though, and it was not waiting for Dunne. It felt wrong. Something there had gone terribly wrong.

He turned back to the south, half expecting to see the dark miasma from the city now spreading between the coastal hills, but there was nothing save the same ruined suburban landscape yawning at him. He'd cross it on the elevated highway and work his way just a few kilometers south to the floating docks where some of the island's wealthiest inhabitants kept their ships in private slips.

Dunne's hand itched again, and he scratched it without thinking. This time, his fingernail caught on something hard embedded in his skin and pulled it out. He felt only a small twinge of pain and looked down at his hand to see that his ChipIn had become dislodged from his flesh and had fallen to the ground with his scratching. The plastic and metal looked much smaller than he had imagined when he ran his fingers over it when it had been embedded under a thin scar. He abandoned it there in the dirt and began walking again toward the south.

Even as production costs fell, profit margins were driven higher by the insatiable need to fill bottomless pockets. These modern dragons were simply real men who didn't see the dragon in Beowulf for what it was.
The Politics of Illiteracy
Hanes Shamey

XXIII

Down in the city, things were moving. In the factory where Nix's corpse festered, gray-skinned, stone-like figures circled his body.

"This one, we can use," said the fish creature, crouched on two man legs with flipper feet standing in the clotted pool of Nix's blood.

"We need Cymidei, the Cauldron of Regeneration," the dog-headed one replied.

"Can it be here?" asked the third, a grotesquely emaciated dwarf.

"It will," replied the footed fish.

The stone-skinned creatures bowed their heads. Behind them, forming from dust that gathered and blew in small whirlwinds grew a great black cauldron. Steam rose from the dust-made construction, and the fish man dragged his flippered feet to the side of it, trailing Nix's thickening blood. He peered in.

"Bring him."

The dog-headed creature and the dwarf took Nix by his feet. His broken boots fell apart as they dragged his body from what should have been his final rest. His head left a smeared

red trail. They hoisted his body over the side and threw him roughly into the cauldron.

A dark plume of mist rose out of the great, black pot as the body sunk into the black ichor it contained. The blackness in the cauldron swallowed all light, and swallowed Nix's body completely. Inside, it looked formless and endless, like an absence or a hole in the world instead of a simple cauldron.

"Six weeks, they always said," said the withered dwarf.

"He'll not have six weeks. The sun will move a quarter length across the sky, and we'll pull him out. It will be enough to suit our needs," said the dog-head.

The fish man spoke up, "If the other one is a puppet of the *Tuatha Dé Danaan,* this one will be our counterbalance. The *Fomóiri* will have their own man in this world.

They stood in a semi-circle round the cauldron as it boiled Nix, its steam rising up out of the ruins and darkening the sky.

Hours passed and the cauldron seethed heat and foul odors. The beings from the depths faded, losing color with the light until becoming shadows and disappearing entirely. The cauldron melted into the air soon after, leaving Nix's body flat on his back.

Nix's leg twitched. A garbage rat the size of a greyhound yearling wobbled up to the corpse's leg and sniffed it. It squealed, huffed, and then beat a hasty retreat through the broken door.

Nix sat up rigidly, folded in half at the hips with the slouch that had been his habit for his whole life. There would be new habits making their way into his existence alongside the old ones. He was different now, and that meant some substantial changes.

His head hurt, but it felt light, as if he were almost drunk, but without the burning in his gut or the foul taste emanating from behind his molars. Instead, he could only smell a faint coppery odor, like burnt wiring, and he wasn't sure if he could feel those molars.

He shook his head. It still felt light and airy, as if it were less than it should have been. His tongue felt swollen. He ran it around his front teeth. They were still there, but he felt a space in the back where his wisdom teeth had come in so painfully. He felt his face with both hands. It was normal. Nothing wrong so far, but when he ran his fingers through his hair, something was off. He got to the back of his head and felt a dry crusty edge. His sense of spatial awareness must have been off. There shouldn't have been an edge there. It felt like his fingers dipped into a space where they had never been before, not even on a drug-induced trip.

There was a sizable hole in the back of his head.

Nix reached both hands back now and felt the crust-caked sides. He could feel the jagged, broken angles of his own skull plates. The crust he felt was his own dried blood. He recognized the feel of it from some of his victims. He shook his head again. The strange sense that he couldn't place earlier was the feeling of air circulating inside his head.

Objectively, he should have been dead, even though he was congratulating himself on merely "knocking himself out." Nix didn't understand the severity of his wound. If he could have, even with his whole brain intact, he would have marveled at how his head was even still connected at all to his neck with a portion of the rear of his skull missing.

Nix couldn't remember firing the gun. He remembered the moving man-shape that came nearer and nearer to him. He remembered the fear that he felt, but then nothing else until he awoke on the floor with a hole in his head. That other man must have done it. The other man shot him.

Nix didn't feel angry. He felt nothing at all. He did not know that the part of his brain that was necessary to feel anger was missing. He knew that he was going to find that man and kill him. It was his destiny and his duty. He didn't know what had happened to anyone else, but he did know that man had something to do with it. He knew things in a manner that was impossible.

Nix walked over the broken stones of his hiding spot and surveyed the world around him. He felt strongly and deeply that he had to do something. This feeling had all the power of an instinctual response. There was an undeniable drive to find the man who had forced him into his current state. When Nix thought about that man, the one who had attacked him and wounded him, he was overcome by a sudden white-hot heat that burned in the center of his back, deep behind his lungs and centered in the bundle of nerve tissue that ran up his spine. It wasn't the same as anger. He'd felt anger before, all the times that he'd been treated "unfairly" by his commandant, all of the times that he was rejected by the upper class women that he felt he was entitled to have sex with, all of those times that he was denied the bits and pieces of life that should have been his as a man and an Orangeshirt. This was more than anger.

This was a biological drive. An instinctual, predatory sense of purpose. Nix would wreak violence upon that dirty brown devil that put the hole in his head. It was as sure a thing as knowing that anyone who crossed him would feel his violence. He felt a pressure in his groin and was not surprised to find that his feelings of vengeance and power had excited him. They always did.

He was going to do so many terrible things to the man who had hurt him. He wanted to watch the man suffer. Nix would make him beg for his life before ending it. And Nix was going to enjoy it so much.

He was sure of it.

"There was no reason to remain on the island for any man. To remain on the island was to admit defeat, to admit that you were no one and nothing and would never amount to anything."
The His Story of Man
B. Koffee Altiere

XXX

Dunne looked out over the lowlands that he had to cross to reach the town by the docks. From the hilltop, this side of the island still resembled the land that he had walked through to reach the once busy metropolis. He could not remember how many days had passed since he first awoke in the underground den and trekked into the city to search for other survivors.

Dunne scanned the horizon in the direction that he was moving and heard the sound of movement to his right. He turned to find a man sitting on a flat stone pondering a pile of sticks. The man was dressed in shining robes that radiated a pure white light the likes of which Dunne had never seen before, not even in the cave. His skin was similar in color to his dress— an almost electric white. Dunne walked closer to him over the newly lush and green ground.

The man was seated on a pile of broken stones amidst some gorse, and when he was closer, Dunne could see his features through his radiance. He had straight, golden honey-colored hair and a neat beard that perfectly framed his face and lips. Dunne recognized him immediately from the paintings, statues, and prints lining the walls of churches and hives wherever the President for Life's face was absent. He was the old vision of the savior, from the days before the President for Life claimed the mantle of "savior."

The man showed recognition of Dunne's presence in his body language but didn't yet look at Dunne, instead focusing on a shaped piece of wood that he held in his hands.

He spoke, still focused on the wood. "I was a carpenter once, a very long time ago…" He sighed and swept his eyes across the landscape, through Dunne and out to the sea. "But I've always been a student too. My mother and father taught me to read at a young age, and I often went about quoting the books I had read to impress people older than I was. They said that they'd never seen the like. Usually memorizing the sacred texts was the task of older men." He looked wistfully into the distance toward the sea. "I wanted to impress them."

Dunne crouched down on his haunches across from the man and tilted his head quizzically. He knew what to expect from some of these visions now. They had something to teach him. He asked, "What did you have to prove?"

In response, the man looked deeply into Dunne and sighed. "There were things that my father wanted to prove to them."

"Why didn't he simply tell them?"

"No one believes anything that you tell them. They have to experience it themselves."

Dunne thought about the things he had learned from the telescreen and from listening to his fellow workers. He remembered that people often believed things without any experience simply because believing those things made them feel good. They believed whatever they wanted to based on convenience rather than fact. He remembered how many people talked about the importance of the Bible.

"Didn't we have a book that everyone was expected to know and obey? A book that told us how to behave?" he asked.

"Yes. There was —" The bearded man paused and looked at Dunne without speaking, as if waiting for him to say something more. Then he added, "Ofttimes, people used a mediator between them and the book. They didn't understand the metaphors or the parables. That clouded the material and the meaning for many of them. It introduced biases and misinterpretations that broke the messages."

Dunne responded, "Perhaps that had something to do with the original message?"

The man tipped his head back and laughed unexpectedly. "Perhaps. That happens. Things are rarely as clear as we imagine them to be. It was lost so long ago. You can't imagine in your wildest dreams what will happen after you go. Most of the time, people simply forget you. The real problem is when they don't. You would not believe what these people did with their stories of me — even with the best of intentions. It was pure madness."

The shining bearded man reached into the pile of sticks and started working them together, molding the wood that shifted shape within his very hands into the form of a cross.

"I think it may be time for me to move on. Too many people have done too much evil in my memory."

Dunne nodded in agreement. "I too now understand when it is time to move on."

The brilliantly white man nodded in assent. "Yes, you do. You're a reasonable person, aren't you? People can choose evil or goodness when they are abused, but you've seen the bad and chosen goodness for yourself. That's the way that people are supposed to work. That was the way that my father made them—" He paused here, his face fell in shadow. "Supposedly. I'm not sure of that anymore. Are you familiar with the story, my story?"

Dunne nodded again. Everyone was familiar with the story of the first son of God and how he was made in the perfect likeness of his father with his shining white skin and perfect blond-brown hair and anglo-centric features, and how the father was stern and unforgiving and held his children to unreachable standards of perfection. Everyone also knew the prophecy of how his son would come again with an automatic rifle to deal with the sinners and the non-believers.

"You know, you have to be very careful who you ally yourself with. Very often, people will simply lump you together with others because they don't know any better."

Dunne nodded. He had seen the crosses everywhere. Some of the corner bodegas and shops still sold them in the days before everyone was gone. Crosses littered the ground now in cemetaries around the city, broken into fragile pieces. The man continued staring quietly at the cross in his hand. Dunne looked around. Nothing moved. It was as though the scene was frozen in time, but an uneasiness in his gut told him to move on. It felt similar to the days when he waited for the Orangeshirts to turn on him.

"I have to go," he said to the bearded man.

The man looked at him, shrugged his shoulders and replied, "Before you go, here's a tip for you — A little something that I learned the hard way: never leave anything written down behind you after you leave."

Dunne looked at him quizzically.

"I mean that. Everything you write, even everything you say can be twisted and turned and manipulated to mean something else. The more you say, the more that people can take what you said and turn it back on itself to disprove the very idea that you were trying to advocate for." He sighed through his trimmed beard and after a moment smiled radiantly at Dunne.

Then the man grew brighter and brighter, his radiance seeming to glow from within like a sun. Dunne had to close his eyes and shield them with his arm. Then the light faded and Dunne opened his eyes. The man and all traces of him were gone.

Dunne knew that it was time to leave. He'd been told often enough that no man ever became anything at all by staying on the island. To leave though, he needed a bigger boat. Now that all of the people were gone, all he had to do was find one of their big boats. Except that wasn't all that he had to do. He had to learn how to sail it too.

Sailing had been one of those things that he had seen and never done. He'd seen big races with giant sailboats on the well-televised Presidential Sailing Classic. He'd even seen sailboats out on the sea, often sailing up the coast from the harbors of Dunstones and Gray just down the coast.

He wasn't sure if the boats would still be moored now: if they'd gone adrift, if the tides had washed them out of the harbors without their men to maintain them. So much of the land seemed to be changing even before his very eyes. Man's industrial excesses were being reabsorbed and broken by the landscapes into their component parts, then locked away below the ground or washed out to the very reaches where they'd someday be loosed again in a Wagnerian operatic cycle of death and rebirth.

Dunne watched the water and the waves from the side of the hill. It was amazing how the water seemed to remain still, even as the hill-like waves washed through them from horizon to shore. He had never seen the water like this. Sitting on the hillside to the south below the mansion gave him many new perspectives that he could not have guessed at before.

He watched the sunlight glisten on the water. It shimmered like a sea of broken glass. He could imagine himself out there, floating on the waves and gently moving across them even as the water itself seemed immobile. White lines of reflected light moved with the currents across the deep sea waters, showing him the tops of the waves as they gently rolled ever lazily through the tableau before him.

Moving just below the surface of the shimmering sea before him, he saw a pinkish red line moving through the water. It was like an electric arterial flood, a thin snake of a river moving through the sea, drifting sideways through the depths. It twisted and turned as it rose and sank, increasing and decreasing in clarity as it wove its way through the waters.

His first thought upon seeing it was that it was a rope lost from a fishing trawler, one that swept the deep cavernous ocean with plastic cables and weighted nets. And even though that is very much the thing that it resembled, he knew almost as soon as it drifted into his view that it was nothing he had seen before. It was a coagulation of clone bodies, a creature that created itself and grew in size to fit the abundance that its environment provided for it. Somehow, the works of men often resembled the very things they usually destroyed in the ecosystem. It was an odd act of replacement.

The paths down from the hill were cracked and beginning to grow over with thorns and bracken. It felt like the heath was breaking through them in a reversal of the island's history. Thorns had taken root in the broken pavement and they threatened to block Dunne's path down the mountain at different points, catching and pulling at his clothing.

Below him sat the small seaside town of Ratmichelle. It bordered the sunken town of Gray which was swallowed by the rising waters. Dunne walked slowly down the hill. The only sounds were the waves washing the ruins of the former town as he traversed the seaside road. The private beach ahead of him was bulldozed to the sand, and no ruins remained to mar it, only high fences with gates left open and guard shacks unmanned. Dunne walked through the open main gate and came to the last hill before his transition to the lowlands and their docks and bays. It was here where he might find the boat that he needed.

There were more ruins on that last hill, ruins that were for a short time a Pentecostal church for the saved heathens of the island's burned over heather. It was one of the American Evangelical churches that had taken root and sprung up like weeds. A century ago, it had simply been a large cross erected on the peak of the hill, but in the short period after the island achieved statehood, the church was built on the formerly public land to celebrate the president from across the sea. It was then decorated with murals that combined the stories of the president's life with the sufferings of the New Testament Jesus Christ.

The church had burned in the "Great Immigrant Spring Uprising" the year before. The conflagration was blamed on the island's immigrant workers imported from the Middle East to clean sewers, and an investigation undertaken by the Orangeshirts had determined that the fire had been the start of a national uprising led by immigrant leaders and their sympathizers in the capital city. Dunne remembered it because they had taken a handful of the darker-skinned workers and shot them against the back wall of his factory in retaliation for the fire.

Dunne walked through the ruins that remained. Years ago, the church had been celebrated on the telescreens as one of the great artistic and architectural endeavors of the modern age. Dunne looked at the remaining walls and the golden murals of the edifice, now damaged and stained. Dunne thought that the character of the President-Savior was too orange, that the lines filigreed with gold paint were too thick. There was no beauty to be found there.

Pieces of an unburned mural remained, crumbled and lying in one corner of the ruins. They depicted red and blue rays emanating from the heart of the leader and bestowing wonderment and wisdom upon his followers, clad in the brown security uniforms that marked his best men on the island at the time. The mural was broken at the golden hairline of the leader, and his left hand of benediction was missing too, burned away or broken off.

Millions of dollars had been donated by the loyal citizens from their own debt and designated for the church's repair and restoration. But the restoration work had never begun. Committees were convened to study and plan the work necessary, but it had not yet occurred when the world Dunne knew collapsed in on itself.

Dunne pondered the ruins from his vantage point within and arrived at the surety that the repairs never would have begun regardless. The money would have simply disappeared as if it had never existed at all. It would have become another giant sailboat in the harbor, or another mansion somewhere on one of the island's many hills. As Dunne looked at the rubble, more paint curled and fell. The winds coming from the sea captured it and rolled it away over the heather, and Dunne saw it turn to dust before his very eyes. He left the ruined church behind and continued south.

The waters crashed upon the rocks a meter from the low path ahead at high tide, and Dunne set upon his final walk to the docks. As he descended toward them, he found some of the gates broken and rusting. The black wrought iron was falling apart before his very eyes. The green plants grew and twisted tendrils up and through, winding and gaining strength even as the iron crumbled to rust in the salty air.

For hundreds of years, the island had been home to gates and walls, but the pace of sectioning and walling grew vastly during the reign of the President for Life over this fifty-first state. The land had become more valuable and was held as investment by the wealthy, even as the inhabitants declined in value.

As Dunne descended into the docklands, he found that many of the super-yachts were in various states of disrepair. Those closest to the entrance seemed to be the most dilapidated. Those closest to the deep water looked the most sea-worthy. Walking up and down the floating docks, some of which were not as floaty as they should have been, he could see that the waters below had cleared as well. They were no longer fouled with leaking oil or petroplastic waste.

The cliffs known as the Gray Head offered some shelter from the storms that came from the east and south, hence the location of these bouyant plastic docks. The moorings and walkways floated above the skeletal ruined remains of the seaside resorts of old Gray, sunken now below the waves.

In the rays of the sun passing through the water, he could see the ruins of the old town below him. The water was clear enough to allow him to see the remaining stone foundations from before the sea level rise. The brick and concrete foundations waited like some ancient octopus god to re-emerge as if from a long and deep slumber.

The waters of the sea here were calm and mirror-like. Dunne gazed downward from his floating dock into the water at his own reflection. It was recognizable as himself, but dramatically different. His hair was growing back. His skin was clear. The changes that Dunne could see in himself mirrored those that he also saw working through the land before him. Restoration was taking place.

He could not see the future, but he could see a future. It was the first time in his life that could remember having that kind of vision. He had always lived only day to day, looking forward no further than his own immediate future. He still could not remember much of his past, but things were becoming clearer, much the same as the sky and the air that he breathed.

Dunne had no idea how to navigate by sailboat and had little time to learn, but he felt no desire to attempt to pilot one of the greater diesel powered or coal burning ships that he was sure were still in the dockyards of the old capital city to the north. He had no faith that he'd be able to take the controls of one of the sensor ships anyway. It was far beyond the abilities that he had been able to master while he worked at the rending factory. A sailboat was in his future. He felt optimistic that as long as the boat was watertight, he could figure out the techniques of sailing in the strangely calm waters that surrounded him now.

The first boat that he found was a huge three masted affair. Dunne didn't know it, but it belonged to the son of the man who owned most of the island's major western port. The ship was huge, overshadowing the other boats bobbing in the light waves moored to the plastic docks. It would never do for his needs.

Sailing was a still a marker of social status to Dunne, and only the richest citizens sailed ships of such magnitude. The smaller paddle boats or the motored autoboats were rented to the poorer tourists who lacked the disposable income to own ships such as these. Yacht clubs here and around the island maintained the upperclass exclusivity of sailing. Their costly memberships were far beyond the reach of anyone in Dunne's debt classification, and the clubs were separated from their surroundings by the same tall iron gates and fences that gave the expansive manors their seclusion.

Dunne reflected again how everything in this world was sectioned off — the haves and the have-nots were the only real social classes, and the mirage of mobility from the lower to the upper was maintained by and through the Orangeshirts. As in everything else on the island, Orangeshirts were the intermediaries between the richest and the poorest., even though they had little political or financial power of their own. Those class divisions had finally been lost in the world that Dunne inhabited, but their remains littered the landscapes as well as the sea. This ship would always belong to someone who ruled the seas. It was far too big for Dunne's purposes.

He needed something that would get him across the ocean without being too big for him to handle. Something that could get him to his destination unnoticed if there were other dangers yet to be met.

In all of human history,
it was only violence which
brought any sort of lasting
societal change.
The Truth as It Is
A.J. Rebbew

XXXI

Nix picked up a piece of broken steel rebar from the rubble. It was as good as anything else for what he had in mind for the man he blamed for his injury. He would enjoy crushing his skull and bashing his brains out, watching his face disintegrate under the force. Then Nix would shower in the splatter as he pounded every part of the man's body on a stone. He would beat his corpse until it was bloodless, until all the bones were shattered into hundreds if not thousands of splinters. He would pound the man until he was a paste, and then he would defecate and urinate on the paste that was left. He would do these things because he knew without doubt that they were the right and proper things to do.

He looked up and down the river. Twilight was moving in swiftly. There were no signs of movement. Not even the carrion pigeons were flying overhead looking for garbage and scraps. He held his hand to his ear. The whole world had gone silent around him. Even the flow of the river seemed to have silenced itself.

Nix imagined that all of creation was afraid of him. He was a new class of super predator, an "Super-man." Like the savior of all men of the West, he had been reborn, become more powerful. Except he would not find his doubting Thomas and allow him to probe his wounds. He would pulverize him.

His hatred bubbled in his chest, and he spit a mouthful of blood on the ground. It was frothy and dark. clotted and thick. He saw a light to the south where there was nothing logically left to make a glow that white on the horizon over the hills. He thought that must be his target. It looked like the video games he played that indicated the player's next goal with a light or a change in color over the mapped landscape. His enemy was trying to escape him, trying to avoid Nix's nearly divine retribution.

He felt a sense of almost-euphoria that was constant. He imagined he could hear more sharply, he could see farther and with more clarity. He could feel the vibrations of the universe through his skin. He felt more alive with this hole in his head that he'd ever felt without it. He would never have imagined before in his life that carrying a mortal head wound would make the whole world louder and brighter. Closer to death, he was more alive.

He crossed through the streets of the city purposefully, a hunter stalking his territory following the scent of his prey. He walked through the ruined suburbs without slowing. His pace was now inexhaustible. Silence traveled with him as he walked, and the island was silent so as to not attract his violence. There was nothing left to stand in his way of running the whole island now, except this man who had tried to kill him. Once he had revenge, he would be free to own everything. It was going to be his kingdom now.

He left the outskirts of the main city and drew south. He could feel his strength increasing. As he walked, he swung his rebar like a sporting hurl, striking down everything standing near him. He collapsed walls and bashed in doors as he went. He cracked rock, shattered plastic, and splintered wood.

As he went along, he remembered that there was a dedicated Orangeshirt armory nearby. He'd forgotten about it all this time. Perhaps he could break in using the rebar. His steel bludgeon would be a good weapon for close quarters — it would be his killing blows, but he wanted something better for long range, something to hit the man with when he first saw him, something to knock him down from afar so that Nix could successfully stalk him to the ground for the killing blow.

As he thought about loading up the weapons, he thought back to the drugs. He didn't need them anymore. He was permanently high now. He could feel it. Everything the drugs did for him before was happening to him right now without them. He wanted to feel the man's death on his hands, wear his blood on his clothes even before the man crossed over into Hell.

Nix located the armory in what had once been an exhibition space. Art fairs and business conferences had once been held there, back when the island state was yet a nation. The thick stone walls dated to an age before the world became disposable. Its main entrance doors were heavy steel, but they were rusted where the hinges welded on. Nix bashed the doors twice before they burst open, breaking off the rusted hinges and collapsing.

In the armory were many weapons, including machine guns, assault rifles, and electric ceramics that were the next generation of weapons used for crowd control, intimidation, and suppression during large-scale security events or conflicts. There were large caliber, high-velocity railguns waiting for an owner to imprint upon their security measures, and these were the first to catch his eye. He'd never had a chance to use one before.

The first one he took crumbled in his fist. The petroplasticine weapon had become brittle and dry in storage. He dropped its remnants on the floor and broke the other three it was shelved with with a hard kick. Any of them would have exploded in his hands had they been fired.

He huffed in anger and moved deeper into the depot. All the steel weapons were corroded and rotted, broken and steeped in decay in their slots and crates. But then he found a case of the ceramics. They looked untouched by corruption.

He seized a large caliber ceramic rifle from its crate and pulled the trigger. Nothing happened. The small plutonium batteries were dead. The electric ceramics were as useless as the steel or the plastic weapons. He threw it to the floor, shattering it into small pieces. His hollow head started throbbing. The euphoria had passed and something he didn't understand had replaced it.

He picked up his chunk of rebar and used it to smash everything in sight. He smashed the crates, bent and broke the weapons, scarred the walls and bashed every door and window. He stalked back out through the smashed door and strode across the battered, deteriorating street. The hole in his head throbbed slightly less — only his acts of destruction lessened the sensation that shook his every step. He smashed brick and stone and fence row, but the dull throb continued. He blacked out and collapsed on the ground.

He awoke a while later. His head throbbed only lightly now, like a barely noticeable heartbeat. The hole in his head felt like an echo inside him. It was a space that things reverberated in. He sat up and rolled over to his hands and knees. He took the rebar bludgeon from the ground and stood up, using it for balance like a cane.

He scanned the landscape. He could feel the throbbing in his skull lessen when he looked toward the southern coast. Beyond the hills where he had seen the white glow. He had to go there to lessen the throb. He had to use violence to lessen the throb. He had to use violence on something that was there in the distance. He put the ideas together in his head, then he swung his bludgeon over his shoulder and walked. That was where he had to go.

He could go in that direction until he could find the man that he blamed for his state. He would find the man no matter where he hid, and he would kill him.

*"Advertising came to its full power
when it merged wholly with sports
and celebrity as a tool of fascism.
This too, began in America and
spread like a petrol-fueled inferno."*
The Governing Principal
Irulan Prince

XXXII

Dunne found a small yacht tied to a much larger one, a three decked mega-yacht. This smaller boat was less than fifteen meters and still had a small cabin. Compared to the larger boat, it was a lifeboat. It would suit his purposes well enough and was the boat in the best shape of any that he had seen. The giant white three-decker tethered to it was already starting to list, and corrosion showed in orange lines down the hull. The barnacles that crusted it at the water line were thick. Somehow, the smaller yacht had none.

Dunne took stock of the harbor. The small boat was the only vessel in the docklands that looked to be still seaworthy. It was as though some force was saving it for him. He climbed aboard the greater yacht and looked out to the sea from its high bow. It looked flat and beckoning to him again — an endless field of sparkling jewels. He had to go west. He felt compelled to find the cause of the illness that had wiped almost clean of people his home island. He knew that he had to leave his home to become something, and America was the place to go.

He remembered the little bit of history that he had been taught, how millions of the island's inhabitants had gone to American to become greater than they were throughout the existence of the island nation. It was a natural part of God's plan that this island nation become an official part of the country across the sea. Or so he was told.

He climbed aboard the larger boat to reach its small, tethered partner. The large boat's once highly polished wooden decking was rotten and degraded from the salty air and the lack of maintenance. He carefully stepped where he could see fastener marks on the planks to avoid weak spots and gingerly walked to the head of a ladder that led down to the smaller boat. From there, he clung to and used the tethering line to draw the bow of the small watercraft closer. He brought it in and stepped down to the deck of his new sailing ship. Safely onboard, he tugged at the weather-beaten tether until it broke and fell into the water.

The smaller ship was not anchored, and without the rope, it began to drift. Dunne found the cabin door unlocked. In the small galley cupboard he found some dried fruits and meats bundled with breads in plasticine shinkwrap. The boat was already provisioned with a few tin cans and plastic boxes, but not with enough for a transatlantic voyage. He needed to search the galley of the larger ship for more provisions but found that his small boat had already drifted free of the docks and into the sea while he took stock of the cabin interior.

The ship gained power and speed even as he looked around to take his bearings. The sun was now at his left. He went on the deck and pulled the sails from their storage. The halyards and the jib were on top. At first he was confused, but he looked at the cloth and then the rope and pulleys on the mast with shackles. He chose a sail that fit the shackles and ran it up the mast. There was no wind, and the sheet ran up without twisting. He secured the mainsail as best he could with his scant experience of having seen sailing races on the telescreen. Then he moved to the back of the boat to check the tiller.

It was stuck. He tugged and pulled on it to no avail. He put his hip against it and pushed. He threw his weight into it and pulled. It stayed in one position. It seemed to present no danger though, and he could see that he was safely rounding the head of the coast and moving to put his back to the sun. The boat was slowly shifting itself west and moved with greater speed now that the sails had been set.

The water grew rougher as he went farther from his former home, and the boat's movement in the waves began to lull him into sleepiness. It was no longer a glittering plain of diamonds, but now he could see swells and currents reflecting white in the eastern sun. It was calming and he fought against drowsiness. He sat back against the cabin and let his mind drift.

He thought back to working in the factory, but found that those memories had become less and less painful each day since his departure, and now they were fading like an old nightmare. As he sat on his boat moving westward, he felt the books hidden in the pocket of his cloak and pulled them out. Now he had time to read. The boat was keeping its own course, although he found none of the electronics needed to self-pilot.

His mind drifted back to the kindness, the mam figure he had kept locked away for so long like a balm in the safest regions of his dim memory. It was this kindness that had taught him to read so long ago that he had forgotten it.

He thought forward to the sickness and his reawakening. He remembered being as sick as he had ever been, and he remembered the light of the open door as he returned to life. He thought of his deep loneliness when he found his old haunts empty. Even though he was lonely in his past life, there had been people around him to fill the spaces. Then he remembered the horror of the decomposing bodies floating near the Poolbegs.

He took a deep breath of the clean sea air and pushed his thoughts to more positive things Those people had passed into a better place. Even if it was nothingness, it was better than the rending factory. Nothingness was at least an absence of pain and hurt. He felt certain that even though their transitions had been painful, that their transformation into energy had been something like his experience. Either they became the same nothing that they had been before they were born, or like him, they entered into a new world of their own.

He settled with his books on his lap, using the boat's life vests as cushions. He would read. He opened the first book and allowed the boat to take him west.

To be continued in *The Last Literate Man: Book II.*

www.ingramcontent.com/pod-product-compliance
Lightning Source LLC
Chambersburg PA
CBHW020910200626
46814CB00001BA/270